Sovereign

The Revelation Trilogy
Book Three

T. E. Burrell

Sovereign is a work of fiction. All of the names, characters, locations, and events are products of the author's imagination or are used fictitiously. Any resemblance to actual persons, places, or events is entirely coincidental.

DEDICATION

The Revelation Trilogy is dedicated to the two women who made it possible.

My mother Mickey, FORCED me to read for an hour every day during my summer break between first and second grade. It started an obsession that I am forever grateful for.

My wife Becky supplied an amazing level of patience and understanding along the journey. Those who know me well can attest this is no small feat. Without her advice and support this story would still be rolling around in my head all by itself.

CONTENTS

ACKNOWLEDGEMENTS

My thanks to Jordan for his insightful feedback, questions, ideas, and encouragement during the writing of this trilogy. His developmental editing was incredibly helpful.

Thanks also to Jess and Emmaleigh for their help with the cover art. Their advice, energy, and creativity is greatly appreciated by someone who is significantly artwork challenged.

Sovereign

CHAPTER 1

PALATIUM

Tee woke without opening his eyes or moving. His Guard training kicked in just like it had on the slave ship. His first thought was that he was dead. Whatever he was lying on was warm and unbelievably comfortable. He thought it smelled lightly of lavender. Then he noticed a headache intruded on his comfort. He decided the afterlife should not be a mix of comfort and headache. It should either be wonderful or horrible, but not something in between. Given the things he had done lately, horrible was likely the proper judgement. He could hear someone softly breathing a few feet to his left. After a few minutes, the person sighed as if impatient and moved slightly. Perhaps getting more comfortable in a chair? Curiosity overcame his paranoia. He opened his eyes, turned his head, and found Forti sitting in a chair by the side of his bed reading a book. Tee was in the biggest bed he had ever seen.

He swept his eyes quickly around the room and was stunned by what he saw. He had never seen anything so extravagant. At first he thought it might be a one room home given its size. However, he didn't see a kitchen so perhaps it was in a separate room on the other side of the door. If so, this would be a very large home. The ceiling had three dimensional features with a large mural painted on it. The walls were a soothing color with artwork adorning them. There was a full set of plush parlor furniture arranged around an elaborately decorated fireplace. Opposite the fireplace was a large desk made of almost black wood placed in front of ceiling to floor glass windows. Bright daylight was streaming in. It made no sense to him.

Forti was patient while Tee looked around trying to get his bearings. When his eyes wandered back Forti said, "am glad to see you awake. The doctors always worry with a head injury."

Tee remembering his last moments from the Arena reached up and felt the back of his head. There was some sort of bandage there. Touching it lightly he immediately identified this as the source of his headache.

"Sorry about your head. I was a step too late," Forti said grimacing a bit in empathy.

"Where is Victor?" Tee asked.

"I'm sorry Tee," Forti said with compassion in his voice. "He didn't make it. It's the stuff of legends, but he's dead." After giving Tee a few moments to absorb the bad news he continued. "I have a lot to tell you and it's going to be hard to accept."

"How do I know I can trust you?" Tee said bluntly. He couldn't imagine why he was in such an opulent place. Even more confusing was Forti saying he was going to explain it to him.

"Excuse me for just a second Tee," Forti said as he got up. He walked over and cracked the door open and spoke quietly to an unseen person on the other side. He came back, sat down, took a moment, and then said, "Victor thought we should have a conversation with just you and me. He wanted us to establish trust. He told me to apologize for not telling you everything about the assassination plan. His apology will make sense later. The important thing to know is that you were successful. The emperor is dead. You are safe."

Tee forced himself to bury his grief over Victor's death. He needed to worry about self-preservation for now. He pushed himself up into a sitting position and was immediately woozy. His headache increased adding nausea to his list of 'not in heaven' ailments. He gritted his teeth and propped himself up by leaning back against an elaborately carved headboard. He waited for his head to clear then looked at Forti and said, "why I should trust you?"

Forti smiled and said, "Victor told me it would be difficult to explain this if he didn't survive. The short answer is that 'I am of the Guard, and we are brothers.'"

This was a formal greeting ritual used to start briefings. It communicated the close relationship between all Guard members and the need to trust and believe in the presenter. "What?" Tee asked, clearly stunned by the reference, especially given it was said within its intended purpose. In disbelief he said, "you can't be a member of the Guard."

"Victor told me he is the Master Sergeant of the Guard. He said that since he has not been notified of a change in status he has the authority to invite, test, and approve new recruits. He said he was convinced I could provide capable service below the Wall. Whatever that means. Perhaps you can explain it to me later. All of this came out early in the morning before the two of you entered the Arena. When he gave me that phase to say to you he said he also has the authority to graduate you into full Guard membership. You're not a Newbie anymore," Forti said.

It sounded like something Victor would say. But why? I'm supposed to be dead along with Victor Tee thought. The plan was to make them pay. There was always a hope that their actions would spawn an uprising, but Tee never put any faith in that.

"Why am I still alive?" Tee asked in an angry voice.

"Now that's where this gets really interesting. Do you remember the call for uprising that Victor made you memorize?" Forti asked.

"Yeah, 'overthrow the tyrant' or something like that," Tee said confusion deepening. "It was supposed to encourage the crowd to overthrow the emperor and his family."

"Well, he lied. It was a clever lie because in a sense it's true. You shouted out 'Provoco ius Imperandi,' correct?"

"Yes," said Tee with a questioning look on his face.

"The correct translation is 'I challenge the right to rule'," Forti said. "By ancient custom anyone can challenge the emperor's right to rule on his ascension anniversary. In Arista this is also called New Year's Day. That' why he was so heavily guarded. It originally meant personal combat in the Arena. Centuries ago, one of the early emperors successfully argued that an emperor's weapons included his army, guards, family, servants, and slaves. So, if challenged, all could be utilized for the emperor in 'personal combat'. The other key change was that a weapon of the emperor cannot be used against him. This guaranteed safety from those closest to him."

Tee held up his hand at that point and in frustration said, "please just tell me what this means."

"It means that you are the Emperor Theron, First of his Name." Forti said with an amused grin.

Tee just stared at him. He couldn't believe what he had just heard. Although he had lots of questions one thing needed to be resolved before anything was going to make sense. He furrowed his brow and asked one more time, "why should I trust you?"

Forti's face showed a mild frustration, then it took on an amused expression and he said "Victor said you would be a tough nut. He admired your 'pig headed ways' as he put it. He told me two things that might help. First he told me to remind you to balance your stance."

It was the very first thing Victor had harped on in their training sessions. He had pointed out that Tee took on a defensive posture even when positioning for an attack. Victor had likened him to a little girl confronting a mouse. In typical Victor fashion he insulted him brutally in creatively colorful language before telling him why it was important. In this case Tee was limiting his options while telegraphing weakness. Tee considered this and then said suspiciously, "anyone who watched our early training sessions might come up with that."

"The other thing he told me was what happens between a mentor and a newbie before the newbies first battle." Forti walked over and whispered the call to victory along with the correct response in his ear. "Victor told me he said that to you just before you entered the Arena for the Harvest Festival."

Tee just stared at him. It was all too much to process. Victor would never have given Forti that particular piece of Guard lore if he hadn't met Victor's stringent requirements. That meant Victor trusted Forti without reservation. It meant Tee had to trust Forti with his life. He was trying to make sense of it all when Forti said, "If Victor didn't make it, I was to tell you he would like you to call him Vic the next time you see him."

To Tee's horror his eyes formed tears and as one started running down his face, Forti thankfully turned away. Tee had to get his control back. There had been way too much death this past year to say nothing of having his freedom taken away from him. After gaining control Tee said, "what else do I need to know."

Forti raised his eyes and said, "Senator Cereo is someone to trust and he's waiting just outside the door."

Once again Tee was caught speechless for a few moments. Then he said "You have to be kidding me. The man who thinks he owns me is someone Victor wants me to trust?"

"Senator Cereo doesn't believe in slavery any more than you do. And yes he's trustworthy. It's a long story. Let's have him come in. It's important that we pull a plan together for the next few days. You are the emperor, but it's a very dicey situation and much needs to happen before it all falls apart," Forti said.

Tee thought about that for a few moments and then nodded his head. Forti rose and went to the door. Then he paused and turned back around, "Victor knew you had succeeded. Your first arrow severed the carotid artery and the second pierced his heart. Both were kill shots. I was told Victor clearly recognized this and smiled just before he died."

Caius could hear them talking as he waited with Leo just outside the door. The doctors had been worried about the head injury and all three of them waited nervously all night hoping he would awaken. Not only had Theron awoken, Forti said his mental faculties were intact. He still couldn't believe the two Pacifica gladiators had pulled this off. Forti had come to him the week before with his confession of helping Victor plan the emperor's assassination. He explained that he had kept it from Caius so there was deniability if they got caught. He pressed Caius to take control if they were successful. By sheer luck, his son's 2nd Legion was in the barracks right next to the Arena. They were days away from transport to Liberty. His efforts to delay that invasion had ended in failure and he had accepted it. After a tense 30-minute discussion with Leo they decided to throw the dice. Leo was aware of the ancient law of challenge by combat. They would risk everything if Victor and Theron were successful. Leo was the one who really pushed for this decision. He still remembered his plea. "Caius, we have a chance to make a difference for millions. We can free everyone in our family. This opportunity will never happen again. We can't turn away from this." It really wasn't all that hard to convince him. Caius had always been known as the risk taker in the family. But Leo now wore that crown. They purchased all the remaining New Years Day tickets still available that were across the arena from the Emperor's suite. Those seats had been filled by Forti's security team and selected members of his son Vincent's legion.

Waiting patiently, Caius reflected on when this crazy path in life started. It was almost thirty years ago, and he had just turned sixteen. He had been terrified. His parents were dead, and he had no idea what to do. He was deeply ashamed when he realized he wasn't overly upset about them being dead. It was the uncertainty of how their deaths would affect everyone he loved that haunted him. The overseer, a brutal alcoholic who did nothing unless his parents were in residence left as soon as the news arrived. He pulled Caius off to the side before leaving and said, "make a few examples of the slaves if you want to live. They'll slit your throat by the time I get to the front gate if you're not tough on them."

His parents had left him when he was just a baby at their remote villa with June, her daughter Oly, his half-brother Leo, and June's father Sage. His half-brother was only a month older than him, and June had been recruited to be his wet nurse. His parents rarely visited and when they did it was a horrifying experience. His father was always drunk and at some point, would say horrible things to June and drag her into his bedroom. His mother would act as if nothing were happening. He despised them both for it. When he was 12 he told his father to stop doing bad things to June. His father just laughed, grabbed June's arm, and drug her towards his bedroom telling Caius he could come watch if he wanted. Caius picked up a walking stick and hit him with it. His father responded by beating him mercilessly. After exhausting himself his father calmed down and said with a smile, "OK, she's getting a bit old anyway, you can keep her for yourself if you want." Then he laughed as Caius lay humiliated on the floor.

Later, with his face flushed red he haltingly told June he only wanted her to be safe. June with a warm but sad smile said, "Caius, you are not your father. You are the good-hearted young man I've always knew you would be."

The first night after receiving the news they sat around the dinner table and June informed him that, "all of the slaves not part of my family left the villa this afternoon. We gave them food but didn't let them steal anything."

Caius just shrugged and announced his plan, "I'm going to free everyone, sell the ranch, and split the proceeds."

June smiled, hesitated a moment, and then gently asked, "and then what are you going to do?"

"I don't know. I guess I'll go to Roma and find a job."

"What kind of job Caius? What skills do you have?" June asked softly.

"I haven't really thought it through yet, but that's what I'm going to do," he said and glared defiantly back at her.

"You know if you sold us and the villa you could probably afford to go to college. You would have to be frugal, but you could do it," June offered.

"NO!" Caius shouted. "That's disgusting! It's insulting you think I would sell you, my brother, my sister, and grandfather!"

"Well, Oly isn't really your sister, is she?" June countered.

"She's my brother's sister which makes her mine," Caius said with his lower lip protruding outward and his body language conveying an immoveable conviction.

June concerned look turned into an amused grin, "you've always been a headstrong and stubborn child. You would be easy to dislike if you weren't so sweet." Her smile flattened and mist formed in her eyes. Caius blushed and looked down. Then with tears welling in her eyes she said, "since you were a baby, I have loved you as my own. You are a loving brother and treat all of us as family." This stunned Caius, June NEVER cried. "Your stupid, doomed to fail plan just confirms we really are a family. If so, we're going to keep our family together. We have land and we're going to work it."

A calmness and determination fell over Caius. He would free them all. If they wanted to continue to live at the villa with him as a family it would be a dream come true.

The only hope they had of paying their real estate taxes was the one-acre hobby vineyard his mother had ordered planted. She knew the owner of Gold Coast vineyard, the most renowned winery on Arista. She had been sold cuttings from their Pinot Noir stock at an outrageous price. Gold Coast never shared cuttings or any other secrets about their wine business. But the owner liked Jenny and was confident that nothing would come of it. His mother insisted she was going to be a vintner. She purchased a library full of books on grape growing and wine making but never got around to reading more than a few of them.

Years ago, this had initiated a 'family meeting' where it had been decided they had to produce drinkable wine. If they didn't, they would be blamed for sabotaging his mother's vineyard. It was decided that Sage, Caius, and Leo would grow the grapes and Oly would learn how to make wine. Oly was the natural choice because she possessed an uncanny sense of taste and smell, critical in winemaking according to one of the books. Caius's participation in this was of course voluntary, but he put in as much effort as anyone. It was incredibly hard work as there wasn't an irrigation system. The vineyard had to be watered by hand.

This was in addition to the daunting task of growing enough crops and livestock to feed everyone. His mother, again, had the opinion that her refuge from the world had to be disconnected from it. It had to be self-sustaining. Much like the vineyard, his mother's only contribution to this was supplying an extensive library of books on sustainable agriculture. Mixed in were books on agri-business. With wet winters, and bone-dry summers, it was challenging but possible. His mother's 'live off the land' fantasy was the reason they would survive.

The hobby vineyard was currently in its sixth year and its first harvest had been the previous year. They had produced 250 cases. His parents had been delighted with that first year's wine. His parents had expensive tastes so if they liked it might actually be good. Leo said that if they could sell two hundred cases for ten credits a bottle they could pay their property taxes and have enough left over to cover their other expenses. Even then Leo was the brains behind the business. He had devoured the business-related books in the library. He was passionate about building a successful winery business. Leo immediately pushed for expanding their vineyard. He told them that with only one acre a bad year could break them. For this they needed a more reliable source of water than a single well. With no power available Sage came up with the idea of building a gravity flow irrigation system. This was eventually done by forming a reservoir in a large ravine uphill of the farmable area of the property. Of course, this just added more work. But because it was their collective future the familial bonds grew stronger.

If they were going to successfully sell their wine Caius thought they had to have a gimmick. Caius's mother had been extremely popular, even if she was considered a bit of a crackpot. She had a natural charisma combined with a way of making people around her feel comfortable. He suggested they name the wine Jenny's Acre and combine it with Sage's suggestion of Dry Brook Vineyard. The latter being an inside joke about their plan to build a reservoir based on a brook that was dry most of the year.

At first Caius had been hesitant about using his mother's name. He had not forgiven her for his father's abuses. She should have stopped him he thought. After mentioning this to June she sat him down and said "You will never be free if you don't find a way to forgive. It will control you Caius. Honoring your mother by naming the wine after her is the right thing to do. For whatever reason, she was not strong enough to stop your father. But she was always pleasant, kind, and considerate to everyone in the villa. She is the reason we will survive. What is most important however is that she is your mother. You have an obligation as her son to honor her."

Caius had spent little time in Roma. But he had spent a whole summer there when he was fourteen and knew many of his parents' friends. So, they gambled. Money was extremely tight. They strapped two cases of wine to one of their two plow horses and sent Caius off with blankets, a handful of credits, and a lot of prayers.

When he finally arrived in the capital he hesitated. An entire week of sleeping by the side of the road meant he looked and smelled a bit rough. He knew his parents' best friends but was hesitant to knock on the door of an elegant domus while holding the reins of a plow horse.

His father and mother's best friends were avid wine collectors. Not an unusual hobby for the elite. The File's had a reputation for offering the best Arista had to offer at their parties. Deciding this was the best place to start he gathered his courage, tied up the horse, then walked up and knocked on the massive front door.

The butler took one look at him, wrinkled his nose, and said politely, "the service entrance is around back young man."

As the butler moved to close the door Caius put a hand up and said, "Jeffery, it's me, Caius Cereo."

Jeffery looked shocked. He wasn't used to seeing a member of the elite looking like a lost farm boy. Recovering, he took a few moments to respond. He knew the Cereo family had been broken with Adrian and Jenny committing suicide. While no one cared much for Adrian, Jenny was loved by everyone, including himself.

"I'm sorry. I didn't recognize you Caius. What can I help you with?" Jeffery assumed Caius was looking for a handout and if his master didn't give him one Jeffrey would do what he could. Unlike most wealthy citizens Jenny had always been very kind to him. She didn't treat him like a servant. He wasn't alone in this regard as other members of the staff had shed a few tears when the news about Jenny had been delivered.

"My parents built a vineyard at the villa, and I have wine to sell. I was hoping Mr. File could help me find a buyer," Caius asked with desperation clearly in his voice and manner.

Jeffery considered this for a minute then said, "go around to the service entrance and I'll meet you there."

When the servants entrance door opened, Jeffery was there with a man Caius didn't recognize. Jeffery smiled and said, "this is Oliver our sommelier. Can he sample what you have?"

"Sure," said Caius holding out a bottle he had pulled from one of the cases. He watched them both closely as Jeffery supplied a wine glass and Oliver carefully removed the cork. Oliver smelled the cork and then poured a small amount.

Oliver tentatively took a sip and after a moment looked surprised. He then swirled the wine in the glass, sniffed it, and then sipped again. He let it stay in his mouth longer this time. He smiled, handed the glass back to Jeffery and then raised a brow. He turned to Caius and asked, "How much are you asking for your wine?"

"15 credits a bottle," Caius said. The question had surprised a higher price out of him. The plan was to sell individual bottles and perhaps a case. With enough sales they could then bring the rest of the wine to Roma and hopefully sell it all.

Another look of surprise crossed Oliver's face, and he asked, "do you mind if Jeffery and I take this to Mr. File for his opinion?"

"Of course not. Do you want me to stay here?" Caius asked.

"Why don't you do that. I'm sure he would be pleased to see you, but he might be in the middle of something," Jeffery said. He then hesitated a second, and then turned to one of the servants and said, "would you ask Gloria to make master Cereo something for breakfast?" He then turned back to Caius and said, "we'll be back in a little while."

Jeffery politely knocked on Jovan File's office door and waited for a response.

"Come in," Jovan called out.

Jeffery and Oliver entered with Jeffery quickly saying, "begging your pardon sir, Adrian and Jenny's son is in the kitchen asking to meet with you. Jenny's hobby vineyard has produced some wine, and he would like you to help him sell it. I didn't want to put you in a delicate situation, so I got Oliver to give an opinion."

Oliver leaned forward and said with excitement, "it's not just good sir, it's exceptional. For new wine it's unusually smooth, like velvet on the tongue. The fruit is a complex mix that is in my experience unique. It's quite delicious. I need to spend some time with it to fully understand its complexity. But with age it will only get better."

"It's from Jenny's vineyard, really? I thought that was just a fantasy," Jovan said. "Do you have some of it with you?"

"Yes sir," Jeffery said and produced a wine glass with a small amount in it. Jovan swirled the glass, sniffed it, and then took a sip. His gaze quickly rose to look at Oliver with a pleasantly surprised expression on his face.

Jovan came down and greeted Caius warmly just as he was about to start in on an amazing breakfast. "Caius, it's so good to see you." He hesitated and his face took on a sad expression and he said, "I am so sorry about your parents; Jules and I loved them."

"The card you sent was very much appreciated, thank you," Caius replied. One of the reasons he had come to the Files was the thoughtful card they sent. Few of his parents' friends had bothered. They had even invited him to visit them the next time he came to Roma. It was that offer that emboldened him to knock on their door.

"So, you want to get into the wine business? Oliver tells me you are offering to sell it for fifteen credits a bottle. How many cases do you have?" Jovan asked.

"200 cases, most of this year's vintage," Caius answered.

"Is it here in the city? Your villa is quite distant," Jovan said with a slight frown on his face.

"No, I just have two cases with me," said Caius.

Jovan thought for a minute. "How about I buy all of it from you for ten credits a bottle. I'll pay to ship them. As soon as I find a buyer I'll send you the credits. Of course, I'll give you 240 credits right now for the two cases you have with you. Jules will be delighted to have your mom's wine in our cellar."

Caius was ecstatic but tried not to show it. 240 credits in hard cash was double what they found squirreled away in the villa. One of Caius's gifts was the ability to read people. He knew Oliver had been very impressed with the wine; he also knew Jovan was going to make a good profit on the deal offered. His dad always said Jovan was an excellent negotiator. But the offer on the table was their minimum asking price and they didn't have to pay for shipping. Deciding not to look like a rube he said. "If you buy all 200 cases, and pay for shipping, I'll settle for 12 credits a bottle." Caius was proud of himself for not taking the first offer.

"Done," said Jovan immediately, a bit more enthusiastically than Caius expected. He pulled Jeffery off to the side and whispered something to him. Then he turned to Caius and said, "I hope you can join us for dinner tonight. Jules would love to see you and I would enjoy catching up and hearing all about your vineyard." Smiling he waved and exited the kitchen.

Jeffery smiled at Caius and said, "Mr. File would like you to stay here tonight so you can rest up for the trip back. I'll show you to one of our guest rooms and let you rest and freshen up. Dinner will be at eight o'clock. Don't worry about your horse. We'll brush him down, feed him, and find a spot in the stable tonight.

It was the start of a wonderful day. He had a hot shower and was given clean clothes to wear. He ended up spending much of the day in the library marveling over the selection of books the Files had. Leo would be in heaven here he thought. He ended up writing down titles of books on business that he thought Leo would like. Perhaps someday he could surprise Leo with one of them as a present. Dinner at the Files was fancy, lengthy, and reminded him of the summer he had spent in Roma as a young boy. His parent's home, Domus Cereo, was large, elegant, and that summer was one long endless party. While he enjoyed people, and they liked him, everyone young and old seemed pretentious and uncaring. The Files were no different, although he did like them both. Seeing them now with a more mature eye he decided they just didn't understand what life was like for ordinary people. After some reminiscing about his parents Mr. File asked, "you said the two hundred cases were most of the vintage, how much more do you have?"

This increased his suspicion that the wine was worth much more than twelve credits a bottle. He considered his answer and said, "we have another fifty cases in storage but I'm going to hold onto that for a rainy day." Leo had insisted they hold onto the additional cases because he said if their wine really was good it would grow in value. It was Leo's opinion that they should never borrow money to fund their business. He said they were used to living modestly and they should salt away as much as possible for unforeseen expenses and future investment.

"Well, let me know if you would like to sell them. Be happy to give you the same price," Mr. File said with a smile.

That offer convinced him he had not gotten as good a deal as he could have. Oh well, compared to expectations he was very happy with the way the day had worked out.

The next morning after another amazing breakfast Caius said goodbye to the File's and left feeling like the world was indeed a wonderful place. He was wearing clean secondhand clothes, courtesy of Jeffery. He had a bag filled with fancy sandwiches from Gloria their chef. But best of all was the 288 credits he was on his way to deposit in the family's bank account. He couldn't wait to get home and tell everyone.

The conversation Caius had with Leo when he got home set the stage for their future business dealings. Everyone was thrilled he was able to sell all the cases. But Caius could tell Leo was not completely happy with how the negotiations had played out. Leo took a deep breath, and seemed a bit hesitant, but ended up saying gently, "Caius, you should have asked them what they thought it was worth instead of offering up a price."

"Sorry, you're right. I guess I got excited that they wanted to talk price so quickly. I knew it was a mistake at the time. I won't make that mistake again," Caius said sheepishly.

"You also should have told them we would take care of the shipping and payment was due on delivery," Leo said.

"Why do it that way?" Caius asked, confused, but with a facial expression and tone indicating he was honestly interested in the answer.

"Basically, they got three credits per bottle for shipping which comes to 7,200 credits. We could have shipped all 198 cases for around 2000 to 2500 credits total. In the future we should think about buying a cart and some oxen so we can do our own shipping," Leo said calmly.

"I'm sorry! I didn't realize that cost us so much money," Caius said feeling horrible.

"We're learning Caius. We'll make mistakes. It's ok as long as we learn from them," Leo said in a soft voice. "I just realized I made a mistake in saying we ought to charge ten credits per bottle. I did that based on how much money we needed instead of what the wine was worth. We should have investigated that. I'm really impressed you were able to sell the whole lot, and for more than our minimum. We thought you would sell the first two cases bottle by bottle and then come back for more. Your trip turned out much better than we dreamed it would," Leo said complimenting him. He hesitated, and then continued to explain. "There are two reasons for getting cash on delivery. The first one is the scenario where one of the cases falls off a shelf and bottles break. Who pays for that if the agreement is that we get paid when they are sold? The second is that with this agreement we are basically loaning them money at zero interest to stock their inventory."

Caius pondered this for a while. Then he said, "you

should be making our business decisions. But you're legally a slave so we can't present you as the head of the business. I know many of the elite families in Roma, and that is our customer base. So, I can act as our salesman." Caius stopped catching his brothers' eyes and said, "I have an idea. How about you go everywhere with me. I will present you as my valet. You will sit in on all the meetings and tell me privately what decisions need to be made. It's a bit odd, but if anyone asks I'll say you're providing security. You are quite a bit larger than I am." Then he stopped and looking embarrassed said, "You're not my servant Leo. I hate asking you to act like one."

Leo brightened and smiled, "that's a brilliant idea. We both know we complement each other. I'm no good at selling. Not really good with people. And you're not really interested in the business details." He hesitated and then said, "I've never felt like anything other than your brother Caius. I can play any role the family needs me to play. You would do the same."

It was just like Leo, pretending Caius didn't care about the business details. The truth was that he knew he didn't have the business sense and good judgement that Leo did. "Truth be told, the family needs you more than they need me," Caius said.

"Truth be told, you're full of shit Caius," Leo said, and they both laughed. Leo's expression turned serious, and then he said gravely, "I'm really worried about whether we can pull this off. I just have to look stupid. But you're going to have to convince people you're smart." Leo's frown turned into a sly smile and they both laughed again.

They found out later that their wine had sold for upwards of one hundred credits a bottle. Jenny had been well known and loved by the partying elite. Her orphaned son selling Jenny's Acre wine had a certain cache driving up the price. However, the real reason for its success was that it was a truly exceptional wine. The owner of Gold Coast Winery was outraged with their success. Dry Brook was a new competitor at the highest end of the wine business. He decided to try and take some of the credit by letting everyone know that Jenny's Acre was based on his root stock. Instead of diminishing Dry Brook Vineyards' reputation it had the opposite effect. Most wine connoisseurs agreed that Jenny's Acre was a superior wine to Gold Coast's pinot noir. Knowing they used the same root stock resulted in the conclusion that Dry Brooks soil conditions and wine making skills were superior. What still caused an emotional reaction for Caius was Mr. File's treatment of the increased price. He decided to split the increased price instead of pocketing it. While it was motivated by charity for the son of his good friends, it was the best investment he ever made. Jovon File was, and always would be, the sole distributor of Dry Brook Vineyard wines.

Caius was yanked out of his nostalgia when the door opened. Forti stepped through the door, looked at the two brothers and said in an amused and mildly sarcastic tone, "Theron, First of his Name, will see you now. As predicted, he's more than a little suspicious and very confused." They all shared a grim smile and walked in together.

CHAPTER 2

GENERAL HARRIS

Jack had informed Lord Druango a few days before that Trajan had been assassinated. They had gone over the details several times already and Jack was getting frustrated. The man seemed to be having trouble accepting that Trajan was really dead. That it had happened in the arena by one of the gladiators made it all the more unbelievable to him. Jack could tell the man was traumatized by his experience on Arista. Druango did not understand how anyone could get into the emperor's suite much less carry out an assassination. Druango was visibly relieved once he finally realized that Trajan was truly dead. But he was terrified by the fact that General Eastbrook was days away from overwhelming his rebel coalition.

"Lord Druango, we need to stop discussing the past and move to time critical matters. You are most fortunate that General Harris just completed a contract in Sector 26 and is relatively close to the wormhole. He can have troops on the ground in less than a week. To expedite matters, I took it upon myself to invite him for discussions. He will arrive late this evening. I expect you will want to hold a meeting with him first thing in the morning."

"Yes, of course. We are fortunate that General Harris is available. I understand he is considered the best of the mercenary generals," Lord Druango said.

"He has a reputation for quickly and efficiently defeating his enemies. He has never failed to collect full price on a contract. That makes him unique. It also makes him expensive," Jack said emphasizing the last comment.

"What does he want?" Druango asked.

"I don't know," Jack lied. "As you know the Commonwealth doesn't get involved in colony negotiations beyond providing mediation. Our role is to maximize trade across the Commonwealth. We do not interfere in colonial affairs."

The price for Harris was astronomical. It would impoverish the planet for decades. It would spike tax revenues due to contract payments. But it was a bad deal for Sector 27 in the long run. Julie being so supportive meant she must be getting some sort of kickback. It also meant the deal was being supported all the way to the High Council. Jack was amazed at how quickly Julie could recover in a crisis. He cringed a bit internally realizing his failed plans had caused more than a few crises for her recently. Arista having control of Liberty was clearly better for Sector 27 financials. But she didn't hesitate to change course when it became clear the Arista plan had failed.

"I guess it doesn't matter at this point. We really have no other alternatives," Lord Druango admitted revealing he had no bluster left to expend. "We can start at 10AM if he is available that early. I really don't want to waste time getting this done."

Jack had never been impressed with Druango, but this further degraded his opinion. He thinks ten o'clock is early! The man is weeks, perhaps days away from the gallows and he wants to sleep in. Unbelievable! "I will have him in your command tent at 10AM," Jack said. With nothing further to discuss he nodded his head indicating an end to their discussions, turned around, and headed back to his shuttle. No need to rough it tonight when he could have the conveniences of his space yacht. It would also be good to go over the plan with Harris one more time. The man was a narcissist and Jack needed to insure he didn't go off script.

The next morning General Harris and his staff had taken over the command tent by the time Lord Durango arrived. They had been pouring over his battle maps and grilling his army staff. Jack had agreed to touch down at 5AM so that Harris and his senior staff could get a better idea of what they were up against before the meeting started.

"Lord Durango, let me introduce you to General Harris," Jack said with a tight smile.

"A pleasure to meet you sir. I've heard much of your abilities and am anxious to see them in person." Lord Druango gushed.

"A pleasure to meet you as well my Lord," Harris said respectfully. "I am not in favor of non-combatants actually witnessing the fighting as you might well guess. I like to keep the person promising to pay me safe," he continued with a smile.

"We have common goals General," Druango replied with his own smile. Hesitating he ventured a question, "I understand your men have already spent a good many hours poring over the battle map."

"Not only that. We have a battle plan that should turn the situation around rather quickly. But before we get into that I would like to agree on payment terms," Harris said with a penetrating look.

"I'm glad to hear this should be an easy campaign for you. I hope that lowers the cost for this venture," Druango said before he even knew what was going to be asked.

Harris seemed irritated by the clumsy attempt to negotiate. "It doesn't," Harris said bluntly and sternly. "Our price is non-negotiable. My men just finished one contract and are due their normal rest and relaxation between campaigns. I have to pay a large bonus for each and every one of them to compensate for having no rest between campaigns. Even if that weren't the case you are not in a position to negotiate."

Druango was used to being in charge. He was clearly

angry at the tongue lashing he just got. But given the circumstances he could not afford to insult General Harris. With his face bright red, he gained control of himself and asked, "What do you propose?"

Ten million credits up front. After we suppress the revolution you will award us 80% of Liberty's portion of increased tax revenues for twenty years. There will be a twenty million credit completion bonus. It is customary that my army gets 30 days of free rein in the areas under rebellion. In addition, we will receive one thousand slaves from the rebel areas with the first choice in their selection. We will pay a fair price for property damage, or any slaves killed or permanently disabled during that time."

Druango was stunned. He had not envisioned this costing that amount of money, and for twenty years! He finally spit out, "That is an outrageous sum sir. How do you justify this highway robbery."

Turning to Jack, Harris said, "First Minister, can you take us back up to your ship so we can coordinate our travel home? I'm wasting my time here."

"No, wait!" Druango said in desperation. "I'm sorry, I don't mean we won't pay. I was just surprised at the cost. If you've looked at the battle map you know we don't have other options. We are forced to pay and pay we shall."

Harris stared at him for an uncomfortable amount of time. He was clearly driving home the reality that he didn't need this contract and could simply leave at any time. "I accept your apology. Papers for you to sign have been prepared. I expect to have signed copies before I leave this tent."

"I can facilitate getting the documents being signed and apply the Commonwealth's notary stamp. You can have the legal part of this wrapped up this morning," Jack said. Harris was a little full of himself he thought to himself. I hope he's not overconfident with Eastbrook. Too many have made that mistake already.

"Agreed," Druango said still collecting himself. He took a deep breath and said, "My men are prepared to review the current situation and offer advice on how to proceed."

"That won't be necessary my Lord," Harris said with clear distain. "Eastbrook's army is unsophisticated and have never gone up against a credible opponent. This isn't unusual in the backwaters of the Commonwealth. In addition to greater experience and expertise we outnumber your rebels significantly. As I said earlier, this won't take long."

"Eastbrook is very devious. He does things you don't expect. His armies have a history of overcoming larger forces. He has extensive knowledge of geography and how to take advantage of it. I implore you not to underestimate him," Druango said with great concern showing on his face.

Harris's senior staff broke into raucous laughter. After they quieted down Harris said, "We don't mean to be insulting, but your concerns are unnecessary. The best thing you can do at this point is relax and wait for us to remove your problem. My men will make landfall in three days. Just make sure you hold on that long and all will be well."

Later as Jack walked General Harris back to his shuttle he said, "I know your reputation. It is very impressive and unblemished by failure. I've watched General Eastbrook's tactics closely these past few years. I have no doubt you will prevail. But I would caution you to be wary. The General has done some rather remarkable things."

Harris looked at him with amusement and said, "I know you're not a military man First Minister. Let me assure you there is nothing to worry about. I know what I'm doing. You can tell the governor this contract should be closed out in a few weeks."

Jack would relay Harris's message to the governor. He would also caution her that the man was overconfident so she shouldn't be surprised if it takes longer than predicted. Jack hoped the man was right. If he wasn't, Jack knew she would ultimately blame him for the failure.

CHAPTER 3

THE SENATE

Tee had been in meetings all morning. He retained his sanity only because he had worked out with Forti early and then went for a swim. He was still amazed that he had his own private pool. It was unbelievably large and the one thing he truly liked about living in the Palatium. The extravagance of the Palatium boggled his mind. When he woke up he thought his bedroom was an entire home. It disgusted him knowing how many of Arista's citizens struggled simply to eat every day while he lived in outrageous luxury.

Listening to wealthy people complain about money was not something he enjoyed. His butt was sore. It was not the first time he had longed for the black and blue of Victor's training sessions. And it likely would not be the last. In his opinion getting the crap beaten out of him was much better than the life of an Emperor.

His frustration of having to participate in these ridiculous meetings was offset by his appreciation of Leo's and Caius's ability to manipulate these people. They were masters at preparing Tee for these small private meetings. He knew what decisions needed to be made before the meetings began. Caius guided these sessions without seeming to be the one in charge. While not everyone was happy with Tee's decisions today, no one seemed unduly offended. He guessed that meant a successful morning. Caius had explained how the power structure worked. His guiding advice was that the powerful had to be fed. And fed they were. It was disgusting to approve decisions resulting in riches being given to people who didn't seem to need or deserve them. God, he just wanted to be back on Pacifica with family and friends. His obligations from being a member of the Guard hadn't changed. He had committed his life to protecting Pacifica. This was the only way for him to do that for now.

Next up on the agenda was his first meeting with the Senate. He had already met Pluta, the magistrate of the Senate. It had been one of his first private meetings. At that meeting Tee informed the magistrate that he required the Senate to loan him Senator Cereo as an advisor. He explained that he needed the senators' help in acclimating to his role. It was a very tense meeting given Pluta claimed that honor should be his as magistrate for the Senate. Tee had to get forceful and demanding before Pluta relented. Tee could tell this man was going to be trouble.

With Forti's team surrounding him, Tee was suddenly outside the Palatium for the first time since becoming Emperor. It was strange to be outside again. No jailors, no shackles, but still not free. He walked down cobblestone streets past multi-story granite buildings. There was even a fleeting look at a large ornate marble fountain down one of the side streets. He would have enjoyed being a tourist for the day. But the harsh realities for this planet's citizens soured his enthusiasm. It was clear this was a paradise only for the privileged few. Several times during his walk to the senate he saw those who appeared to be beggars. Barefoot slaves in thin worn-out clothing were also evident. This might be a wealthy planet, but it was clear that the necessities of life were hoarded and withheld from those who desperately needed them. So different from Pacifica.

The Curia Julia was a reproduction of the senate meeting hall commissioned by Julius Caesar and completed by the Imperator Augustus. The choice was symbolic as its construction represented the transition from a Republic to a Monarchy. Tee had learned from Leo that democracy had disappeared since the collapse of democratic forms of government on Earth. He was told that Pacifica's republican government with elected officials was out of favor across the Commonwealth. Why this had happened was a mystery for Tee. From what he could see Arista's form of government wasn't working very well for its people.

As Tee walked into the senate building he felt uncomfortable once again. He towered over everyone. It was strange to be unusually tall and muscular. To have others think of him as physically imposing. He was much more comfortable just being part of the crowd. A low murmur had arisen as he entered the building. A hum of whispered conversations as they all stared openly at him. He stepped up on the dais, sat down, and per Caius's instructions turned to Magistrate Pluta nodded his head in greeting and said. "You may proceed Magistrate."

Magistrate Pluta gave him an oily smile, held his hands out to the assembled senate and said, "thank you all for responding to the compulsory order to meet today. As Magistrate I declare this meeting to be in session. First on the agenda is a proposal for a special vote from Senator Ricci. Senator, you have the floor."

Senator Ricci walked to the open area between the rows of senators. He was a robust man for those of Arista's stature. He was a warrior by training and a senator by birth. He stuck his chin out and said, "thank you Magistrate. Fellow senators. I propose a vote negating the succession." He stopped for a few moments to let the gasps die off. After the room became dead quiet he continued, "as you know the man currently calling himself Emperor is doing so under the pretense of archaic legal interpretations. Legal succession requirements have changed over the centuries. This is a fact. Succession by combat is not legal. The changes to the laws of succession over the years have been a natural evolution. Our society has matured. The colorful and brutal history of Arista leadership is valued by all of us. It is part of our inheritance. But it is far in the past. A sense of pride motivated previous senates to alter the law of combat rather than remove it entirely. They did so because they wanted to honor our glorious past. The alterations they made were clearly meant to eliminate personal combat as a legitimate avenue for succession. And rightly so. Limiting it to Ascension Day and declaring that the emperors' own weapons cannot be used against him was clearly meant to disable this as a method of succession. I also think it worth noting that the man calling himself emperor is not even from this planet. He is a slave, nothing more. We do not have to accept this. I do not accept this."

Tee marveled once again at Caius's prescience. Or perhaps he simply had a good spy network. In any case, he had predicted accurately what would be said, and who would say it. Tee had been waiting for the personal declaration. Caius had said it would come and he rose to play his part. "I accept your challenge," Tee declared loudly as he stood up and pulled his large ceremonial knife out of its sheath. As he stepped off the dais striding in the direction of Ricci. Caius stood up and moved to intercept him with one hand raised and said, "Your Eminence, I'm certain Senator Ricci did not intend to challenge your right to rule."

Although a military man, Ricci turned white. He gripped his own ceremonial knife but left it in its sheath at his belt. He had terror in his eyes and appeared to be getting ready to flee. He slowly composed himself once he saw Tee had halted. Then in a shaky voice he said, "what is this Cereo? I did not challenge Theron."

"Your confusion is understandable senator. A careful review of the law was performed after the events of the Accession Day celebrations. As head of the justice committee, I had intended on delivering this information today and apologize for not requesting that the magistrate let me go first. Just this morning the Justice Council came to a unanimous decision that Theron was within his rights to challenge the emperor Trajan. In addition, it was determined he did so within the legal guidelines. One of the conclusions from that analysis is that anyone who questions the emperor's authority is considered to have challenged him to personal combat." Caius explained patiently. He hesitated a few moments and then said, "I would also recommend you refer to him by his title instead of his name to avoid the appearance of a challenge. You are not family after all." Cereo then looked to Pluta and smiled. His subtle reminder of how Trajan used to refer to him obvious to all.

Pluta flushed at the last statement then turned to the bench where the Justices sat and asked, "Justice Wright, is that description accurate?"

"Yes Magistrate. The law is old and the legal language archaic, but its meaning is clear. The emperor can be challenged at any time. Acceptance of a challenge is only automatic on Ascension Day. Senator Caius is correct that questioning the emperor's authority in public is legally considered a challenge to combat. The Senate floor is considered a public place."

"Your Eminence, can you please forgive Senator Ricci this once. He clearly did not understand that his motion constituted a personal challenge. His confusion is understandable. I can vouch for his personal integrity."

Tee delayed long enough to peak the tension in the room, as Caius had instructed him to do, and then said, "I've been educated on my authority and responsibilities as Emperor. I understand that my authority can be challenged and am happy to defend it." Tee glared at Senator Ricci. "During my education I have also come to appreciate the complexity of Arista law. It is reasonable to assume Senator Ricci was confused. Given your assurance of his personal integrity Senator Cereo, I will forgive it this once."

You could feel the senate breathing a sigh of relief. They were accustomed to sitting safely in the stands while gladiators cut each other to ribbons. They were not used to being physically threatened in their hall of power. They had all watched Tee in the games and had no illusions about what would happen if he perceived a challenge. Magistrate Pluta paused a few minutes to confer with one of his lieutenants and then said. "Senator Ricci, do you withdraw your motion to vote based on the legal guidance from our Justice Council?"

Ricci couldn't get his response out fast enough, "yes Magistrate, I withdraw my motion."

"Good then, that matter is closed," Pluta declared and then he turned to Caius. "Senator, would you please lodge your requests for floor time before the meeting? Following our standard process would have avoided unnecessary confusion today."

"I agree with you Magistrate, and beg forgiveness. I will endeavor to be more diligent in the future," Caius said as they looked knowingly at each other. They both knew Caius had created this confrontation to shut down questioning of the validity of Theron's rule.

"That would be much appreciated Senator Cereo. Let's move onto the next proposal for a vote. Senator Potts, you have the floor," Pluta said.

"Thank you magistrate. With the approval of the Emperor, I'll read the motion." Potts looked over to the emperor's dais and received the traditional head nod to continue. That this courtesy had been missing from the first motion proposal was obvious to all. Caius had counseled Tee to ignore the initial minor insults because it would make his sudden challenge all the more dramatic. "The sudden nature of the succession has caused unease in Roma. Malicious rumors are flying around with regard to the intent of the 2nd Legions proximity to our capital city. There is a growing fear that property and lives are at risk. While the Senate believes these to be false, we must face the reality of the current mood in the city. I propose we direct the 2nd Legion to remove itself to a minimum of thirty miles from Roma. The proposal being that this requirement is in place until the senate votes to revoke it. As always, our vote is dependent on the emperor's approval," Potts said looking to Tee, who nodded approval.

Magistrate Pluta asked, "are their comments before we proceed to vote?"

"Magistrate, might I have the floor?" Caius asked.

"You have the floor Senator Cereo."

"I want to voice my strong support for Senator Potts proposal. We must do what we can in these times to calm everyone down. There are no immediate threats that require any of our Legions to be within thirty miles of Roma. Given that, let's put this requirement on all our legions. A minor change to what Senator Potts has proposed," Caius said to the surprise of the entire Senate. Everyone knew that Pluta's supporters wanted to separate Caius from the legion under the command of his son. Caius had lost some of his support with the succession. Many were suspicious that he instigated the entire thing as a means of grabbing complete control. It was rather obvious that he had something to do with it given Tee's insistence that his former owner become his key advisor. A role traditionally held by the magistrate.

Pluta looked pleased with this turn of events and quickly proposed, "if there are no further comments from the senate I move that we vote on Senator Potts proposal." It passed unanimously.

Caius raised his hand and said, "Magistrate, I have one more motion for consideration by the senate."

"Proceed Senator Cereo."

"I move that we vote to confirm Theron, First of his Name, as Emperor of Arista. Having the Justice Council announce their accension decision helps, but nothing would solidify public confidence and reduce fear like a clear public statement from the Senate."

You could see the wheels spinning as Cereo's foes looked for a way out. If they argued against confirming, Theron could rightfully view that as a challenge to his authority. Nobody wanted to die today. On the other hand, voting to confirm would publicly commit the entire senate to serve under Theron's rule. Pluta recovered first and said, "we all recognize His Eminence's legal right to rule. I think we can dispense with having to vote on it."

Tee was again impressed with Caius's premonitions. Pluta pushed back but used an honorific instead of his name. He glared at Pluta and recited his lines, "given the earlier confusion I think a vote would inspire public confidence. The only argument against a vote would be one that questions my right to rule."

The motion passed unanimously.

The rest of the afternoon was boring as seven other votes on mundane topics were made. As Tee walked back to the Palatium Caius whispered that he had done an excellent job. While Tee was gratified by the praise he was disgusted by his role. He disliked bullies and that was the role he played today. The political intrigue and positioning disgusted him. But he knew he had to fulfill the role laid out for him. He just kept reminding himself that this was truly the only path he currently had to protect Pacifica.

When he returned to the Palatium, Tee walked to one of the smaller courtyards in the large central garden. This courtyard was surrounded by a grove of dwarf trees. It was his favorite place in the Palatium. It was the closest to nature he could get these days.

Next on the schedule was something he had been looking forward to. A reward for the long and frustrating weeks of playacting. He waited patiently until Dobler was led in. Expecting a smile, he was surprised to see Dobler looking frightened, maybe even terrified. Tee mentally kicked himself. He was the God cursed emperor. Dobler was a slave. Not only was he a slave, but he was also Tee's previous jailor.

Tee stood up, smiled, and held his hands out wide in greeting, "Dobler, you're safe here." When the tension eased slightly Tee added with a grin, "you have given me no reason to harm you."

That got a nervous laugh out of Dobler remembering their first conversation. "I thought you would be merciful. But I did have the keys to your cell for quite a while," he said. Tee noticed Dobler had visibly started to relax. Then Dobler smiled and said, "I remembered on the way over here that I once threatened to hose down your cell with you in it." To which they both shared a laugh.

"Let's take a walk," Tee said as he beckoned Dobler towards a winding path heading deeper into the garden. Tee could see Dobler's head on a swivel as he took in the gross grandeur of it all. Perfectly manicured stone walkways with beautiful flowering plants all around. Hummingbirds flitting from flower to flower made it seem like something out of a dream. They eventually came to an impressive set of double doors with guards stationed at each side. With a nod they quickly unlocked the doors and ushered them into a mantrap corridor much like the one used in the gladiator residence. The purpose of this one was obscured by marble designs on the floor, flower stands, and gilded artwork on the walls. The painted mural on the ceiling was inappropriate in Tee's opinion. The nude woman that was its centerpiece was shocking the first time he had seen it. Tee was sure most would not guess the corridors' true function. He was sure Dobler would.

When the iron gates at the other end of the corridor were locked behind them by a second set of guards Tee stopped and said, "this is my personal residence. A good portion of my hometown of Apple Valley could live here in luxury." He smiled and shook his head still amazed by it all. "The tables are turned Dobler. I'm now your jailor. But before I explain why I asked you to come here I'd like you to meet your fellow prisoners." They turned down a hallway and Tee continued, "there are three guest apartments. Trajan used them for visiting family members. They are quite large, and you'll have to share yours." They walked down a long hallway and out into a small courtyard garden with a pair of small fruit trees and a fountain gurgling in the middle. Tee turned and walked over to one of three ornate doors positioned along the outer walls.

Tee knocked and the door opened immediately revealing an attractive woman with blonde hair that was starting to turn white. Her eyes were vividly blue and lit up with excitement. There was a younger woman standing behind her. Those blue eyes locked onto Dobler searching. After a few moments she whispered, "Dobby? Is it really you?"

Dobler froze with his mouth slightly open in stunned silence. When he recovered he said with recognition and deep emotion in his voice, "Jessie." He stepped briskly towards her and wrapped her in his arms. They just held each other for a long time. Then he stepped back, took both of her hands in his and just looked at her. "I can't believe it. It's really you." Then with tears streaming down his face he turned towards the other woman and with sudden recognition said "Sally?"

"Yes Dad, we got here late yesterday and have been waiting all day to see you." Sally pointed to Tee and said, "we couldn't believe it when he told us what was going to happen. I didn't even know if you or mom were still alive." And then she broke down crying as Dobler scooped her up into a bear hug.

After it all settled down a bit Tee said, "I can't free you and your family Dobler. At least not yet. You know my thoughts on slavery, so I won't say more about it now. Politically I can't do anything in the short term. You'll have this apartment within my private residence for your extended family's use. I would like you to be my personal valet and your family to help provide services in this private area of the Palatium. It won't be difficult; you know I have modest needs. I'll pay for any work your family does. I need those closest to me to be people I trust. Is that acceptable?"

With eyes still glistening, and voice choked with emotion Dobler said, "there isn't anything I wouldn't do for you Tee. We can never repay you for this. Whatever you want we'll be happy to provide." And looking for approval from his wife and daughter he was rewarded with enthusiastic heads nodding up and down.

"We'll talk more when you're ready Dobler. Until then take all the time you need with your family," Tee said. Then he turned and walked away.

As they walked into the apartment together he heard Jessie say, "you have three grandchildren and a son-in-law to meet." And with that they disappeared into their apartment and closed the door.

Tee was delighted. This couldn't have worked out better. Tee remembered explaining to Forti, Caius, and Leo that he wanted his private quarters to be a sanctuary. That it only be accessible to those he trusted. After some debate they agreed to pull Dobler from the Arena and search for his family. Caius was supportive but warned him, "it may be more painful for Dobler than not knowing Tee. But I agree, he has a right to know. Years ago, we searched for Leo's mothers' husband and found he had been murdered by his overseer. We also searched for Leo's uncle. In some ways that news was worse as there was no way to free him. He still toils in slavery today. This was all very distressing for Leo's mother. That was the bad news. The good news is that we discovered Leo had a half-sister. His mother views her as a daughter. Eventually I fell in love with her, and we married. My family is a tangled web Tee. But I could not have asked for a better one."

Walking back to his quarters it was the first time since just before the last GEM war Tee felt a measure of happiness. He was going to spend the rest of the evening enjoying that feeling.

CHAPTER 4

PARTIAL MOBILIZATION

As soon as Jennifer started the Committee meeting Del held up his hand, "You'll all find this hard to believe, I certainly did. Tee Stone is now the emperor of Arista."

They all sat and stared at him for a few moments until Griff said sternly, "that isn't funny Del."

"It wasn't intended to be. It's simply the truth," Del said with a slightly bemused expression.

Jennifer knew Del was a bit of a practical joker, especially when Griff was around. In fact, when they were together it was sometimes hard to distinguish them from twelve-year-olds. However, she could tell Del was serious.

"He's finally lost his mind," Griff said looking around at the other committee members.

"Perhaps. Always possible," Del said. "But we have intercepted communications that lead me to believe what I just told you. I have copies for everyone so you can judge for yourselves."

The room was quiet while they all read through Del's materials. Jennifer started reading and her disbelief slowly lessened and was replaced with amazement. The further she read the more she agreed with Del's conclusion. It was unbelievable. But it was hard to refute. No doubt something drastic had happened on Arista. One of the communications simply claimed Trajan had been assassinated. Another claimed that Trajan had been killed during the Arista New Years games. A third reported that a gladiator had killed

Trajan. That same communication claimed the event had triggered an ancient rule by combat clause resulting in the gladiator being named emperor. Multiple communications referred to the new emperor by his title. Theron, First of his Name, Emperor of Arista. Theron was a name unique to the Stone family according to Del's write up. It had been passed down for generations. This had to be Tee!

Griff put his report down and said, "if there was ever anyone who could have pulled something this crazy off its Tee. But if true, what does it mean?"

"It means there is a ray of hope. It means we might have someone on Arista with our best interests at heart. It doesn't mean he can do anything about it." Del said.

"If he's the emperor why can't he do whatever he wants?" Griff asked.

Jennifer spoke up and said, "we don't know what their actual form of government is. A monarchy can range from complete and total control to merely being a figurehead with no power. We believe Arista is more the former, but we don't know for sure."

"And, to top it off the Commonwealth has ultimate control of Pacifica. It may not matter what Arista wants," Del added. "The good news is that it appears Tee is still alive and might be safe. Although it's just as likely he's in greater danger now than when he was a gladiator. We just don't know."

They all sat for a while musing over the implications until Jennifer spoke up and said, "Let's move to our agenda as we don't have a lot of time. Del would you keep us updated on this situation?." Jennifer asked and with a head nod of agreement from him she continued, "Our agenda item is to discuss the massing of GEMs just over the horizon. You've all seen the report, so I won't go into specifics. Griff has a recommendation. Griff?"

"At the end of the last conflict, we were preparing to retreat back to the Landfall Dam. The force coming up against us is much larger. We need to recognize that we cannot stop the GEMs at the Wall. My recommendation is that we do two things. The first is to call for partial mobilization. If we strip the coastal forts and backfill with volunteers we can execute a retreat with only Guard and Wall Archers. It's critical the retreat be well planned and executed. Confusion or panic at the wrong time would result in a massacre." Griff stopped and looked around the room, "any questions so far?"

Kevin spoke up, "what happens to all the materials stored below the dam?"

Griff nodded his head and replied, "that's the second recommendation. We should move everything not needed for the retreat to storage facilities in Landfall City."

Jennfier let out a soft breath, steadied herself, and said, "once we start moving war materials people will quickly figure out we're giving up on the Wall. We're going to have to go to the Pacifica Council with both of these recommendations. We need their support to keep everyone calm. Any attempt to do this quietly will result in chaos."

"Del and I can talk the CGG into proposing both of these," Griff said with a slight frown. His face then took on a mischievous grin and he said, "Del can create another bullshit report. That and his ability to lie with a straight face will convince everyone it's real."

Del looked down at the table then and when he looked back up he appeared to have been hurt by Griff's remark. He took a breath and said, "my grandfather told me he would always be proud of me for telling the truth, no matter what it was. I'm not sure what he would think of me these days."

Griff went stone faced. He hesitated for a few moments and then said with conviction, "I think he would be very proud Del."

Wasn't it just like men to apologize without an apology, Jennifer thought to herself. All this craziness must be getting to Del. He's never shown weakness before. It was so out of character. That made it especially disturbing. The last thing they needed right now was for Del to fall apart. Breaking the uncomfortable silence she said, "let's vote. All those in favor of proposing a partial mobilization and relocation of war materials to Landfall City raise their hands." She looked around the room and said, "the motion passes unanimously."

Early the next morning President Malrey was sitting in her office reviewing military logistics. She had been preparing for the two council agenda items she would facilitate today. She had a good view of Landfall Lake and the city as sunlight winked on the horizon to start the day. She took a few minutes to watch the city awaken before taking a deep breath and getting back to work. Jennifer was exhausted. It wasn't lack of sleep or her workload. Although both of those contributed. It was the constant bickering at council meetings.

Today would be emotional. A partial mobilization wouldn't be a big deal by itself. But coupled with a motion to move most of their war materials to Landfall City was going to make for a difficult day. Those two votes coming together would make it obvious they were giving up on the Wall. Barlow would of course propose negotiating with the GEMs again. She would be able to stop that nonsense without too much trouble. His diminished support from the vote of no confidence fiasco continued. She continued to worry that his isolation would eventually cause even greater problems.

She was thankful Pacifica still had one trick up their sleeve. Unfortunately, it could only be used sparingly. After that it was a choice of retreating all the way to the protection of Apple Valley or spurring the Commonwealth into action. It really wasn't much of a choice. Their estimate was that half the population, maybe more, would perish in a retreat of that magnitude. Even if half the population reached Apple Valley, many would likely starve. The only responsible action was to hurl a few black powder bombs towards the GEMs and wait for the Commonwealth to arrive. She shuddered remembering what she would be required to do next.

A few hours later President Malrey opened the council meeting, "Del and the CGG have come today to provide background for the first two motions. Del will give an update on GEM activity and the CGG will offer solutions to counter the implied threat."

Barlow jumped in and said, "whatever is going on we should counter it with an offer for peace. If we're going to abandon the Wall anyway perhaps we offer them Landfall Valley."

Well, that came sooner than she thought it would. Obviously details on the two motions had leaked. Looking around the room she saw nothing but disgust on everyone's faces. Well almost everyone. Councilman Rickets looked like he was sympathetic to Barlow's request. Those two were going to cause trouble at some point.

Jennifer didn't hesitate. She immediately said, "all those in favor of adding an agenda item to discuss negotiations with the GEM's raise your hands."

Only Barlow raised his hand.

"All those opposed?" Five hands shot up. "I'm sorry Councilman Barlow but it doesn't look like there is appetite for that discussion today," Jennifer said crisply and then immediately followed it with, "Del, you have the floor."

The next three hours were completely dysfunctional. Councilwoman Ricks even joined the craziness by calling the CGG a coward. In her opinion they needed to stop the GEMs at the Wall no matter the cost. To his credit the CGG stayed calm. He pointed out once again that they had narrowly escaped a full retreat the last time the GEMs attacked. That retreat would have been a disaster. Children and non-combatants would have been trapped in a mass of people trying to escape. To make matters worse they would have lost all their war materials further strengthening the GEMs. He told them the Guard would stay disciplined and that a retreat did not require as many warriors as holding the Wall. Especially since the GEMs would be surprised. In the end both motions were approved. Unfortunately, they both won by 4-2 votes. Barlow and Rickets had both voted no to both measures. Jennifer could have understood a vote to block mobilization. That cost money. But leaving their vast military stores in a location that was likely to be overrun made no sense. Rickets had her worried. Since his son died he was voting irrationally. She hoped the disease stayed confined to the two of them.

Jay was tired. They had been spending mornings practicing a retreat from the Wall and afternoons moving materials. The Tram did most of the work lifting sacks of grain and armory inventory to the top of the dam road. But it all still had to be loaded and unloaded. He was tired. But not so tired that he wanted to go back to the barracks. So, Jay wandered the streets until he ended up in front of the Blue Heron Tavern. Suddenly remembering it was Friday night nostalgia drove him to enter and look around. To his surprise he spied Hestie and Diana sitting across from someone in a Guard uniform. Before he could exit quietly Diana recognized him and with a big smile waved him over.

"Jay, it's great to see you. Pull up a chair and join us," she said with enthusiasm as she glanced sideways at Hestie.

Diana seemed to do most things with enthusiasm Jay thought. It made it difficult to say no even if sitting across from Hestie was going to be awkward.

"Do you know Glenn?" She said motioning to the man he was now sitting next to.

They just looked at each other for a moment and then Glenn smiled and glancing back at Diana said, "yes we've met. Jay knows some of the members of my squad."

Jay smiled remembering when they met. It was in jail the morning after the brawl with Glenn's squad. He noticed Hestie's mouth had turned up slightly obviously remembering the story. "Good to see you again Sergeant. I've heard we have special assignments from Griff in common."

Glenn laughed and said, "yes we do. At least it keeps us both in good shape."

Jay smiled and turned to Diana asking, "are you staying at moms?"

"Yes, she's incredibly gracious. Arti and I just arrived today, and she insisted we stay with her. Turns out I'm staying in your room," she said.

"You're welcome to it," Jay said. Then with concern in his voice he asked, "How's Arti?"

"She's an incredibly strong person. But it's difficult," Diana said, losing the electricity in her smile.

Jay suddenly remembered what he had been keeping in his pocket. He pulled Tee's insignia out and offered it to Diana. "I took this off of Tee's spare uniform. I've been meaning to give it to Arti. Would you give it to her for me?"

Diana just looked at him for a few moments and with eyes misting up said, "don't you want to keep it?"

Jay took a breath and then pointing at the red stripe on his own insignia said, "this means Tee is always with me Diana. This one belongs with his mother."

Jay had been watching Hestie out of the side of his eyes the whole time he had been sitting there. She had been looking down and avoiding eye contact. As soon as he finished talking she looked over at Diana and said, "I have to go." Then looking at Jay for the first time she said in a soft but shaky voice, "It was nice to see you Jay." Then she simply stood up and left.

Diana looked confused, stood up, and as she went to follow Hestie said, "I'll be right back."

There was a few moments of awkward silence until Glenn said, "I'm sorry about Tee. Everyone I've talked to seems to think he was something special. I'm not sure Diana is ever going to get over it."

"Are you and Diana friends?" Jay asked.

"Not in the way you're asking. But we have become really good friends. We spend time together, but her heart belongs to Tee," Glenn answered, insinuating he would like it to be more.

"Really? Wow! She's all he talked about in recruit training. Claimed she was his cousin's girlfriend. But he did a horrible job of hiding how he felt. It was sad," Jay said.

At that point Diana walked back in and sat down. "Everything OK?" Glenn asked.

"Yeah she's upset. She's leaving tomorrow to go back up to Apple Valley." Diana looked over to Jay and said, "Grammy isn't doing well. With Arti and I down here more help is needed."

"Isn't she in school? Won't that be a problem?" Glenn asked.

"She'll just work out some self-study program and get her professors to approve it," Diana said. Then with the corners of her mouth turned up slightly she said, "she's likely the smartest person you'll ever meet."

Jay suddenly stood and said, "I have to go too. One of Griff's special assignments starts early tomorrow morning."

He started to walk away, and Diana rose saying, "I'll walk out with you Jay." Once they got outside she put a hand on his arm to stop him. When he turned towards her she said with her blazing blue eyes locked on his, "I don't know what's going on either."

"What?" he said, although he knew full well what she meant.

Diana stepped a little closer and said, "Hestie. She's either lost her mind or there is some secret she's hiding. Knowing her it probably involves sacrificing herself for some reason. She and Quinn are both hiding something. She is the least selfish person I know. One thing I am sure of is that she's wildly in love with you. She left because she just couldn't keep up the façade with you sitting there." Diana stopped for a moment and then said, "Don't give up on her Jay. The two of you are perfect together."

The only thing he could think to say was, "I haven't yet." Then he turned and walked off. He was embarrassed a few minutes later when he realized he hadn't thanked Diana for her encouragement. He hadn't even said goodbye. His voice had been cold and angry. It was rude. He needed to think so he took the long way back to the barracks. Diana said one thing he strongly agreed with, whatever was going on probably involved Hestie sacrificing herself. Jay could not imagine what that might be. He decided it was a good thing Hestie was heading up to Apple Valley. The GEMs were coming, and she would be far safer up there than down near the   Wall.

CHAPTER 5

CAVERNS

Colonel Peters came out of his field staff tent to a red sun dying on the western horizon. The cold mountain air was thin, and he was breathing a bit more deeply than normal as he walked uphill towards the command tent. After a few days at high altitude his body was starting to adjust. Putting that minor annoyance away he focused on what was troubling him. The war had been going badly ever since the mercenaries landed. The Royal Army was exhausted and in danger of becoming despondent. It took great effort for Peters to remain enthusiastic and pretend optimism in front of the men. He didn't think they bought the act. It seemed like they had been running and running to no apparent purpose. Occasionally they would stop, backtrack, and perform a surgical strike resulting in a surge of confidence. But then they would start running again. That they had lost few men after all these weeks was a testament to Perry's brilliance. That they were in a strategically perilous position was a testament to Perry's fallibility. Peters had read in one of Perry's military history books that the most brilliant of generals were also the ones most likely to make disastrous mistakes based on overconfidence. Perry had perhaps proven that observation these past months.

The worst of the blunders was allowing General Fedral and about a third of their army to get split off from the main body. The last reports of Fedral and his troops was from a scout who had watched them run away from battle in a panic. He described it as a complete rout. And for God's sake where were the auxiliaries? Fully half of the Royal Army were militias that could be called up and quickly incorporated into the professional army. The mercenaries had arrived so quickly that the process of calling them to duty had been late. The recently promoted Captain Graves had been sent out to assemble as many of the widely distributed militias as possible. He was tardy in returning with them. Was Graves too young and inexperienced for the mission? Did the militias refuse to honor their commitments? Had they joined up with General Fedral's command? Had some of them joined the rebels? Was the army currently under Perry's direction all they had? There were far too many questions without answers.

Thank God they had set up camp three days ago in a defensible valley near the peak of the mountain pass between Druango and the vast flatlands leading to the Royal Castle. The troops desperately needed the rest. But they would run out of food within the week. Now the difficult decision. Do they try and fight their way back into Druango or fight a running battle down the mountain retreating all the way to the Royal Castle. Waiting while their enemy strengthened the two ends of the mountain pass would be a grievous mistake. It was a trap that would close soon. They needed to choose a direction and attack. The only other option was surrender. Reports from the areas under occupation were bleak. Rape and pillage were commonplace. Citizens were being treated as slaves. Surrender was not an option as far as Peters was concerned.

The odd thing was that Perry didn't seem to be overly concerned by any of this. Perhaps he was exhausted, perhaps he had given up. Peters didn't know what they should do but they would have to act soon. Generals had been taken out of command by their staffs before in these sorts of situations. If Perry didn't start making rational decisions soon something would have to be done. The thought was deeply troubling. Perry was like a father to him. He could never repay the man for what he had done for himself and his sister. The difficulty, perhaps impossibility, in removing him was that his staff and the common soldiers worshipped him. They would follow Perry to hell. Unfortunately, that seemed to be the direction they were headed.

As he entered the command tent he looked around and saw discouraged faces all around. Perry walked in and looked around seemingly checking for something. He seemed to have found what he was looking for and started the meeting with a stern face. He turned to his head of security and said. "Sergeant Greaves, place Lieutenant Yelling under arrest." There was a sudden surge of movement from behind the staff officer as Yelling was roughly placed in restraints by a couple of Greaves men. "Search his tent. You should find a quantity of spice there and perhaps more evidence of treason. Bring anything you find back here by 2100 so we can hold a field trial." With that the man was pulled roughly from the room his face a picture of terror and panic.

"Gentleman we've had a traitor in our midst," Perry said with his face an angry mask. He looked around the room at all of them, "What do you do when you don't know who to trust?"

"Don't trust anybody," came the chorus. And for the first time that evening the corners of Perry's mouth turned up just slightly.

"I am sorry for the confusion and anxiety caused by my decision to withhold information from you. It's been difficult trying to explain our movements the past few weeks without being able to explain the end game. I trust everyone in this room with my life. Unfortunately letting our actual plans get into the hands of our enemy would cause more than the loss of my life. It would cause the loss of our freedom, of our future, of our humanity. We are literally fighting for our way of life. Our enemy intends to enslave us. They would force our families and descendants into a brutal life of endless work and poverty. All in the name of greed. They would do this without remorse." Perry hesitated then and looked around the table engaging each one of them with his eyes. Then he said, "before I outline our current situation are there

47

any questions?"

Colonel Pike spoke up. "What did Yelling do sir?"

"He exchanged information for spice. He's an addict. He's likely been one for quite some time. As you'll remember we spent months in Druango at the end of the unification war. I'm guessing he was recruited then. As you know spice is an extremely addictive drug that can only be produced by Commonwealth technology. It's not only prohibited by Liberty, but also by the Commonwealth. That makes it extremely expensive. He was hooked and decided to betray us instead of getting help."

Perry's chief logistics officer Captain Lowell then asked, "how long have you known?"

"I noticed early on that our enemy seemed to know details of our general plan. It was small things, nothing blatant. They did a pretty good job of hiding their knowledge. So, I tested my concern and discovered it was valid. At the time, I didn't know who the traitor or traitors were. But I knew we had a leak. It took about six weeks to identify and verify that Yelling was selling information. I did this with the assistance of Bria and sergeant Greaves. Bria's sudden interest in cooking was her way of gaining access to our stores to help with the investigation. Just so you know, she does not enjoy cooking so expect that to stop immediately." The command staff groaned at this news. She may not have enjoyed cooking, but she did produce excellent meals. The corners of Perry's mouth lifted once more. The thin smile disappeared, and he continued. "Captain, we'll talk later on how the spice was hidden in our ration deliveries. It was cleverly done. I don't hold you responsible but think it's a good learning experience. The only good thing I can say about Yelling is that it appears he didn't reveal our royal secret," Perry said. This was as close as anyone ever came to acknowledging that the woman they all called Bria was actually the queen.

Coronel Peters spoke up once more and asked, "so, what we've been doing the past few months has been part of a plan?"

Perry smiled broadly for the first time and said, "Coronel Peters, I can always count on you to ask the question everyone wants to ask. The answer is yes, I have not lost my mind quite yet." This comment caused an outbreak of nervous laughter. They were all thinking it thought Perry. He paused a moment and then said, "if there are no more questions I'll dive into our situation and what we're going to do about it." Perry paused again, looking around the table for any more comments or questions and then said, "gather around the map table and I'll explain. Our movements have led us to this mountain pass on purpose. As some of you know I like hiking in the mountains. As a young man I enjoyed exploring caves. There happens to be two large caves that connect creating a tunnel from one of the minor canyons off of this valley to a hidden shelf just above the valley below." Perry's staff leaned in towards the map table as Perry pointed out the locations of the cave entrances. "From that shelf is a narrow but navigable trail to this minor canyon extending off the valley below. The entrance to that canyon is narrow and well hidden by brush. That entrance is just behind the enemy's defensive position at the bottleneck. Years ago, before the first unification war, I had both cave entrances concealed." Perry smiled and looked around the table. "You could say this plan has been coming together for twenty-five years. As you know our scouts are reporting that the lower valley has been filling up with enemy troops in anticipation of an assault. They would be better served to starve us out but since they see us run at every opportunity they think they can end the war quickly. General Fedral was made aware of the traitor before he split off. Yes, that was a planned ruse. His orders were to retreat and locate Captain Graves. His units along with Graves militias should now be well hidden near the base of the mountain pass. General Fedral will be positioned to either ambush their retreat or attack their rear based on his judgement of the situation. We will leave just enough troops at the mountain pass above to hold off an assault from that direction. Our main attack will be just before dawn. Colonel Peters will take his rangers and slip in behind them by utilizing the caves. His orders are to attack after the main attack has begun or when he judges it most expedient." Perry stopped and looked around the table once more and said, "even with General Fedral and the militias we will be outnumbered tomorrow. Surprise is essential. We must quickly overwhelm them. We get one shot at this." Perry paused and asked, "any comments or questions?"

Then Captain Brush, a brash young man of great potential and a quick wit said, "Welcome back General, we've missed you." The staff laughed relieving the tension. Young Brush was well liked and probably the only one who could have pulled off saying something like that to the General. They all appreciated seeing Perry smile broadly once again.

The staff meeting broke up an hour later after the details of the next day's assault were discussed and finalized. Peters always marveled at how Perry could get each officer to internalize and own their own plan. Perry always let his staff determine the execution details for their units as long as it fit within the overall strategy of the battle plan. A young lieutenant Peters once asked him, "why don't you just tell us what to do?"

"Because you will execute your own plan better than one I give you. I might come up with a better plan, but it's only going to be better for me. As a leader your primary job is to delegate, not direct. Giving and obeying orders is critical, but your role is really one of support and mentorship. You just need to make sure that each one of your delegates understands the general plan and can do their job."

As Perry's staff filtered out of the command tent on their way to organize the assault, Perry said, "walk with me Colonel. I'm going to show you where the upper end of the cave system is." They walked in silence until out of earshot of the others. Perry then said, "you're wondering why I didn't include you in the people who knew we had a spy."

"I admit it's a question I have. It's hard to accept that you didn't trust me," Peters said with sadness in his voice.

Perry stopped walking, forcing Peters to do the same. He turned toward him moving close and said, "it has nothing to do with trusting your loyalty. I trust you with my life. I trust you with the Queens life. I don't trust your acting skills."

"Acting skills sir?" Peters said confused.

"One of the reasons your men admire and trust you is because you're an open book. There are no secrets. If you're angry, they know. If you're proud of them, they know. They aren't wondering if you have hidden opinions or agendas. Everything is there for everyone to see," Perry said. "If the entire command staff were concerned about my decisions and you weren't, Yelling would have known something was up. If you knew Yelling was the spy he would have seen the accusation in your eyes. I couldn't risk that."

Peters gave it some thought and decided the General was right. He was a terrible liar and hopeless at acting a part. He huffed a breath and said, "my sister always said I couldn't tell a decent lie to save my life."

Perry smiled, and as he slapped him on the back said, "it's a strength. I admire and value you because of it. However, it does have its drawbacks given this situation. You're a successful leader because of who you are. Don't think you need to change anything."

Early the next morning General Harris was a happy man as he walked briskly to his command tent. The Liberty contract was almost complete. By tomorrow, the day after at the latest, he could go enjoy the fruits of this planet for a month and then head back home. He was still trying to decide how to spend the money. If he were successful this would be an outrageously rich contract. And success was assured. The famous General Eastbrook turned out to be a dolt. No coherent strategy. Running away at every opportunity. A complete buffoon. He was ineffective at coordinating even simple battle plans. Something any of Harris's lower-level officers could have done successfully. Allowing his army to be split apart was gross incompetence. On the other hand, his focused surprise attacks were impressive. But perhaps that was Colonel Peters and not Eastbrook. It took more than good special forces to win a war against credible military men. He might look into purchasing Peters and perhaps a few of his officers. Decent special forces officers were hard to find. Offered a choice between the life of a mercenary and death by hanging was typically an easy one for his defeated opponents to make.

Harris's command tent was a bustle of activity. He frowned when he noticed Lord Druango and his cronies assembled around the coffee stand. Nothing worse than customers thinking they have something to contribute. They lost their war against this same Army. Any advice they might offer was worse than useless.

Grumbling to himself he said with a tight smile, "good morning Lord Druango. Are you here to witness our victory?"

"Good morning General. We are excited to see you so close to achieving the end of this," Druango said with a smile that didn't reach his eyes. "I would be remiss however if we didn't warn you once more than Eastbrook is not always what he seems. History would recommend caution."

General Harris just stared back at Druango attempting to get his anger under control. This was the worst part about being a mercenary. The customers. If you irritated them they could decide to delay payment. While the Commonwealth would mediate mercenary contracts they could care less about enforcement. That was between the colonies. His home planet wasn't even in the same sector. The only other option was to completely conquer the planet and hold it for ransom. A costly and lengthy process at best. No, he would have to feed this clown's oversized ego. "Your advice is appreciated but Eastbrook is badly outnumbered and bottled up. He is trapped in an indefensible position. The portion of his army we routed has disappeared like the morning fog and their militias never materialized. One good push and he's done."

"As you say, he's bottled up. Can't we just back off and starve him out? Seems the more prudent strategy," Lord Druango said clearly concerned.

"No need, his army is done. This effort has taken longer than I planned. Eastbrook's habit of running away from every battle has delayed the inevitable long enough. I'm happy for your group to witness this final assault but please stay back from the fighting. Getting too close to the action is an unnecessary risk." Just stay the hell out of my way he thought, although it would be amusing to see one of them get skewered. "Now if you don't mind we have a lot of work to do this morning."

To General Harris's annoyance they did not take the hint and leave. They did, however, stop offering advice. As his staff was discussing the order of battle a commotion was heard.

"Probably a localized raid," his chief of staff offered. "They do that sort of thing a lot."

General Harris nodded his agreement, and they focused back on their planning. Suddenly the command tent flap was swept aside, and a wild-eyed young Lieutenant ran in and said, "we are under attack."

General Harris turned to the overwrought young man and said, "of course we are. That's what happens when you decide to become a fighting man." His comment elicited a derisive laugh from his command staff.

The lieutenant was nonplussed by the insult however and continued, "Colonel Beaty said the upper defensive line has been overrun with enemy units attacking it from above and below. Somehow they flanked the main line of defense. He's ordered a general retreat and recommends moving to the other end of the valley to set up a new line of defense."

Harris felt a cold sweat break out. Colonel Beaty was a solid experienced officer. If he took it upon himself to call for a general retreat without discussing it with Harris the situation was really bad. This was obviously a last-ditch effort by Eastbrook. No reason to panic, but every reason to move quickly.

"Gentleman, you heard the report. Execute a general retreat to the far end of the valley and set up a line of defense. You have your orders." And with that the staff members ran out of the command tent shouting orders to their officers.

"General, we warned you about Eastbrook. He's lured you into a trap," Druango said with fury in his voice.

"Shut up and stay out the way Druango. If you hurry you'll avoid Eastbrook's troops who likely don't have a good opinion of you," Harris said as he hurried out of the tent to organize the retreat.

At the base of the mountain pass a scout traveled quickly but silently to the hidden encampment. Giving the correct passwords to the pickets he made his way to General Fedral's command tent. The assembled staff had been waiting all night for his report. "Excuse me sir," the scout said as he entered the command tent. "The attack you predicted has started. It appears to be successful so far. Fighting is heavy and enemy troops are retreating down the valley. They are making efforts to set up a line of defense at the lower end of the valley."

"Any signs of them planning to retreat beyond the end of the valley sergeant?" File asked.

"No sir," the scout responded.

Well, Perry's done it again Fedral thought. If he hadn't known Perry as long as he did he would have thought the original plan crazy. But Fedral had seen too many crazy Perry plans exposed as brilliance. Perry had somehow manipulated General Harris's movement and timing precisely. Right down to the day, location, and situation Perry had told him to be prepared for. The news of the leak had been one of the more shocking experiences in Fedral's life. A punch in the gut. That someone from the inner circle would betray them was hard to believe. Almost impossible to believe. The loyalty of Perry's troops was legendary. His direct staff was more a family than anything else. Regardless of who the traitor was, it would be a sad day when he was exposed.

Fedral shook himself out of his thoughts and said "We're going with Plan B. Captain Graves, hold the 2nd and 3rd militias in reserve a half mile back as we've discussed. Be ready to move up in support on my orders or on your discretion if conditions warrant. Gentlemen, let's move."

Late in the afternoon after a long day of fighting Perry barked out, "Colonel Peters."

"Yes sir."

"We need to break this line before they further stabilize their position. Take your rangers and attack the right flank centered on where that small stream flows through. They don't have earthworks setup properly yet to defend that streambed. It will be hard fighting, but we need to break through."

"Yes sir. Do you want to signal the attack, or should we go when ready," Colonel Peters said.

"Go when ready but Signal as you do," Perry said. He took a deep breath and reviewed their situation. Their initial attack had been a complete surprise. Harris's army had been forming up for an attack and were not prepared to defend. Peters flanking maneuver had been executed flawlessly creating a rout. While they had already captured roughly one third of Harris's men who had been positioned to attack that morning, the rest had escaped the trap. They moved quickly down the valley until facing resistance about three quarters of the way down. By midafternoon they had taken the valley but had gotten stopped by Harris's second line of defense. As always mistakes were made. Perry had given orders for Fedral to either attack if their retreat resulted in them abandoning the valley or wait until Perry's troops reached the end of the valley. He realized now that he should have ordered both ends attacked simultaneously. Given what his scouts on the cliff tops were reporting he believed Fedral had been discovered when he moved into position early that morning. Waiting for Perry had given them time to position themselves to protect against attacks from both sides. Harris had turned the bottleneck at the end of the valley into a fortress. Perry had to admit that Harris was a credible opponent. His army kept their composure and quickly established a defense against both ends of the pincher. It was a shaky but defensible position. These were well led and disciplined troops.

Perry and his staff were standing together on a low hill with a partial view of the fighting. Their growing assessment of Peters heroic charge was that the enemy had pulled troops from elsewhere and plugged the gap. The gambit had failed. Many rangers had been lost.

"Ideas gentlemen?" Perry asked. And as his staff shuffled their feet trying to come up with an alternative plan a messenger ran up the low hill out of breath.

"General! They're surrendering. The mercenaries are surrendering."

Turning to examine the battlefield once more Perry saw that the defense of the stream bed had suddenly collapsed. What was left of Peters' rangers were now pouring into the gap. How and why this had happened was a mystery.

What turned the tide was Captain Graves and his militias. The enemy had stripped defenders from the back side of the stream bed to stop Peter's assault on the front side. One of Graves scouts noticed the paucity of defenders in the area where the small stream flowed through. Graves could hear a major assault that seemed to be somewhere further up the stream bed. He recognized the situation, abandoned caution, and quickly drove right through it. Once the line was breached small mercenary units started surrendering. Graves soon connected up with Peters' Rangers. Harris's defense was cut in half. They now had gaps that couldn't be closed on both upper and lower defensive lines. Isolated groups began surrendering in mass. It all fell apart quickly.

One of Perry's genuine pleasures was awarding battlefield promotions. It was especially gratifying when the promotion was for an unusually noteworthy accomplishment. Captain Graves had thrown the dice at exactly the right time. If he had faltered, if he had exercised caution, they would likely be back to running for their lives. Perry had little confidence he could fool Harris twice.

Captain Graves was standing at attention in front of Perry's command staff. He looked awfully young, Perry thought. He also looked awfully nervous. Perry could remember his own days as a young officer hugging the walls at senior officer meetings. Being called to attention before all of them was intimidating.

"Captain Graves. For your courageous and meritorious service given during this campaign the command staff have approved promoting you to the rank of Major. You are being assigned to Colonel Peters as a Ranger unit commander. Let me thank you personally for your bravery and quick thinking. A lot of good men died creating the breach you so quickly took advantage of. Due to your actions, they did not die in vain."

"Thank you sir," Graves said keeping his features locked.

"My Queen," Perry said turning it over to Olivia.

"Major Graves. At General Eastbrook's recommendation, and my concurrence, army officers of special distinction are awarded the Royal Cross. This is in recognition of the enormous contribution you have made to the kingdom.

Those holding this distinction are rare. You'll find you're in good company," she said as she looked at Perry's Royal Cross pinned to his uniform. "My thanks, and the thanks of the kingdom for your service." The queen then stepped forward and pinned the Royal Cross to his uniform."

"Thank you Your Majesty," Graves finally got out.

Olivia looked him in the eye and with a smirk said in a conversational tone, "You can go back to calling me Bria now." This caused a general low chuckle among Perry's staff officers. Perry smiled thinking his adopted daughter was really stepping into her role. A queen to love and admire.

"Yes ma'am," Graves said with a smile breaking through.

Now that the pleasant portion of the day was complete, it was time for Perry to do his duty. It was a duty he took no pleasure in. A duty that would haunt him. But a duty that must be done.

Lord Durango was led in chains into the command tent along with twenty-two other members of the nobility. This group represented the core leadership of the revolt.

"Lord Durango. You and your followers are being charged with treason and rebellion against your rightful ruler and the kingdom. After the unification wars you all swore pledges of loyalty which you have broken. I am convening this court to dispense justice," Perry said with iron in his voice.

"You can't do that Eastbrook. Only the queen can declare war. She is also the only one who can authorize a Royal Army and name its leader. She is off world. The reconstituted House of Lords found her uncle guilty of treason. He was found wholly responsible for her abduction and transportation to Arista. This judgement voided his authority to act on her behalf. As you know he is still a fugitive. As Queen Olivia's fiancé, I was given the legal authority by the House of Lords to act as regent until she returns. You have no authority. I command you to set us free immediately. If you don't stop this nonsense now you'll hang for it," Durango confidently said.

As he finished talking Queen Olivia stepped out in her royal finery from behind a screened entrance. Durango's eyes grew huge, and his mouth dropped open. Those with him audibly gasped.

"Lord Durango. You are mistaken on a number of topics. Top of the list is the obvious fact that I am not off world. I have directed General Eastbrook to command the Royal Army and put down a rebellion against the crown. He is authorized under my declaration of war to hold military court hearings and dispense justice." Olivia paused and grimly smiled at Durango who was speechless with horror clearly showing in his eyes. "I'll also take this opportunity to break our engagement," she said tossing her engagement ring to his feet. "Now that the legality of these hearings is settled, I'll step out of the way and let General Eastbrook do his job." She left as quickly as she had arrived.

It took all morning to review the evidence, hear pleas for mercy, and pronounce sentence. It was a bit of a farse given everyone knew what the outcome would be. But Perry insisted they follow proper procedure. Executing the sentences, however, was over quickly.

Twenty-three corpses were swinging gently with the breeze as General Harris was led past them and into the command tent. He was clearly angry at being shackled and didn't hesitate to complain about it. "Will you take these ridiculous restraints off? I am willing to negotiate a surrender, but I expect to be treated with dignity during those negotiations," Harris said in a condescending tone. "Trying to scare me with those idiots hanging from the gallows isn't going to work. I have friends in the Commonwealth. They won't be pleased if I'm treated badly."

Perry looked at Harris calmly and said, "this isn't a negotiation. The only option open to you is unconditional surrender. If you refuse, we'll simply mop up the few units you left back in Durango's capital. It won't be difficult."

"I know Sector 27 is far away from the center of the Commonwealth, so perhaps you don't understand how these things are done. My benefactor will offer a reasonable ransom for myself and my army. He'll agree to some restitution, again provided it's reasonable," Harris said softening his aggressive tone a bit.

"I am not the one who's uninformed," Perry said. "Once you landed on this planet you placed yourself under the laws and authorities of the crown. You are not a prisoner of war General Harris. You are under arrest for violating the laws of this nation. A full set of charges await an investigation by our legal system." Perry paused and then added, "you are under a misperception if you think credits will take the place of justice for those who died and those who were abused."

Harris had a cold sinking feeling in his gut. He sensed that General Eastbrook was being completely forthright. He really wasn't negotiating. The general was intent on extracting some form of revenge. He had to admit the man had lived up to his outsized reputation. Underestimating the man was a grievous mistake. But he was clearly a rube. Harris's benefactor was an obscenely wealthy dictator of a collection of the oldest and richest colonies in the Commonwealth. His tentacles reached all the way to the High Council. His reputation depended on fulfilling his obligations. Harris had a contract with his benefactor and could expect it to be honored. The powerful Commonwealth authorities that took his benefactors bribes couldn't interfere directly given the strict non-interference Edicts. But it didn't mean they wouldn't act aggressively to assist his benefactor if properly paid. The bribes would be large, but Harris knew his benefactor's reputation was important enough to him to force payment. This was simply how things were done. He would have to bide his time and suffer this humiliation for now. Justice would prevail. Revenge would be sweet.

CHAPTER 6

COMMAND PERFORMANCE

Caius was intimidated and overwhelmed. Since boarding the Governors space yacht, he had been inundated by technologies denied to the colonies. It was the simple things that were the most appealing. He had spent a ridiculous amount of time turning lights on and off in his suite with voice commands. He kept changing the temperature and humidity just to see what it felt like. His bathroom was a marvel. Being wealthy he was used to indoor plumbing. But his toilet had an amazing range of capabilities from a heated seat to multiple options involving water cleansing. The shower was so complicated he gave up trying to figure it out. He was able to set the water temperature to his liking, which was good enough. Having water come from above and all sides was an experience. His skin was drying out from all the showers he was taking. He quickly became addicted to the information retrieval capabilities and entertainment. This was all accessed through a large screen above the desk in his assigned suite.

After an entire day of playing with technology he realized it was distracting him from planning through his various alternatives. The challenge with lies is that you have to remember all the details he thought. So far he had been able to tell a simple story. That simple story was going to require revisions that made it complicated. He had been a bystander. Now he was a major player. In the beginning he had simply been trying to delay an invasion of Liberty. Now he had to consider the complicated politics of three planets plus the Commonwealth. What gave him indigestion was that he had no idea why the Governor asked for a private meeting. The expense, time, and effort it must have cost to set up a meeting on A27 meant it was very important to her. He knew colonists were rarely invited to Commonwealth planets. What was her game?

The invitation had come in the form of two Commonwealth representatives showing up unannounced in the early hours at Domus Cereo. They explained they were there to escort Caius to A27 for a compulsory meeting with the Governor. Caius was told he had an hour to prepare and that he would be gone for an entire week. He was also told the Governor wanted this meeting to be kept strictly private.

Luckily, Leo had not gone to the Palatium yet. Leo had been in the habit of getting up early and working with Dobler on basic self-defense skills. As his brother had jokingly noted, "with all the crazy things you've been getting us into I thought I better learn how to defend myself." Caius also thought he was using it as an excuse to watch Forti and Tee train. Leo was fascinated by the raw athleticism of the two and enjoyed learning more about the martial arts.

Caius spent five minutes throwing clothes and toiletries in a bag and the rest of the hour planning out the week with Leo. They decided to hide the fact Caius wasn't in Roma. It was fortunate the Governor insisted on privacy. Pluta had observers everywhere and they would need help from the Commonwealth escorts to avoid detection. They would all go to the Palatium together and then the two Commonwealth escorts would appear to leave by themselves. Leo would leak out that the emperor had received a private message from the governor. That same morning the emperor was going to come down with a contagious illness. There would be enough concern that a quarantine would be placed on the private residence portion of the Palatium. Caius and Leo would unfortunately be caught up in it. Leo could navigate all the correspondence that would naturally flow back and forth.

There was a planet plus a business empire to run after all. If something especially tricky came up it would be communicated that Caius was very ill and would be unable to respond for a few days. It would work.

Caius decided the Governors insistence on his visiting A27 was based on intimidating him. The travel was already doing a good job of that. A simple threat to force him to take some sort of action could have easily been communicated through Jack. No, there was more to it. He was still working through his alternative stories when the shuttle from the space yacht landed. From there he was whisked off into an air taxi. Once again he was overwhelmed with technology. Transportation on Arista was simple. You walked, rode on something involving a horse, or traveled by boat. He had flown through space, been transported on some sort of moving walkway, and was now flying through the air in a pod that had whirling blades above it. When he first arrived in his suite on the space yacht the large display above the desk was showing a technology tutorial. It had clearly been created for colonists to enable them to use the common forms of communication, transportation, and personal comfort available on a Commonwealth world. How these things were accomplished was noticeably missing. While he had become aware of these conveniences from the tutorial, it scrambled his brain to experience them.

Taking a deep breath to ease the anxiety of flying through the air, Caius looked out over the countryside. It appeared to be an undeveloped paradise. Colonists believed the Commonwealth always took the best planet in each sector for themselves. What he had seen so far supported that belief. He passed over forests, grass covered plains, a major river, and numerous lakes. Snow covered mountains could be seen on the far horizon. Suddenly the air taxi cleared a series of low hills, and he saw a building sitting in a small, picturesque valley on the shoreline of an idyllic lake. It was the only sign of human habitation he had seen in the past hour. He wondered if the air taxi was the only way to get to this location. He hadn't seen a road in since just after leaving the vicinity of the spaceport. The planet seemed to be almost entirely uninhabited. Humankind had learned from the environmental disasters of the 21st century. Colonists kept their terraformed planets lightly populated. It wasn't enough to limit greenhouse gases. A healthy planet was one that didn't feel the footsteps of its human inhabitants. A27, however, was an extreme case of being kept in a natural state.

When they landed he was led along a stone walkway to what he now recognized as a residence. The formal garden that was off to one side looked almost as extravagant as some of the many courtyards in the Palatium. It was in the garden area he first noticed that servants had thin silver bands tightly wrapped around their necks. Then he noticed they all had blank expressions on their faces. It was creepy to say the least.

"Senator Cereo, thank you for making the trip," the governor said as she stood up from a small table positioned on a covered deck overlooking the lake. "Please join me for lunch."

"You have a beautiful home Governor," Caius said.

"This is my getaway. My main house is in the city, but I wanted to insure privacy, and I thought you might enjoy seeing some of the planet," the governor said smiling with her mouth while her eyes stabbed into his.

"The entire trip has been amazing. Thank you for hosting me," Caius said keeping his warm smile in place.

One of the blank-faced servants shuffled over to the table with a bottle of wine and two glasses. Caius looked up at him and froze. He was unable to hide his shock. Caius glanced over at the Governor, and she had that unblinking stare of hers in place. The corners of her mouth were slightly upturned in a smirk. She turned her head to look at the waiter and said, "I think you recognize Evans Senator Cereo. His new responsibilities are now more in line with his abilities." She turned back towards Caius and gave him a predatory smile. After an uncomfortable pause she continued. "Evans made the mistake of taking bribes from slavers. The Pacifica gladiator you know so well was the result of one of those bribes. That was a minor violation. He would have easily recovered if it were only that. However, being part of a conspiracy to kidnap the reining ruler of a Commonwealth colony violates the non-interference Edicts. Violation carries an automatic life sentence of service. I was fortunate enough to be assigned his caretaker," she said as Evans poured wine for them both and then stepped back from the table. He was the perfect waiter. Caius noticed the bottle he poured from was the original vintage of Jenny's Acre. June was a very good artist and had hand drawn all of the first year's labels. They were unique and very distinctive. It was likely the same bottle of wine Evans purchased at his charity event. The effect was a deeply chilling one.

They both knew Evans didn't have anything to do with the kidnapping of Queen Olivia. Caius knew Pluta had been involved but was likely innocent as well. Pluta was too cunning to take that kind of risk. He must have been trapped into it. That meant Jack and the governor planned and executed it. Caius made a show of thinking about this and then asked, "are all your servants criminals?"

"You're very perceptive, and yes. The beauty of our system is that we create low-cost labor for our society's needs instead of spending credits on prisons. The practice originated from the strict rules governing the separation of Commonwealth and Colony. Colony citizens, even slaves, are prohibited from populating Commonwealth planets," the governor said continuing her icy stare.

"Creative and efficient. I'm not one who likes to waste people or credits either," Caius said pretending to be impressed instead of horrified. "What have you done to make them so docile? It appears Evans doesn't even know who I am."

"He doesn't. It really isn't him anymore. He only knows

you are a guest, and he must do whatever you ask him to do. The process involves permanent changes to specific parts of the brain," the governor explained.

"What's the purpose of the collar," Caius asked.

"It's for training purposes. Pain and pleasure are useful tools for optimizing their contributions."

"Interesting. Is the process exportable to the colonies?" Caius asked.

"No, it involves prohibited technology. It's only used for the needs of Commonwealth planets."

"A shame. I could get more output from workers who aren't burdened by emotions and thoughts of things that will never be," Caius said with a conspiratorial smile. The governor relaxed a little and Caius could tell he had passed some kind of test. While he couldn't be sure, he thought she was unaware of how disgusted he was by this practice. This was evil beyond even slavery.

The governor looked at him for a few moments with her intense stare, seemed to come to a decision and said, "I asked you to come to A27 because I have an offer. I want you to be Sector 27's First Minister." The governor gave him a warmer smile, although her smiles never reached her eyes. Even her smiles were chilling.

Caius just looked back at her for a few moments thinking through his carefully constructed set of alternatives. While this specific situation wasn't on his list of possibilities one of his alternatives fit it reasonably well. "I'm stunned and flattered governor. I didn't know colony citizens could take on administrative roles in the Commonwealth."

"They can't. Part of the process is making you and your immediate family Commonwealth citizens. This is extremely rare and involves patronage from the Commonwealths High Counsel. Fortunately, I have connections, and this offer has already been approved."

Which meant corruption went to the very top of the Commonwealth thought Caius as he asked, "why me governor?"

"When you drop the façade you get right to the point. I like that," she said keeping her smile in place. "You started off being an annoyance and graduated rather quickly to a significant disruption. I decided to support Senator Pluta because I was concerned you would keep out maneuvering my First Minister. Then suddenly your gladiator slave becomes emperor though an archaic succession law and you now control the planet. To say I was outraged is an understatement. Next the Liberty Royal Army was successful against the best mercenary army in the Commonwealth. More plans up in flames. That this was something you warned me about made it all the more aggravating. After giving it quite a bit of thought I decided I needed a fresh start. I decided your creativity and ability to manipulate people to benefit yourself needed to be harnessed by the Commonwealth. So here we are."

Caius wondered what was going to happen to Jack, but he knew better than to ask. It would either be seen as worrying about trivial issues or worse having concern for the young man. Caius didn't trust Jack but there was something likable about the man. Dangerous as a scorpion, but likable. "What's in it for me? I already control a planet."

"Control of Arista is child's play compared to what you can do in the Commonwealth. I have meetings in the city this afternoon. I'll leave a compensation package for you to examine. I think you'll be delighted. Evans will give you a tour of the house while I'm gone as well. I'll answer any questions you have when I get back. I will want an answer tomorrow morning when you leave to go back to Arista," she said.

"Greater wealth is attractive, but it isn't my primary motivation. I'm interested in how aggressive you want to be in the sector. I wonder whether we can agree in principal on priorities and strategy. I'm not impressed with what Jack has been attempting to do. I assume that has been at your direction," Caius said with a frown. He knew it was a risk confronting her but thought she would respect rather than resent that kind of approach.

"You do have a rather large set of balls; I'll give you that," She said with her smile turning feral. "I am interested in your thoughts, but I will set priorities and strategies. What do you think Jack should have been doing? If we agree on that we are likely going to be in alignment longer term," the governor said with her most intimidating stare.

Caius made a show of coming to a decision. He huffed out a breath and said, "Ok. First of all, the strategy for Liberty has always assumed a military solution. This is unwise. The planet has been in a state of war for twenty-five years. The army is battle hardened. General Eastbrook was going to have a prominent place in military history books before this latest fiasco. He is a brilliant military strategist, and his men will follow him anywhere. His victory against General Harris just reinforces his reverence with the population. You want to harness that not go up against it. There will be a way in, but it must take the form of a trojan horse not the launch of a thousand ships," Caius said. When the governor nodded her head in agreement he continued, "but that isn't what's interesting in the sector. Pacifica is the prize. While its natural resources are attractive all on their own, its human resources are special. The people there can be utilized for heavy planet labor. Also, the wars they have been fighting against the GEMs for almost a thousand years have created a military that makes Liberty's Royal Army look like children playing. Can you imagine what a mercenary army of Pacifica warriors would bring in fees? My guess is that you benefit when services from your sector are paid for by another. " Caius stopped and got a head nod from the governor, he continued, "Jacks' attention would have been better utilized on efforts to turn Pacifica into a colony."

"It's easy to make that observation but do you have a plan that could achieve it?"

Caius sighed then took a deep breath and said. "I guess I might as well go full disclosure." He looked at the governor once more and taking another deep breath he said, "my plan all along has been to control Arista as a steppingstone to convert Pacifica into a vassal state. Theron is a member of their Guard. That has great prestige on Pacifica. I did some research on the original colonist manifest and their Ship 3 captain was a man with the last name of Stone. Theron's last name is Stone. All of their technology and most of their history was lost in the original GEM war. That means we can create a history and claim he is the rightful hereditary ruler. Now that he is officially the ruler of a Commonwealth colony he can make requests of the Commonwealth. What if he requests admission to the Commonwealth for his home world? The key here is that he is now aware of Commonwealth technology and has a legitimate claim as ruler of Pacifica. Under those conditions I imagine approval could be obtained. My attempts at developing a relationship with Evans was for that purpose, not just to be annoying," he said and gave her a mischievous smile.

The governor was clearly surprised by this idea. She gathered herself and considered it for a while. Finally, she said, "that might be possible. I'll need to investigate and perhaps have a conversation with my mentor on the High Council. Conquest of one colony by another is allowable but having one colony pull another out of its protected status isn't straightforward. There has to be evidence of industrial technology or second-generation warfare. But an argument could be made that knowledge of either of those is sufficient. It would take a while to prepare, and longer for the bureaucracy to approve, but perhaps possible." She stopped and thought some more and then said, "what would be your plan to increase revenues from Liberty?"

Caius gave her his best sneaky smile and said, "our trojan horse is a marriage between Theron Stone and Queen Olivia. He saved her from abuse onboard the slave ship and then they spent weeks living side by side. They think they are in love," he exclaimed with a smirk. "The first step is to orchestrate a marriage between the two of them. However, this does not unite the planets. Theron would only be

Queens Consort. All power would reside with the queen. If attempts to change Liberties constitution through her fail then we will need to assassinate the queen, her uncle, and General Eastbrook. It would then be revealed that rebellious members of the House of Lords paid for an assassination. Outraged, Theron lands with the Pacifica Guard and lays waste to the government. A new constitution encompassing all three planets is then approved. That new constitution would be based on Arista's. Timing of events is critical, but I believe it can be done. However, this cannot be done quickly. A complex scheme like this takes time to develop. I strongly recommend a focus on Pacifica and to deal with Liberty later."

She nodded her head in approval and asked with a puzzled expression, "if you are First Minister then who would have ultimate colony control?"

"Pluta."

"Pluta? I thought the two of you were sworn enemies," she said again clearly surprised.

"We are. But as I mentioned before I don't like to waste credits or people. He would be an efficient if unimaginative dictator. If you study his business practices he is very good at maximizing profits. He enjoys the detailed process of squeezing them out of every nook and cranny. He would initially hate being under my control. But once he realizes the vast power he can wield he would get past it," Caius said smiling.

"Document your plan and we'll review this evening. I have to admit I'm impressed, and I'm not easily impressed. It should be obvious by now that I don't handle disappointment well. If you can deliver we'll work well together."

"I'll put something together for you to review when you get back. By the way, what happens to Jack?" Caius said.

"Jack is a useful emissary but lacks the creativity and ruthlessness to operate at a first minister level. His family is wealthy. He will be sent back to enjoy a simple life of luxury. His father will attempt to disown him. He is a vicious little climber and will attempt to maintain his own career amidst this embarrassment. His motivation for his son's success is a selfish one. His mother will win the argument and make sure Jack lives a comfortable life," the governor said with a smirk.

"He's young and stupid. No question about that. But I think he did a passable job executing his plans. I agree he is acceptable in the role of emissary. Given those two attributes I might have something he could add value with," Caius said.

"Ok, we can discuss that sort of detail later. Will let you know when I've returned." And with that the governor got up from the table and left.

Caius spent the rest of the afternoon sitting at the small table trying to enjoy the spectacular view. He alternated between writing up his bogus plan and being paralyzed by sheer terror. The compensation offered was staggering. It included high paying careers for his son and daughter. It all amounted to an obscene amount of generational wealth for his family. The governor's get away was part of the package. She really knew how to sell. On the other hand, she really knew how to threaten. All of the lake house servants came with the property. Evans was obviously intended to be a constant reminder of what might happen if he failed.

Looking out over the placid lake he thought this was much worse than the worst-case scenarios he had imagined on his way here. He had been forced to go with the alternative Leo named 'pure insanity'. Then Caius smiled to himself remembering the governor's reaction when he proposed Pluta as dictator for Sector 27. That threw her off track. Keeping her a little off balance was useful. He knew the job offer was absolute. He either took it or would have an unfortunate accident in the near future. He would likely never get back to Arista if he didn't accept. He might even be added as a servant to her household. There wasn't anything he thought her incapable of. He kicked himself for throwing out the lifeline for Jack. Nothing but trouble could come from that.

How is my family going to survive this? Is it better to adopt Commonwealth citizenship and do the horrible things required with the hope he could make a difference in other ways? Is it better to sacrifice himself and hope his family survived? He knew what June would tell him. It was her mantra for tough decisions. "Just do the right thing Caius. You know deep down what that is." With that in mind he thought furiously on various options scheming away the sun-drenched afternoon.

CHAPTER 7

GRAMMY

Grammy was relaxed and satisfied at the end of the day. Her chores were complete, and she sat on the porch enjoying a spectacular sunset. The sky was a light blue smeared with clouds that were a riot of white, yellow, and red. Her conversation earlier with Hestie had gone much as expected. She could count on that girl to ensure her wishes were honored. Hestie had been reluctant to leave that afternoon, and Grammy had been reluctant to say goodbye. But other responsibilities beckoned and Hestie finally gave her a tight hug and hurried off. Continuing to sit out on the porch as it slowly grew dark Grammy was delighted to be entertained by the first dance of the fireflies that summer. It was her favorite time of the year. Eventually she realized she was nodding off and in danger of falling asleep out there. So, she stood up and went into the house. She changed into her nightclothes and laid down on the old bed thinking of her Pop. As she drifted off she transformed into Gertrude, the young vibrant woman she once was and always would be. Suddenly her younger self was standing at the kitchen sink satisfied that the dishes were done. As she was hanging the dish towel up to dry a handsome young man opened the screen door and peaked in. "Looks like your work is done Gerty, time to come sit on the porch with Tia and I."

"But Tee hasn't come home yet Pop," Gerty said with concern.

Pop gave her a warm compassionate smile and said, "he will Gerty, he will. His work isn't done yet. But yours is finished. Time to come rest."

Happiness and joy filled her as she walked out the door and onto the porch to be with her true love once again. Grammy passed peacefully in her sleep with a smile on her lips.

CHAPTER 8

RETREAT

Diana was on watch which was troubling. It gave her too much time to think. As always she wondered about Tee. How was he? Would he ever return? If he did would he share her feelings? Which led to Glenn's question at the Blue Heron a few days ago.

"I really enjoy your company Diana. Is it possible we could be more than friends some day?" Glenn had asked with an expression she wasn't sure was concern or desire.

Diana hesitated before answering. Glenn had become a really good friend. She liked his ethics, his humor, and his easy-going manner. His quick acceptance of her plan for the archers during the Apple Valley east incursion said a lot about his acceptance of women leaders. This was important to her. Looking him straight on she said, "I'm not interested any sort of relationship Glenn."

"If that changed would I have a chance," he asked probing.

She paused again giving it some thought, "if it changes then yes." And then she gave him a grin and teased him saying, "along with all the other handsome men running around here these days."

"That's all I wanted to hear." he said smiling. Then turning serious he asked, "until then can we continue to be good friends?"

"I would like that," she said and smiled. Then she felt guilty. She was in love with Tee. She was sure he was still alive. Arti and Griff were both hiding something about Tee, and she guessed it was more good than bad. Perhaps he was gone forever. But her heart still belonged to Tee. She wouldn't consider anyone else until she knew for sure he was gone. As she berated herself again for not telling Tee how she felt alarms sounded from sentries on the wall followed by a deafening roar. Torches on the wall were quickly lit and Diana gave the command to the two archers nearby to light the bon fires. Griff had insisted they not be complacent at night. He believed GEMs were intelligent and crafty. While they hadn't attacked at night in many decades he thought it was a ruse. At his insistence they had placed numerous piles of oil-soaked wood far enough out to be barely visible from the wall. They all went up with a whoosh and what it revealed was terrifying. There was a horde of GEMs running full speed towards the wall with ladders and other siege equipment. This was a full-scale attack. She hoped it would be a long night. The alternative was too horrible to contemplate.

Jay was sleeping soundly when the alarms went off. This was followed rather quickly by a horn signaling a full call to arms. This must be a significant raid he thought as he donned his breastplate and helmet. GEMs don't do full scale attacks at night, he thought to himself. He left off the rest of his armor as he didn't think they would go below the wall at night. That was best done when visibility was good. Strapping his round shield to his back, he jogged out the door of the barracks and towards his station on the wall.

"Jay, what's going on?" said a deep voice in the misty night air. Moose had appeared out of the mist and ran alongside him toward the Wall.

Jay recognized him and said, "I don't know Moose. We've never had a full call out in the middle of the night. Wouldn't surprise me if Griff decided we had gotten lazy and wanted to shake things up a bit. They took the stairs two at a time and when they got to the top they stopped and stared.

"Jay recovered first and said, "better get to your station

Moose. This is a full-blown attack."

"I wish Tee were here," Moose said before he took off running. Tee, Moose, and Rilla had been constant targets of Dee during recruit training. It had forged a bond between the three of them. He knew what Moose was thinking. Tee would figure out something to stop the GEMs. As Jay watched Moose running to his post he thought he was never going to accuse Griff of going overboard again. Everyone knew the GEMs didn't attack in the dark. He had been grumbling about the nighttime drills Griff had forced them to do. He even forced them to practice a full phalanx retreat in the dark. Lots of people were grumbling after that one. Never again he swore.

Arti had given orders for the Wall Archers to slow their rate of fire. This was so they could randomly limit their exposure in the arrow slits. With the height advantage of the Wall the archers had always prioritized GEM archers. The goal was to never let them get close enough to be effective. The GEMs had put out the bonfires almost immediately and had successfully moved their archers into effective range. They hid their archers in the gloom while their targets were well lit up by torches on the Wall. It was suicide to stand in front of the arrow slits and shoot continuously as they normally did.

"Arti, Griff says the Guard is slowly leaving the Wall to form up in the courtyard for the retreat. He apologizes but says we need to keep the GEMs off the wall," Diana said clearly concerned.

"Ok, signal the girls to double their rate of fire. Have the arrow monkeys bring us three sheaves of arrows and then head for the Dam Road. Tell them to run and that we'll be right behind them," Arti said. She was deeply worried. They had held the Wall so far, but the GEMs had not yet retreated. These were experienced warriors not the untested ones that usually came with the first wave. The plan had been to retreat as the GEMs were retreating and hope they didn't notice and turn back. Although they had practiced a retreat while still engaged, they always thought of it as the unlikely worst-case scenario.

Her arrow monkey looked terrified as she dropped off the extra arrows. Arti gave her a confident smile and said, "everything will be OK Louise. Run for the Dam Road and don't stop until you get behind the fortifications. You've done a wonderful job. I'm proud of you." That seemed to bolster Louise's spirits as she gave a faint smile and then took off running.

Arti took a deep breath and disobeyed her own orders. She stood tall and proud in her arrow slit and took down as many GEMs along the Wall as fast as she could. Almost through her second sheaf she was knocked off her feet with intense pain in her shoulder. When the shock from the blow lessened she looked and saw an arrow sticking out of her and blood spurting out from the wound. As her eyesight failed she thought, I hope Louise makes it. Then she passed out.

"There're on the Wall," came a chorus of voices up and down the length of their fortifications. Jay and Kale had ended up fighting side by side. While their section of the Wall was still under the control of the Guard it was clear the time to leave was now. "Let's go," Jay said, and they headed to the stairway with GEMs starting to come over the Wall behind them.

They bounded down the stairs and sprinted towards one of the openings that had been set up in the Phalanx. They were assigned to be part of one of the roving squads who would protect the ends and plug gaps as they emerged. Kale tapped Jay on the shoulder and said, "look, Moose is in trouble."

Jay's immediate thought was that Moose was on his own. In a full retreat they were ordered to go immediately to their new stations. Anything else just created chaos. Looking back, he saw that Moose was carrying someone. Another violation of the rules during a full retreat.

"Who is he carrying?" Jay asked just as he recognized the long braided red hair. It was Arti. Jay stopped and out of the corner of his eye he saw Rilla charge into the mass of GEMs that were starting to swarm around Moose. Jay couldn't help himself and charged into the fray as well.

"I couldn't leave her," Moose said in a weak voice. That's when Jay noticed he was bleeding profusely from several wounds. He had obviously fought hard to get Arti this far. Then Moose collapsed and Jay thought to himself this is the end. Kale had followed him and so far they had held the GEMs at bay but were starting to get surrounded.

That's when Griff showed up with the rest of Jay and Kale's roving squad. They quickly opened up a corridor for retreat. Rilla had forgotten all his training and turned into an out of control killing machine. He wasn't responding to the retreat order. Griff yelled. "Rilla, drag Moose back behind the lines." Hearing his bunkmates' name and a promise of safety for his friend he stopped moving even deeper into the GEMs and did as Griff ordered. "Jay, Kale, right and left. On my cadence."

Jay got safely back behind the Phalanx just in time to see Moose breath his last. Rilla was sitting on the ground next to him holding his hand. He turned to Jay and Kale and said, "he was the best bunkmate ever. Thanks for helping. At least those bastards won't abuse his body. I know Griff is going to be pissed but I'm forever grateful."

Jay looked for Arti and saw she was being tended to by a medic. Griff was standing over her with a look of desperation on his face. That was new. Griff exchanged some words with the medic and seemed satisfied by her answers. The anxiety melted away and determination took its place. Griff turned and hurried off shouting orders. As Jay glanced back at Rilla an image of Tee flying up and over the training Wall suddenly entered his mind. Moose and Rilla, what a pair. He was going to miss Moose. But this was not the time for nostalgia. The Phalanx was backing its way towards the Dam quickly, and thankfully it seemed to be working reasonably well. Time to get back to work. "Rilla, get your ass over here we have work to do," Jay shouted bringing Rilla out of his grief. He and Rilla then chased after Griff who was plugging yet another hole in the line.

It was mid-morning, and Del was standing on top of the Dam with President Malrey and Griff. They were looking out over the mass of GEMs in the valley below the Dam. They were clearly trying to bring equipment in to undermine the Dam. If successful it would leave Landfall Valley indefensible. Eureka Valley would fall quickly as well. Tourists he decided. It made no sense for them to have any more of their warriors in the valley below than it took to destroy the Dam. Such was the unorganized chaotic nature of GEMs. They were celebrating. Well, that was about to change he hoped.

When the Landfall Dam had been constructed it was done with all the technology available to the original colonists. Advanced metallurgy had enabled gates to be placed near the bottom of the reservoir for the purpose of cleaning out sediment. They did this every few years at night on the ocean spillover side which hid it from view. There was another route that followed one of the original bypass tunnels when the Dam was first built. This one emptied out in the valley below. They had never opened this one. Much was riding on it working after all these years. If opened, the valley below would quickly and dramatically flood. They heard it before they saw it. Suddenly the rock camouflage covering the old tunnel entrance below exploded outward with an impressive torrent of water. Panic ensued as the GEMs realized they were all about to drown. As predicted, the Wall created a barrier and a dam of sorts at the far end. Thousands and thousands of GEMs flailed in the rising water and died. This was even more catastrophic than lighting the moat had been.

"Signal them to close the gate," Griff said as he looked

over his shoulder at the alarmingly low level of Landfall Lake. "We might be able to do this one more time even if they quickly regroup. Hopefully, this slows them down enough to refill but we shouldn't count on that." Griff hesitated a few moments and then said, "They're even worse at swimming than we are." It was a good attempt at humor, but it only elicited a few strained smiles.

"We need to be realistic." Jennifer said quietly. "We owe it to the people of Pacifica to consider executing our alternative. Even if none of us want that."

"If we're going to be realistic we need to consider what happens to them if we do execute that alternative. I'm not convinced we should do that until all our options are exhausted. They are likely to be enslaved rather than saved," Del said in a whisper. "In any case I agree it needs to be discussed."

Griff huffed and said, "We are a long way from being defeated. Once the waters recede we'll reclaim the Wall. My hope is they will decide the retreat was merely a ruse to drown them. Given enough time we'll be back to a full lake. They will tread carefully approaching the Dam after this."

"Tomorrow morning we'll regroup and discuss the way forward. Griff I want to thank you for the tremendous job the Guard did fighting off the nighttime attack. You're mostly intact even though losing the CGG is a big blow. For now, you are the acting CGG," Jennifer said.

Griff respected Jennifer too much to make a scene here. He would not join the officer corps even if he were temporarily in charge. She would have to make it a political position of some kind. He was proud of Nate. On the other hand, he was disappointed in himself. Perhaps his training had been insufficient. The man had never learned to retreat properly. But, he had gone down fighting taking quite a few GEMs with him. That was what every member of the Guard aspired to do.

It had been a busy couple of weeks for Griff. The Guard had been working long days and nights to clean up the mess. The dead GEMs had been a horrible clean up job. The stench of the burning bodies had choked Landfall City for days. He was glad that part was over. Getting the Wall back in shape was much easier than he thought it would be. There was sand everywhere but that was much easier to deal with than mud. Not that there wasn't a lot of back breaking work to do. The bad news was that the moat was now partly filled with sand. At this point they weren't going to risk anyone trying to dig it back out. It was still deep enough to be serviceable.

Arti was out of the hospital and convalescing at the Phillips residence. She had almost died from blood loss and was lucky the arrow didn't cause permanent damage. She would be back on the Wall eventually. That was a big relief to Arti. Griff had visited her in the hospital as soon as they would allow visitors. It was so good to see her out of danger. He had been beside himself with anxiety when he first saw Moose carrying her across the battlefield. Then he had rushed in to help, breaking his own rules. Later, he lectured Jay and Kale on not following their retreat orders. They had just stared back at him incredulously until all three of them broke out laughing.

He intended to just check in on her given that she had made it clear she didn't want to see him anymore. He should have stayed away but couldn't help himself. He remembered their conversation with a smile. "Just wanted to make sure you're OK and see if you need anything," Griff said stiffly. He was alarmed at her appearance. She was shockingly pale and looked completely exhausted. Her shoulder was heavily bandaged up. It was obviously painful from the way she was holding it.

"Come sit on the bed beside me," Arti said softly. Griff dutifully sat down. "I want to apologize for getting angry with you over whatever is going on with Tee. He's my only child and his disappearance has torn me apart. I took that out on you and I'm sorry. I realized after giving it some thought that you must have a good reason for keeping whatever is going on secret. I know you. I should have realized you would tell me if you could." She smiled weakly and then said, "I would like to be friends again if you'll have me."

"You don't need to apologize," Griff said firmly.

"Yes I do!" Arti said even more firmly with color rising in her face. "Accept the apology with some grace instead of telling me I don't owe you one."

This was the Arti he knew and loved. "Yes ma'am. I accept your apology. You are forgiven." Griff said softly with a half-smile breaking out on his face.

"That's better," she teased, her voice soft again. And then they spent the next two hours talking about everything and nothing at all until the nurse showed up and kicked him out.

Griff arrived early in the evening at the Phillip's home. It had become a daily ritual. Pam greeted him at the door. "Good evening Griff. Am guessing you're here to see Arti again," she said smiling with just a hint of a smirk.

"Yes. Sorry to be interrupting your household Pam," Griff said.

"You are never a problem Griff. Arti loves your company and I'm rather fond of you myself," Pam said warmly.

They talked for hours until Griff finally blurted out. "There is something I've been wanting to ask you." He could feel his face reddening. "Well, I um, I mean we've been seeing a lot of each other and um." And then he was at a loss for words.

Arti looked at him with a mixture of pity and amusement. Then she said simply, "Yes, I will marry you." Griff was dumbstruck. This wasn't how this was supposed to happen. He sputtered and tried to formulate a response when she added, "that is what you were working yourself up to ask?"

Griff just stared at her for a moment and then stuttered,

"Yes, but I mean um."

"Griff, we're too old to be wasting time. Once I saw the real you, I fell in love. It's hard to tell, but I'm guessing you feel the same," Arti said with a smile.

At a loss for words Griff lunged forward and kissed her pulling her into a bear hug. "Ouch, I'm still healing Griff," she said sharply but with good humor. "Goodness, you are going to have to work on the 'sweep me off my feet' part of this."

Griff grabbed her again, but more gently this time and they both laughed with joy.

CHAPTER 9

RUINED

G rant Parsons was ruined. He alternated between bouts of deep depression and outrage. How could the survey's engineering team have missed the hidden bypass tunnel? How could they not see such an obvious way to protect the dam? His job as an anthropologist did not include making those kinds of assessments. This was entirely the fault of the engineers.

His bookie didn't care. Grant had gambled everything. More than everything. The worst part was that he had been so confident he borrowed from loan sharks. All his legal means for borrowing money had been exhausted. So, he had utilized the not so legal means. These people would not accept a bankruptcy filing. His debt would never be easily wiped away by the justice system. Those who lived in the shadows would take nothing less than his life if he didn't agree to do what they demanded. Grant would be working hard the rest of his life with all of his money going towards paying interest on a debt he would never be able to pay off. The major financial institutions of the Commonwealth were all powerful. They had made borrowing money from unauthorized sources just as illegal as providing the funds. They completely controlled the business of credit. While those who had loaned him the money could disappear, he didn't have the knowledge or means to do the same. The bastards would gladly provide evidence of his avoidance of borrowing from legal sources if he tried to turn them in.

What was even worse is that he was blacklisted. These people were well connected with the bookies. None of them would take his bets, even small ones. Perhaps it was a good thing he was stuck out here in the middle of nowhere. His luck would change. This run of bad luck would turn. He just had to be patient.

CHAPTER 10

ACQUIESENSE

Pluta was aggravated as he walked up the stone walkway towards a deck overlooking the lake behind him. It had taken three days aboard the governor's wasteful space yacht to get here. Three days his business managers were free to make idiotic decisions. He told Henry to inform his callers he was on a weeklong vacation. The man had just stared at him for a few moments. He finally accepted the explanation and simply said, "yes sir."

Surprising the unflappable Henry had provided Pluta with some entertainment to offset his foul mood that morning. After Henry recovered, he hurried about packing Pluta's personal effects. At least his butler could do simple jobs reasonably well. He had written out detailed instructions for Henry to deliver to his managers. He didn't trust any of them to execute those instructions correctly, but what other option did he have? A bunch of idiots he thought. The worst part of all was not having access to his business records. Those were all contained in handwritten journals too voluminous to bring. He was told in no uncertain words that he could only bring one bag. He did discover once aboard ship that he had access to his bank accounts. So, he contented himself with watching the financial transactions for his businesses as they were taking place. He took detailed notes on these transactions so he could grill his idiot business managers when he returned.

He was pulled out of his ruminations by a cold voice, "Magistrate Pluta, welcome." Looking up he saw two differently colored cold eyes staring at him. He kicked himself for not paying better attention on the walk up.

"Thank you for inviting me Governor. It's been a very pleasant experience," Pluta replied while trying to smile convincingly. Her stark white hair and disturbing eyes made him uncomfortable. The trip so far had not been pleasant. But, it had been illuminating. Pluta guessed most would be impressed with the conveniences provided by technology. He was disgusted. They indicated an indulgence in wasteful activities. The Commonwealth was obviously soft.

"Please join me for lunch," she said sweeping her hand towards a small table on the deck.

After sitting down, she dispensed with small talk. "I know you dislike wasting time as much as I do. So let me get straight to the point. All of your plans to increase Commonwealth taxes and trade revenues have failed. I've watched Senator Cereo systematically outmaneuver you at every step along the way. What excuses do you have to offer?"

Pluta was not used to being treated this way. He hesitated, turned beat red, took a shallow breath to try and calm himself, and in a fit of panic decided to blame Jack, "it's not my fault your First Minister can't do his part." He was trying to hide his fear with false bravado. It was clear from her expression that it wasn't working.

She nodded her head to herself as if verifying what she already knew. Then after a few uncomfortable moments she said, "my First Minister did fail to perform. That doesn't excuse your incompetence. The plans relied on you having the situation on Arista in hand. You obviously had no clue what Cereo was doing and were completely unable to stop it once you did."

"I can hardly be blamed for a gladiator killing the emperor. I'm not responsible for Arena security. Who could have guessed that an archaic succession law would make the slave emperor. I will admit Cereo moved quickly to take advantage of the situation. For that I am guilty," Pluta said after deciding she wanted a confession.

"Well, I'm glad you take some accountability. Perhaps there is hope for you after all," she said sarcastically. Then she just stared at him.

Finally, Pluta gathered his courage and said, "what can I do for you governor?"

"I hesitate to ask you to do anything." Then pointing a finger at the waiter she said, "I might as well ask Evans." For the first time Pluta looked at their waiter and noticed the blank expression. He also noticed the thin silver collar around his throat. He recognized the former Chief Justice with alarm. A sharp stab of fear hit him in the stomach as he realized the implied threat. He either performed or he would end up performing similar tasks to Evans.

Fear turned into anger, and he blurted out, "I have nothing to fear from you. I am a colonial citizen. The Commonwealth protects colonial citizens if they haven't broken any laws." Pluta immediately regretted what he had said.

She just stared at him some more. The long silence was extremely uncomfortable. Then she said, "I'm afraid you have broken Commonwealth laws. You paid a large bribe to the Chief Justice to kidnap the ruler of one of our colonies. That violates the non-interference Edicts. Being a colonial citizen does not protect you from complicity in that crime."

He was trapped. There was nowhere to go except to accept his fate and do whatever the governor wanted. She would not have paid to have him travel here just to murder him. Would she? So, if she wasn't going to murder him what did she want?

"I am at your disposal governor. What do you want me to do?" Pluta asked contritely.

She looked at him with an unblinking stare for another uncomfortable minute and then said, "I want to you to be dictator over all the colonies in Sector 27."

Pluta just stared back at her longer than was polite before

recovering from the shocking statement. He swallowed hard and said, "I would be honored governor." He hesitated a few moments and said, "how am I going to accomplish this?"

"That's the first intelligent thing you've said. Recognizing your incompetence to figure this out on your own is a good start. Given your business success I assume you can implement better than you can plan," she said, then waited for his submissive head nod to continue, "We are going to set up your good friend Senator Cereo to fail and then you'll pick up the pieces."

"Nothing would give me greater pleasure governor," Pluta said with a real smile on his face.

"Now you're worrying me again magistrate. I don't care about your childish competition with Cereo. The only goal should be an increase in tax and trade revenues. Are you capable of maturity?" she said sarcastically.

"Yes governor, my apologies," Pluta said. She made him feel small. Something he hadn't felt since he was a child. It made him angry and desperate for revenge. He stopped himself from that train of thought when he realized she just offered him dictatorship of the sector. This was beyond his wildest dreams. Perhaps he could kowtow to this bitch long enough to gain control of the colonies. That damn bribe to get a Pacifica gladiator was the worst of disasters. She had banking records and the ship manifest to burn him anytime she chose.

Another long silence with her eyes locked on his. Then she said, "this is strictly private. Jack will have his role, but he has been told to support what Cereo is doing. He does not know you and I are having this conversation. You will remain in the background for now until I give you instructions. Instructions I expect to be followed to the letter."

"Yes ma'am," was all he said.

Her face took on a thoughtful expression and she said, "what assets do you have within Cereo's businesses or residences?"

"None. The man is incredibly private with his slaves. His business associates are heavily compensated. I have been unable to turn any of them," Pluta said with a straight face. He hoped she didn't see his lie. He did have one deeply entrenched operative. He was very proud of how he had accomplished it. The assets value was too great to reveal.

"Well, I guess that aligns with your general level of incompetence on anything not strictly business related. Keep trying. Even a fool gets lucky sometimes," she said dismissively.

"Yes ma'am," he said, thinking it was the only thing he had said to her so far that hadn't resulted in demeaning criticism.

"Finish your lunch and then get back to Arista. Wait there until I tell you what to do. Do not take any actions against Cereo in the meantime." She stared at him until he nodded his head once more. Then she slid her chair back and without saying goodbye stood up and walked into the house.

He just sat there for a while somewhat in shock. He felt he had come out of this better than expected. Being handed the dictatorship of the sector was better than any of his guesses at what this meeting had been about. The downside was that he didn't trust a word she said. He had to admit that Jack delivered everything he said he would deliver. So perhaps this would all work out in his favor. If the only thing that happened was the destruction of Cereo he would be satisfied. So, given the situation he needed to consider how he could increase the rate of receiving intelligence from his agent. It had to be done without jeopardizing the situation. Reports once a month were not sufficient given what he had just been told. Something to ponder on his way back.

CHAPTER 11

VILLA CEREO

Against her better judgement, Bria felt at home. She and Gloria had ended up on a country estate that reminded her of her father's ranch. June, the head housekeeper, had greeted them warmly that first day. She moved them into an older, medium-sized, no-frills home that was on the other side of a very large vegetable garden from the big house. Bria was told they would live with June and her father. They were each given two small but clean rooms next to each other.

June was an older woman with hazel eyes, short grey hair, and a slim figure. She obviously spent a good part of her day in the sun as her skin was tanned to a caramel color. What struck Bria the most however was June's warmth. Although she was Bria's captor, she instantly sensed that June was a good person.

The next day June sat the two of them down and said, "all slaves are well treated here. Senator Cereo expects everyone to do their job, but he doesn't allow mistreatment." She turned to Gloria and in a soft voice said, "I heard you had a horrible experience during your travel from Liberty. That won't happen here. If anyone makes you uncomfortable, tell me, and I'll take care of it."

"What is expected of us?" Bria asked defiantly.

"Nothing from you. We know you're not used to physical labor or housework. Gloria can continue in her duties as your servant, and if she agrees, I could use some help redecorating the senator's villa. I heard she was responsible for redecorating the Royal Castle in Liberty. Senator Cereo told me reports from our ambassadors say it's spectacular. We aren't fancy here, but adding a little flair for the main house wouldn't hurt," June said smiling.

"I'm going to need something to do. We aren't idle in Liberty," Bria said.

June frowned, considered what Bria had said, and then offered. "This is a working villa. We grow our own food. There is a large vegetable garden, fruit trees, and a small vineyard the household staff manages. The villa also raises animals but that's done at another location. Senator Cereo doesn't think our guests from Roma would appreciate the smell so it's well away and downwind from the house," June said with a grin. "If you want to help me in the garden and vineyard that would be greatly appreciated."

This is not what Bria had expected when she left the auction house. Senator Cereo had a calculating smile that didn't reach his eyes. The other man bidding for her seemed cold and angry so she guessed she should be grateful he didn't win. Gloria had been quite upset when they were separated from Tee. He was going to the oft-mentioned Arena, which sounded horrible. Bria had to admit she felt safer with Tee around. Even when he was chained up. A few days after his murder spree the new guards started making lewd comments. Tee firmly told them to stop being disrespectful. Even with him locked behind bars, the threat emanating from him was enough to change their behavior. She wished she knew what had happened to him.

Life at Villa Cereo was predictable and peaceful. She rose early and joined Gloria, June, and June's father Sage for breakfast. Sage was an ancient but agile man. He was consistently polite and considerate. It was an easy household to blend into. After breakfast Gloria would go off with Sage on her main house redecoration project. Gloria had confidentially told Bria that the main house was plain and drab. That it desperately needed a makeover. Gloria was given a modest but adequate budget and between herself and Sage she was transforming the place. Gloria had slowly relaxed and was happy to be doing something she enjoyed. This helped lower Bria's anxiety over their situation.

Bria and June would spend mornings in the garden and afternoons doing house chores. Months of working in the garden had tightened her muscles and slightly darkened her pale skin. She actually had a tan which delighted her. Not that it was all that noticeable to anyone but herself. At first June tried to give her tasks that were easy to perform. She soon learned that Bria could match her work output. They fell into an easy companionship that was comforting. Perhaps too comforting. While June had informed them that she and her father were slaves, everyone treated them as if they owned the place. It was actually hard to believe any of the people she came into contact with were slaves. June mentioned one morning that she had known Senator Cereo since he was a baby. Another time she had casually mentioned that her son was Senator Cereo's valet. What was somewhat odd is that when talking about the senator her voice was always warm. It was understandable that she might avoid speaking badly of her owner. Nothing good could come from that. But it seemed like she admired and cared for him. Perhaps her family held a special place within his slave hierarchy. It was a little suspicious, but then Bria knew she tended to be a bit paranoid.

She wasn't the only one with suspicions. One morning a couple of months after Bria arrived June said in an offhand manner, "Your Majesty, If I didn't know better I would think you grew up on a farm."

They had visited the villa's livestock fields and yards the previous afternoon. Bria had asked a few questions. Thinking back on the conversation she realized they were questions someone with livestock knowledge would ask. Bria hesitated and then said, "please call me Olivia. There is no need for formality in the garden." Bria paused and held up her dirt covered hands smiling. "I told you we keep busy in Liberty."

June just nodded an acknowledgement. But her face clearly showed she had doubts. She liked that about June. Questions were common, but Bria's answers were never questioned. Her adoption of Grace perhaps had something to do with June's suspicions as well. While visiting the fields one of the field hands told June, "the runt of the litter isn't going to work out." He pointed to a young Australian Sheppard. "she has a good temperament but she's too stubborn to be useful."

"What's she stubborn about?" June asked.

"She's really smart and great at herding. But she herds the sheep where she thinks they ought to go. Not where anyone else wants them to go," he said with a smile. "Would be a good family dog if you want another one up at the Villa."

"I'll take her," Bria said quickly. She couldn't help herself. It was tricolor and beautiful. It appeared happy and friendly. She was used to having working dogs around her on the ranch. "I mean I'll look after her if that's ok."

June had searched Bria's face until it was almost uncomfortable and then said, "Ok, she's yours." And that was that.

Late in the afternoon June slipped away and went to the main house. She walked in the back door and wrapped her arms around Leo and then Caius. "I am so glad you're both here. Sorry but the two of you will have to stay here at the main house. I put Queen Olivia and Gloria in your bedrooms. I wanted to keep a close eye on them. Cara has blended in nicely with the household staff as well. She's staying in the women's bunkhouse."

"Is Cara still terrified of everyone?" Leo asked.

"She's better. But she still looks at your shoes when she's talking to you. Probably just the trauma of it all. Imagine being kidnapped and sold into slavery on another planet.

95

Then she gets thrown into that Pacifica gladiators' cell as a prize. That he treated her kindly doesn't change the horror of being told what was expected of her. This was followed by a slow walk to his cell. She was a simple farm girl before all of this," June said with concern.

Caius nodded his head and asked, "how is Queen Olivia going to take our story."

June thought for a few moments before answering. "She's smart, courageous, stubborn, and levelheaded. The big issue is going to be trust. Living with Grandpa and I these past few months will help. I think she does trust the two of us for the most part. When it's clear we're slaves in name only she may feel she's been lied to. That won't help. She's a good person. We should eventually get her to a good place. My concern is that we don't seem to have much time."

"You're right, things are quickly spinning out of control," Leo said. Then turning to Caius he asked, "if we can get agreement on a plan can we delay the Commonwealth?"

Caius shook his head slightly in the negative and said frowning, "if we can get agreement on the plan proposed to the governor we can only slow its implementation a little. Anything else is going to cause her to change course. I can't predict what that new course would be."

"Let's meet with Queen Olivia in the garden tomorrow morning. Since you're going to expose everything we need to be careful we don't get overheard by the house staff," June said.

Bria had gotten in the habit of taking Grace on a long walk each morning before breakfast. Instead of her usual path she decided to go take a peek at the main house. Last night the main house had been glowing brightly which was new. She wondered if that meant Senator Cereo was in residence. As she rounded a corner she almost ran into Leo. "Excuse me Your Majesty. I didn't see you."

Bria was startled but recognized Leo from the auction

house. He had been polite but distant, which she had appreciated. "My apologies as well, It's Leo, right?" When he nodded yes she said, "I'm not used to seeing people out early in the morning."

"Well, it appears we both enjoy an early walk. I find it clears my head for the day," Leo said conversationally.

There was an awkward silence until Grace padded over to Leo and gave him a good sniff. He held his hand out to her, and she licked it. Bria couldn't have been more surprised. She wasn't sure why, but she had expected Grace to dislike Leo. Grace had strong opinions about people. She mostly liked everyone, but those she didn't Bria had learned to be cautious of.

Leo bent over and petted Grace for a few moments and then said, "Senator Cereo came in last night and would like to talk to you this morning. June thought right after breakfast would make sense."

"I look forward to it," Bria said cutting off further conversation. She had to stop and motion Grace to follow her as she was obviously enjoying Leo's attention. I'll never figure that dog out Bria thought to herself.

Breakfast started out uncomfortably as Bria waited for June to bring up the morning meeting with Senator Cereo. After everyone had served themselves June said, "Senator Cereo came in last night and asked to meet with you this morning. I hope you're OK with that."

"If he's here to set me free then I'll meet with him. If it's anything else he might as well go back to Roma," Bria said briskly. She had given the meeting quite a bit of thought since she had run into Leo. She decided she needed to make a strong statement about her displeasure at being held against her will.

June looked at her with sympathy for a few moments and said, "that is a reasonable stance Olivia. Can't say I would feel any different if I were in your shoes." She then took a deep breath and let it out. "Would you do me a personal favor and just listen to what he has to say?"

Bria looked at her for a long while thinking it over. June had been nothing short of wonderful to her given the situation. While it galled her to give in, this was a small request given the relationship they had built. "Ok, I'll listen. But I won't promise to be polite or compromising," Bria said sternly.

June grinned and said, "I would expect nothing less."

Senator Cereo was sitting with Leo on a bench up against one of the covered garden boxes. It was a popular place for private conversations. Bria and June sat down across from them. "Good morning Your Majesty."

"Good morning Senator," Bria said coldly. Grace was acting odd. After sitting down, she pressed her body against Bria's leg and growled once low in her throat. Grace was looking at the senator while she did this which confirmed Bria's opinion of the senator.

Senator Cereo smiled grimly, then took a deep breath and let it out. "I know you want your freedom and to be allowed to return to Liberty. That is our desire as well," he said motioning around to Leo and June. "However, simply letting you go at this time has serious adverse consequences for three planets. To explain all of this I have to reveal secrets about my family that have been kept for thirty-five years. Secrets that could destroy us. I'm going to trust that you'll keep them in confidence regardless of how this plays out."

"I can't promise that. I will do what is right for my people. If that involves revealing information detrimental to you and your family I won't hesitate to do it," Bria answered with her head held high and a defiant look in her eyes.

Caius hesitated a moment, and with the corners of his mouth upturned slightly he said, "Well, I suppose that's fair. June claims you are a good person, and I trust her instincts. We'll just have to trust you." Taking a deep breath he said, "the story starts 51 years ago when Leo and I were born..."

Two hours later Bria was in shock. That was the only word for it. Everything she thought she knew about the senator, Leo, and June had been upended. If any of it could be believed. She did admit it went a long way towards explaining the oddities she had seen. Sage and June's authority. The way servants were treated. The affection for senator Cereo June had been unable to hide. The story made all of these make sense. That Tee had somehow become emperor of Arista was simply impossible to believe. Could this all be some kind of elaborate ruse? The wonderful news, again if it could be believed, was that her father had defeated Lord Druango who had been backed by Commonwealth funded mercenaries. Eliminating the threat from Lord Druango and his cronies was almost too good to be true. That her father supposedly hung the whole lot of them saddened her. Not because of who had been executed, but how she knew those deaths would haunt her father. She knew he would feel he had failed somehow. The hope that her father and Olivia were safe lifted her spirits. If the war was won, why hadn't they admitted the wrong person was kidnapped. This meant there must still be a threat to the kingdom. It was possible they were simply concerned for her welfare and waiting to play that card. If Tee truly was the emperor, she couldn't imagine him doing anything other than letting her go. If everything is true then the threat from the Commonwealth was real and the answer to all her questions. Only time would solve this mystery. Until then she would follow her father's advice. "If your enemy makes a mistake, don't correct them."

"You must have some plan in mind." Bria asked.

"Any plan for dealing with this must ultimately come from you and Tee. You are the legal decision makers for Liberty and Arista. I am happy to share ideas once we can include Tee in our discussions. For now, I would like your agreement to travel to Roma. Gloria will also be asked to join us. She can go home as soon as we can secure transportation," Senator Cereo said.

"I need to give all of this some thought," she finally said. "Can we meet again tomorrow?"

"Thats fair," Senator Cereo said. "Your head has to be spinning from our crazy story. If you have questions just walk over to the main house. We will answer any questions you have. Just remember that the house servants think we're reasonably nice slave owners. They don't know we are anti-slavery revolutionaries." He smiled at Bria, stood, and started to walk past her towards the main house. Grace stood up and approached him. He held out his hand and she gave it a sniff. Then she licked it and sidled up to him. After a few pets she turned back towards the bench where Senator Cereo had been sitting and growled low again. Crazy dog she thought. Crazy or not she seems to like Senator Cereo after all. In Bria's mind this was no small thing.

"Maybe there's something in the planter. Grace doesn't normally act like that," June said. "I'll have someone clean it out later."

As they walked away, a small figure hidden under the tarp shifted slightly. Hours of lying motionless had left Cara stiff and sore. That was all forgotten in her excitement. She knew this might be a place they would meet to talk and had decided to gamble. This was better than her wildest dreams. Now what to do with the information? Should she go directly to the Commonwealth with it? If so, how can I do that safely? Should she sell the information to Pluta and let him go to the Commonwealth? Given what she had just learned about Pluta should she blackmail him? Maybe a combination of both? She would think carefully through her alternatives before acting. This was the opportunity of a lifetime. One thing was certain. She needed to escape and be well hidden before revealing anything. She had dealt with men like Pluta many times. They had a habit of killing those they thought knew more than they should. She would need to disappear for good. Turning to more immediate concerns she gritted her teeth. That damned dog almost ruined everything. Cara hated dogs. They were simpering parasites. She should have poisoned the mutt weeks ago when it was obvious it didn't like her. Her motto was to eliminate anything that could cause a problem. However, at this point she needed to lay low and escape as soon as possible. Her escape would have to wait until the courier showed up. They had an extraction agreement. Pluta knew nothing about that alternative plan. Cara always had a backup plan. Then she smiled again thinking about what she would do with the enormous sum of money that was surely coming her way.

CHAPTER 12

MEMORIAL

Griff and Del were sitting in a quiet corner of the Blue Heron having a whiskey. Del took a sip and asked, "you hungry?"

"You buying?" Griff responded in his typically blunt manner.

"You get the drinks, and I'll get dinner," Del replied.

"Then I'm hungry," Griff said.

Del smiled seeing his old friend's brusk manner return. Griff had gotten almost solicitous after his emotional outburst in the committee meeting. He was embarrassed that he had lapsed like that in front of everyone. Perhaps he needed more sleep. That had certainly been lacking the past few weeks. It had touched him when Griff seemed to care that he had hurt his feelings. Del had been brought up in a strict household where lying was simply unacceptable. He had prided himself on honesty as a young man and resented the circumstances that led him to develop the ability to lie convincingly. He put that talent to use frequently these days. He knew the lies were necessary, but it bothered him anyway.

"Have you given our earlier conversation any more thought?" Del asked

"I've been thinking about it all day." Griff shifted in his chair and leaned forward, "In battle sometimes you just have to say screw it and charge. You might not have enough knowledge of your enemy. They might be uphill of you and well protected. Command might be clueless, they usually are.

Sometimes the only answer is an immediate all-out charge," Griff said,

"Well, I haven't thought of it in those terms, but it's an appropriate analogy. What about asking command for direction first?" Del said taking the analogy further knowing what Griff's opinion was of asking for direction.

Griff actually smiled. "You know my opinion of whether it's better to ask for permission or forgiveness." Griff hesitated then said, "In this case it's a reasonable question. Like Hestie's secret, this one will wipe us out if the wrong people find out." Being in public they really couldn't discuss this openly. But Griff had cleverly delivered his decision on the difficult question posed earlier.

"So, you agree we keep this to ourselves and perhaps even execute without telling the rest of our group," Del said thinking that even referring to the Committee was something best left unsaid in public.

"Yes," Griff said and then asked, "I know Quinn is fully briefed but how many more need to know."

"Hestie and four more. They will all need extensive training. I already know who they are. As you can guess they're already doing work in the Dungeon." Griff had dubbed the secret shielded tunnel system under the university the 'Dungeon'. The name had caught on. Del continued, "if we decide to execute then a total of twelve more will be required. The skills needed for those responsibilities can be trained quickly. You and I can fill in if we run short," Del said.

"Griff grunted and said, "I don't like keeping this from them. But I'm convinced it's the right thing to do." They both examined their whiskey for a few moments until Griff asked, "I heard Hestie is back from Apple Valley."

"Yes and thank God for that. She's as smart, perhaps smarter, than her brother. She just isn't as obvious about it," Del said.

"Perhaps she just has a healthier ego," Griff said with a

grin.

"Contrary to what some people think, Quinn does not have an oversized ego. He just loves to discuss what he knows and thinks everyone else is equally excited and knowledgeable," Del said. He had been getting progressively more paternalistic with Quinn. His earlier frustrations had turned into admiration for the boy's simple outlook on life. He identified with how being the smartest kid in class can create jealousy and resentment. He had been that kid once.

"Knock it off," Griff said loudly glaring at him. "Stop being so touchy." The glare softened a little and he continued in lower voice, almost a whisper, which was good because people had turned around and were staring with worried looks at them, "This isn't like you. Besides, I like the kid. He's honest, hardworking, and never complains. Unlike some people I know," Griff said referring to the fact that Del had been giving in to a little grousing lately.

Griff was right. He needed to get ahold of himself. Anxiety over what was going to happen to the people of Pacifica was going to disable him if he didn't toughen up. Del just nodded his head in agreement.

Dinner was served and they moved onto more mundane topics. Griff was a good friend Del thought. He was uncomplicated. He wasn't full of himself like so many of his colleagues in academia. Best of all he told simple truths. Sometimes they were truths you didn't want to hear, but they were truths.

Hestie was walking with Quinn to the Phillips house. She was going there to fulfill her obligations to Grammy. There had already been a small gathering in Apple Valley with the list of people Grammy said were family. Grammy did not limit her interpretation of family to blood relatives. She and Quinn were examples of that. She was really nervous about seeing Jay. Scared she might give in. The surprise meeting at the Blue Heron before she left for Apple Valley had shaken her badly. She had barely made it out the door before she broke down in tears. She had held onto Diana and sobbed just outside the tavern until she grew concerned that Jay might come outside. Then she just turned and walked away. And then there was Grammy's letter.

"Did you finish your simulation?" Quinn asked pulling her out of her internal turmoil.

Hestie took a breath to clear her head and said, "I did, but we didn't match. There is something wrong with our initial conditions. I noticed that when the target has unusually low density our simulations differ by a set value. It's a three-dimensional matrix of whole numbers so I think it's built into one of the two programs to jettison unrealistic locations."

"Ok, I'll take a look at it after Grammy's service," Quinn said frowning.

Hestie knew the frown was sadness over Grammy, not her simulation results. "It's not a service Quinn. Grammy was very clear that she wanted laughter not tears."

Quinn looked sideways at her for a moment and then smiled with all his teeth and said, "I don't think Grammy is going to get what she wants today."

Hestie was once again surprised by her brother. It was easy, even for her, to fall into the belief that he was socially clueless. You could even convince yourself that he was terminally happy because he didn't recognize what was going on around him. Then he would surprise you with an insightful comment. It was good to see his smile back in full force.

The front door opened, and Pam greeted them with a smile shooing them inside. Then they were surrounded by everyone. Arti wrapped Hestie in a tight hug and said, "it's so good to see you again Hestie. I can't thank you enough for looking after my mother. I got a letter from her sent a few days before she died telling me how much she enjoyed having you there."

"It was my pleasure. She really didn't need much help. You know how independent she was. I think she helped me more than I helped her," Hestie said. Off to one side she saw Jay looking anxious. To avoid having to talk to him, and also to get the hard part over with, she said, "Would everyone sit down? I have something Grammy wrote that she asked me read."

At first they looked surprised, and then that knowing look invaded everyone's face. Hestie face brightened slightly, and she said, "well you know she had to get in the last word." This caused everyone to laugh. Then satisfied this was starting out the right way Hestie read Grammy's letter.

Dear Family,

I felt the need to write this so I can lecture all of you on the need to stop crying. Remember all the good times instead. I asked Hestie to gather everyone together so she could deliver this.

I have had an incredible life. No person could be more fortunate than to have the love of our dear departed Pop. I'm likely sitting with Tia on the front porch right now, both of us laughing at one of Pop's ridiculous stories. Who could have had better children than Arti and Hugh? Only Ansen, Tee, Pete, or Tia might have been an improvement. In addition to my blood relatives, I've had the joy of expanding my family with Hestie, Quinn, and Diana. Some of my happiest and most fulfilling memories were watching over my grandchildren, which includes the three of them. Lots of laughs, a few tears, and I thank God for all of it.

Now none of this means I feel my work is done quite yet. To finish off my worldly responsibilities I've left each of you a short note. Yes, one more piece of advice from Grammy. Please think about what I have to say. I expect you to follow my advice. I will ask about it later.

Love you all Dearly,

Grammy

Well, if her intention was to get everyone to stop crying she failed miserably, Hestie thought as she looked around the room with tears streaming down her own face. Only Grammy was capable of lecturing and advising at her own funeral. It made her smile. Smiles slowly infected the room and then the 'crazy Grammy' stories started. Perhaps Grammy's letter did have it right.

Handing out the letters caused another round of tears. It was no surprise that she had letters for Arti, Diana, and Quinn. The surprise was that she had letters for Jay, and of all people, Griff. Arti and Griff's engagement happened after her passing. How did she know? Nobody opened theirs in public. More than a few snuck off to see what she had to say. They all knew their letters would contain something very personal and private. Grammy knew everybody's deepest fears and secrets and offered advice on all of it.

Hestie opened hers the day Grammy died. It was a good thing she did because she would have melted if Jay were anywhere around. Hestie had found Grammy tucked into bed with a smile on her face. At least that's how it looked to her. Late in the afternoon that same day Hestie went down to the beach and sitting on Grammy's bench opened up her letter.

Dearest Hestie,

Have loved all of our time together. The deep conversations and the silly ones. You have always been wise beyond your years. I have a special place in my heart for you. For you I have a simple request. Look after them for me.

You have never needed much advice from me. But you know I never pass up the chance to interfere. Look after yourself first. Don't make life decisions based on what you think is best for others. Follow your heart and not your head Hestie.

Love Grammy

P.S. That Jay is a keeper.

How did she know! Perhaps Tee or someone else had told her they were dating. She had wondered why a letter had been left for Jay. She had been tempted more than once to open it. But no, that would be a violation of not only Jay but Grammy as well. It had been horrible the last time she saw Jay. When he pulled Tee's insignia out and handed it to

Diana she almost lost it. It was just like Jay to be thoughtful. A tremendous gift for Tee's mother. God she loved that man.

Grammy was spooky. At an early age she had called out Grammy for her fortune telling. She would hold court at the table on the front porch with her deck of cards and give them all their fortunes. Her fortune telling was always vague enough that they would invariably come true.

"You're just making all this up," Hestie had said accusingly.

"Well don't go spoiling it for the others Hestie," Grammy had scolded her. "They are having fun with it and so am I." Then Grammy had winked at her and said, "it will be our secret."

Not for the first time, Hestie wondered if she was wrong about Grammy's fortune telling. Her predictions always seemed to have a lesson embedded in them. They always did seem to come true. Grammy seemed to just know things. Jay had been on the top of her mind the whole time she had been taking care of Grammy. One benefit of taking time off of school to help with Grammy was that it gave her time to think. Perhaps there was some truth to the old adage that distance made the heart grow fonder. She wasn't sure her heart could have gotten any fonder of Jay. How did Grammy know Jay was on top of her mind. That she was trying to come to a decision. Or more accurately that she was trying to reverse a decision. She was privately worried she wasn't being rational. She had definitely been swept off her feet and that was scary which complicated things.

Diana approached her whipping her eyes, "you already opened yours didn't you?"

Hestie hesitated a moment and then said, "I did, the day she died."

"Did you follow her advice?" Diana asked with a humorous smirk. A glimmer of the old happy Diana showing through.

"No. Not yet anyway," Hestie admitted. Then she wondered why she qualified her answer the way she did. Then of all people Jay walked up.

"Thank you for delivering the letter Hestie," Jay said. Then he smiled and added, "she just had to get one more piece of good advice in."

"Did you open yours?" Diana asked.

Jay's smile faltered a little and then glancing at Hestie he said, "yes I did. She cautioned me to be patient. She said the best things in life are worth waiting for."

Hestie stomach lurched. More Grammy spookiness she thought as a tickle raced up and down her spine. She steeled herself and said, "well sometimes you do have to move on. You shouldn't wait for something that is never going to happen."

Jay smiled grimly, then continuing to look directly at Hestie he said, "I think Grammy's right. Some things are worth waiting for." Turning to Diana he said, "it's been nice to see you again Diana. Glenn said you're meeting at the Blue Heron this Friday and asked if I wanted to come along. Will probably see you there." Then nodding at Hestie he walked off.

They watched him walk away in silence. Then Diana turned to Hestie and pulled her into a hug. They held onto each other for a while soaking in each other's friendship. Diana stepped back and said, "I have no idea what's gotten into you. I'm on your side even if I think you're making horrible decisions. I know you're going to drop out of Friday night now that Jay is coming. I'm hoping you will explain it to me someday."

Hestie's eyes welled up. Jay had intentionally brought up the Blue Heron to give her an opportunity to avoid him. Thoughtful. Just like him. Her heart was truly broken. Looking at Diana she thought she had the best friend a person could have. She settled herself and said in all honesty, "I hope I can explain it someday too."

Sovereign

CHAPTER 13

BLACKMAIL

Pluta was excited, frightened, and angry all at once. His initial elation at getting Cara placed in Cereo's villa had slowly turned to agonizing frustration. It had been months, and the contract was not yet complete. He supposed this was his fault. He had insisted Caius and Vincentius be assassinated together. The scheduling obligations of the senate and those of the 2nd Legion did not naturally line up. Hard to blame Cara for that.

Now he was being blackmailed. Or was it her way of proving she had a valuable source of information? That had been her claim. Her documentation of a large number of his questionable business practices would cause significant trouble in the right hands. Civil lawsuits at a minimum. With a prosecutor who was in the pocket of Cereo he would stand a good chance of being convicted of fraud. Either could ruin him. She never threatened him in the letter. She didn't need to.

She claimed she had information on Cereo that was even more damaging than what she had on him. That was exciting. The frightening news was that it intersected in some way with the governor. She claimed she could sell the information to the Commonwealth for a fortune. After his visit to A27 he was committed to having as little interaction with the governor as possible. Trying to sell information to her would likely backfire in dramatic fashion. She would assume he should just give it to her. It was also possible that Cara would reveal to the governor that he had been hiding things. His blood ran cold at the thought.

Cara was a highly respected and prohibitively expensive assassin. In the criminal world, she had a reputation for efficiency and integrity. As Pluta started to calm down he realized his anger had quite a bit to do with her competence. She had disappeared with no notice from the villa. Then she had compiled and documented evidence from public sources on his indiscretions. After receiving her letter Pluta had searched frantically for a few days before giving up. It wasn't even clear she was still on Arista. Cara had covered her tracks well.

A bank account had been provided and his only decision was whether to deposit the demanded amount or not. She had given him ten days to comply. It infuriated him to pay a fortune for something sight unseen. Objectively he knew he had to pay. She had left him no options to negotiate or maneuver. Perhaps the worst part was knowing he could never extract retribution for the way he was being treated. Rational people did not try to have top level assassins assassinated. They had their own little inbred world, and the likely result was ending up dead. If you were lucky.

CHAPTER 14

DIPLOMACY

Bria and Gloria arrived at the Palatium late in the day. It had been a tiring trip but their first view of the Palatium shocked them out of their lethargy. The building was enormous. It sat on a hill and was a mix of Roman columns and fortress-like walls. It had clearly been designed to provide security while maintaining an elegant visage. Tee came out to personally greet their coach. His security team was obviously irritated by this. Bria thought their concern a little ridiculous given the large number of armed men guarding the entrance to the Palatium. If anyone got past all of that they would still have to deal with Tee. She couldn't imagine anyone brave or stupid enough to do that.

Gloria flew out of the carriage once it stopped and wrapped Tee into a tight hug. She told Bria that Tee reminded her of her brother. She just felt safer when he was around. It was strange that Gloria who was generally suspicious of men was so trusting of Tee. The poor woman had been through hell. Orphaned at sixteen it had not taken long for her vulnerability to be noticed. A local pimp kidnapped her and took her to a neighboring kingdom where he sold her into prostitution. Gloria's last name was Peters. Her brother, the now Captain Peters, had searched frantically for her. But at thirteen it was well beyond his ability to do more than search their hometown. Starving he had joined the military to get enough to eat. But he never forgot her. He searched for her everywhere he was deployed. Bria's father had noticed sergeant Peters taking a few days off every time they deployed somewhere new. Otherwise, he never took leave. Worried about what might be going on he had him followed. It turned out that Peters was searching for his sister. Having sisters himself, Perry took an interest and used his surveillance network to track down what had happened to Gloria. Although slavery had always been illegal in Liberty, she was basically a slave in Druango serving the high and mighty. Once found, Perry gave the then Lieutenant Peters permission to take a small group of volunteer rangers into enemy territory and rescue her. Once freed, her father talked Olivia into taking the woman on as a servant. So perhaps Gloria saw Tee as a replacement for her savior brother.

"It's good to see you both," Tee said warmly turning to catch Bria's eye.

"Are you really the emperor?" Gloria asked.

Tee grinned and shaking his head in disbelief looked back to Gloria said, "that's what they tell me Gloria. It does seem crazy doesn't it." Disengaging with Gloria he held his hand out towards Bria and said, "let's go inside and get you both settled. We have a private apartment for the two of you. If you are up to it we can have dinner later and catch up. I'm sure you have as many stories to tell as I do."

Leo showed up the next morning and escorted Bria to a covered roof top patio with a view of Roma's city center below them. It was magnificent.

"Tee is finishing his morning exercises and thought you might want breakfast before we begin," Leo said.

"Is he going to join us?" she asked.

"No, he's been up for hours already. If he doesn't exhaust himself first we can't keep him engaged in conversations. Says he's always done this," Leo said shaking his head.

"He exercised constantly in his cell on the trip here. It got on Gloria and my nerves enough that we had to get him to agree to limit it to certain hours," Bria said smiling.

Contrary to what Leo had just told her, Tee and Senator

Cereo walked in.

"Good morning Your Majesty. I hope you were comfortable last night," the senator said smiling.

"Gloria and I were both very comfortable. The apartment is more than adequate," Bria said with a neutral expression. The apartment was more extravagant than Olivia's quarters in the Royal Castle. Given the poverty she had seen in her travels on Arista, the extravagance sickened her. Tee had expressed the same thoughts at dinner. Bria had stayed up late with Gloria and Tee trading stories. Their stories were bland compared to the craziness Tee had been through.

"If you're OK getting started I would like to reveal more of my conversation with the governor," Caius said.

"You haven't told me everything yet?" Bria asked.

"I haven't told you or Tee everything yet," Caius replied.

Bria looked at Tee and saw he was as angry as well, "this is unacceptable. The deceptions have to stop if you hope to include Liberty in your schemes."

Caius held up his hands in a peaceful gesture and said, "agreed. The secrecy needs to stop. Please accept my sincere apologies to you both for keeping some things hidden. If the governor got wind of what I'm trying to do it would doom all three planets. Hear what I have to say and then decide what you both want to do."

For the next few hours Bria listened in amazement to Cereo's story of discovering her kidnapping and thwarting the governor's plans. When he got to the part of the story where he said he had promised a marriage between Tee and Olivia she had to stop him. "What gives you the right to promise anything that has to do with Liberty," she asked glaring at him.

"Nothing gives me that right. What gives me the motivation is a deeply personal abhorrence of slavery. While abolition is years away on Arista, anything I can do to prevent it elsewhere is something I consider to be an obligation."

He said this with such intensity that Bria tended to believe him. She softened a little realizing she had her own secret and said, "I can't fault your motivation. Please continue."

When he was done explaining all that had happened Bria was speechless. She was worn out by the intricate political intrigues. It wasn't in her nature to be manipulative. But it seemed every path out of this involved playing a role that went against her nature. She wished Olivia were here to handle all of this. Bria, a simple country girl, was a poor substitute for Olivia the rightful queen of Liberty. The saving grace was that Prince Justin and Chief Justice Roberts would be here tomorrow. After that her only role would be to report on what she knew. She didn't have the authority to make decisions. Realizing this she calmed herself and said, "your entire strategy has been a series of delays. You don't have a plan that results in freedom for the three planets."

"Guilty. I don't have a plan. The reason I think delay tactics might work is that the governor doesn't care what happens to Sector 27 after she leaves. This is a career steppingstone for her. If we can figure out a way to make her successful without forcing our populations into slavery we've won. She will leave and we'll hopefully get a better governor. That's the best I've come up with," Cereo said clearly exasperated with their situation.

"Why is Pacifica in danger? My understanding is that we have been designated as a preindustrial civilization and must be left alone," Tee asked.

"With another governor there might not be an immediate danger from the Commonwealth. But it's just a matter of time before the GEMs break through. The Commonwealth would be satisfied with letting it all play out and cleansing the planet for its nature resources. However, Pacifica's human capital is seen as having high value. Heavy planet slave labor and mercenary armies are lucrative. Pacifica's military capabilities would be in high demand. The governor is motivated to find a way to step in before the GEMs succeed," Caius explained.

"You're plan is to help the Commonwealth turn us all into slaves?" Tee said clearly angered.

"If we do nothing that is exactly what the Commonwealth will do. I am hoping we can agree on a plan to keep as many people free as possible. If the Commonwealth doesn't need to force us to do what they want, they won't care how it's done. This is about power and money. A hard life for many? Yes. If we can stay in control it's one that can evolve over time into the free societies we all want," Caius said.

Tee thought about that for a few moments and then said, "I'm not sure how I'm going to talk my government into naming me king."

"You won't have to. We'll go to Pacifica and reveal the reality of the situation to them. They already know the GEMs are going to break through. Our proposal would be that they accept a constitutional monarchy. That means you're a figurehead for the Commonwealth to justify naming Pacifica a colony. They view democracies as barbaric remnants of the past. They believe they are dangerous to the Commonwealth. If successful, your form of government stays intact. Unlike your status on Arista, you would be king in name only," Caius explained.

"Your plan is to announce a betrothal but delay the marriage as long as possible?" Tee said.

"Tee, it's our plan. You both have more control of it than I do," Caius said looking back and forth at them both. "But you're correct. My proposal is to do exactly that. I will do everything I can to delay or change the plan so the two of you aren't forced into marriage. If I fail, you both need to accept that the marriage will happen," Cereo said firmly. "I don't want you to think I can work miracles. The governor is capable of all sorts of horrors. The reality is that we may all regret whatever decision we make," Cereo said.

Later that afternoon Bria was sitting by the side of an

117

enormous pool with Tee. They were watching three children squealing in delight and splashing each other. They were Dobler's grandchildren. Tee had been teaching them to swim. His rule was that they weren't allowed in the pool unless he was with them. Tee had been walking Bria back to her apartment when the three children had spied them.

"Tee, Tee, Tee," they clamored and came running. The eldest eventually asked in a pleading voice, "Can you watch us swim?"

Holding the smallest who had jumped into his arms, he had another hanging on his leg. Tee laughed and said, "sure, let's do that." Turning to Bria he said, "do you like to swim?"

"I do, but I think I'll just help you watch them," Bria said smiling. She had met Dobler and Jessie earlier that morning and heard their tale. They couldn't say enough good things about Tee. The story of him being an imprisoned gladiator under Doblers' control then suddenly becoming emperor had terrified Dobler. The story of their family being reunited brought tears to Bria's eyes.

"I should have known better," Dobler said. "I saw his character every day at the Arena. When he realized the children were terrified of him he made a point of spending time with them. They adore him. I'm ashamed that I doubted him."

Sitting next to Tee by the pool Bria exhaled letting go of her anxiety. She realized she was enjoying herself. Tee was easy to be around. His natural optimism helped her control her anxiety. Like Dobler, she was a little ashamed of herself. She didn't fully trust Tee. She liked him. She respected him. She even admired him. And being completely honest with herself she was attracted to him. Handsome with the body of Hercules wasn't the main attraction, although it didn't hurt. It was his toughness mixed with empathy and compassion. But could she ever fully trust someone who had so thoroughly fooled her. Maybe it was the explosive and efficient way he killed the three guards. She had grown up surrounded by soldiers and had often been in military camps.

She had seen death. She had seen a number of horrible things she wished she hadn't. But she had never seen anything like that. It was over in the blink of an eye. While Bria was still in shock trying to understand what she had just witnessed, Tee calmly unlocked the door to Theo's cell and murdered him as well. Not that humanity would miss any of them. They were animals. It was better described as justice than murder. But, at that instant, she truly believed she and Gloria were next. The experience still made her wary of Tee and she felt guilty about it.

The three of them had shared quite a bit of time talking during the weeks of space travel. There was really nothing else to do. Tee explained what life was like on Pacifica. His family, joining the Guard, what they did for fun, and the latest GEM war. He explained that everyone was a warrior. This included women and children. He talked about the role of Wall Archers. He seemed very proud of his mother. Pacifica had a republic form of government which was odd and interesting. She had been taught these forms of government always devolved into tyranny. It certainly didn't sound like tyranny. What did sound horrible was the never-ending war with the GEMs. While Bria had been subjected to war most of her life, the enemy was human. Their enemies were interested in control and owning property, not committing genocide. She could understand how that environment might produce the sort of violent outburst she had seen from him.

"Do you trust them?"

The question from Tee jerked her out of her inner thoughts. Bria smiled and then said in mock seriousness, "I'm not sure I trust you." They both laughed and she felt another twinge of guilt at the partial truth in her reply.

"Timmy stop! No running on the side of the pool," Tee said in a deep voice. The boy slowed to a quick jerky walk. "That boy pushes all the rules," Tee said with obvious affection. Then with a serious look he turned back to Bria and said, "Honestly, you've been at their villa for almost a year. Do you trust them?"

Bria thought about that for a few moments and then said, "I trust Sage and June. I'm convinced they are good people. Whether Leo and Caius are trustworthy I don't know. June loves the two of them dearly, but you know how a mother's love works."

Tee nodded his head, "I'm in a similar situation with Forti. I'm obligated to trust him. I know that sounds weird, but he is a member of the Guard and trust in each other is absolute. Forti trusts the two of them. I believe his trust is real. I've also come to believe Forti is a good judge of character."

"But you don't trust them yourself?" Bria asked.

Tee hesitated clearly thinking about how to answer that, "I have no reason not to trust them. The situation with the GEMs on Pacifica leaves me with no other option. If I don't support their plan I believe my people are lost," Tee said. "You and Liberty are not in an immediately dire situation. I will completely understand if you decide to take a less risky approach for Liberty."

Tee's head snapped back towards the three children as sounds of distress came from that direction, "Timmy! What did I tell you about sisters?" Tee said firmly. Timmy had been splashing water in the older sisters' face with a little bit too much exuberance.

"I have to protect them," Timmy said looking down.

"Who do you have to protect them against?" Tee asked.

"Everyone. Including me," Timmy said clearly reciting something Tee had obviously made him say more than a few times before.

Bria smiled. That was an interesting way to correct Timmy. Tee was going to be a good father someday. She went back to the difficult question she needed to resolve. They sat in silence for several minutes until Bria came to a decision. Tee's concern for the inhabitants of her planet in light of what that would mean for Pacifica is what swayed her. She appreciated that Tee didn't claim trust when it was clearly in his best interests to do so. Instead, he gave an honest answer. When Prince Justin and Chief Justice Roberts showed up tomorrow she would support Cereo's plan. Not that she really had a vote of course. She was Bria not Queen Olivia.

Bria broke the silence and said, "Even if Leo and Caius are trustworthy, I'm certain the First Minister is not."

"Amen to that," Tee replied.

The next morning the First Minister opened the meeting by saying, "I hope we can resolve the current conflict between Arista and Liberty. Given Arista has a new emperor perhaps there is an opportunity for a resolution that benefits you both. I want to remind everyone that my role is one of mediation. The Commonwealth has no wish to interfere in the internal affairs of its colonies."

And if you believe that… thought Bria. She took on her best impersonation of royal distain and said, "I will go no further with this meeting until I've had the chance to consult privately with Prince Justin and Chief Justice Roberts."

Prince Justin came quick on her heels with, "it's outrageous that my queen has to ask permission to speak with her uncle. While we don't want war we are highly skilled at it. We will stop at nothing to gain her freedom."

"We are not going to release Queen Olivia until His Eminence is convinced she is safe. Lord Durango was very clear in his belief that you Prince Justin do not have her best interests at heart," Caius said glaring at the Prince while pointing his finger. Tee nodded his head in agreement.

"I ask both of you to please step back and remember why we are here. Recriminations are not going to achieve the result you want. I think it's completely within my authority as mediator to recommend that Queen Olivia be allowed a private conference with Liberty's Regent," Jack said calmly.

"Queen Olivia does not have nor need a Regent. She

simply needs to be set free," Prince Justin said snarling.

"My mistake," Jack said showing mild frustration. Then he continued in a lightly sarcastic sing song tone, "I support Queen Olivia having a private conference with her uncle. Any objections?"

When no one spoke up Tee gently said, "please take the morning to get caught up. Feel free to meet anywhere you choose. There are no restrictions." He then looked nervously at Caius until he got a nod of approval.

Bria's regal manner dropped. She showed softness for Tee as she said, "thank you Tee. I'll take Prince Justin and Chief Justice Roberts to my apartment where we can be comfortable." Turning to Jack her manner switched back to stern and added, "given how long I've been gone from Liberty I will need the whole day."

Jack hesitated and then said, "we'll meet again tomorrow morning then."

Well, that had gone exactly to script Bria thought. Even Prince Justin had played his part without realizing he had a part to play. When they had planned this out the day before she had guessed he would show outrage early, and he had. While Justin was ordinarily gracious and calm by nature, he had a hot temper when he perceived injustice. When they had gotten out of sight Prince Justin grabbed Bria and gave her a hug. Being a close personal friend of her father's while she was growing up they had a family-like relationship. Taking a deep breath he said, "it's so good to see you safe Olivia. We've been out of our minds with worry."

She held onto him for a while, then disengaging she said, "When we get to my apartment we can talk. Its private and I believe it's safe there." clearly indicating it wasn't safe to talk in the main garden.

When they walked into the apartment Gloria was waiting for them.

Prince Justin dispensed with a greeting and immediately

said, "the girls are healthy, safe, and as happy as can be expected."

"Thank God," Gloria blurted out before burying her head in her hands and bursting into tears. She recovered after a minute and said, "Thank you Your Highness. That news means the world to me."

"They are at General Eastbrook's ranch and being taken care of by his sister Beatrice. They miss you horribly. I assured them you were ok and that I was going to personally bring you home." He smiled then added, "the last time I saw them they were learning to ride ponies. You'll remember that Aunt B is quite the character. There is a lot of laughter. She loves those two girls and is going to have a hard time letting them go."

Gloria dried her tears and said, "I can't tell you how much it means to me to hear they are healthy and safe. Thank you. I know you have much to discuss so I'll leave you alone for now. If you need anything just let me know. I'll bring some lunch around noon."

Prince Justin stopped her with a look and said, "Gloria, I can't express how much the royal family appreciates your service this past year. If there is ever anything you need you have only to ask." Gloria nodded her head, curtsied, and quietly left.

Once when Tee was asleep, Gloria silently moved to stand at the bars of her cell and said in a soft whisper. "I won't tell them how close you are to General Eastbrook given your friendship to Bria. You know General Eastbrook would do anything for you. If they knew they might try and tempt him into a betrayal. It was Gloria's way of saying she wouldn't betray her. At the same time, it would tempt them to contact her father which might present an opportunity. It was cleverly done. Bria had developed an enormous level of respect for Gloria through the extremely troubled times they had shared.

Once Gloria left Justin said, "Bria and her father asked

me to tell you they miss you horribly and can't wait for you to get home. We are all concerned for your safety."

Bria gave a slight smile and said, "you can call me Bria here. Things are not what they seem. I'm reasonably safe here on Arista. That wasn't entirely true until Tee became emperor. The Commonwealth is the real enemy."

Justice Roberts frowned and said, "how can the colonies be in danger? The Commonwealths non-interference Edicts are strictly enforced. Just recently the Chief Justice for this sector was convicted of violating them and was quickly replaced. He was caught taking a bribe involving your abduction. No one knows what happened to him. But we do know the Commonwealth is brutal with these cases."

Bria sighed remembering her first conversation with Caius. "It's a long story. Be patient and I'll tell you what I know. I'll also tell you what Senator Cereo is proposing as a way forward." Hesitating a moment she added, "the governor is responsible for my abduction and Lord Druango's rebellion. If they hadn't gotten involved Olivia would be married to Lord Druango and we would have that to worry about. Perhaps it has worked out better for Liberty that this happened. But I'm convinced we are in real danger from the Commonwealth. Executing those who committed murder and rape on Liberty outraged General Harris and irritated the governor. Harris is evidently very influential in the Commonwealth. While the governor can't do anything openly, Senator Cereo says she can cause a lot of trouble."

By early afternoon they had finally gotten to the point of discussing their decision. Or more accurately, Prince Justin's decision. There were two options. Go along with Cereo's plan or simply go back to Liberty. Bria had gotten a commitment from Caius and Tee that they would simply let her go. However, they requested Liberty stage a big fight over it. Tee would step in, declaring he was letting her go. The story to the First Minister being that Tee was in love with her. The danger of Arista giving in too soon was that the First Minister might tell the governor Caius hadn't done everything he could to force a three-planet pact.

"Are you really prepared to marry that monster?" Prince Justin asked frowning.

Bria frowned back at him, "Tee is anything but a monster. Yes he's huge. That makes him incredibly intimidating. But warm and compassionate is a better description. Lord Druango was a monster, and Olivia was going to marry him for the good of our people. Can I do anything less? The plan doesn't work without the promise of a marriage."

Prince Justin considered that, "I apologize Bria. He's been nothing but polite and considerate so far. I also know he did what he could to protect you and Gloria on that damned slave ship. And it appears he continues to treat you well," he said as he waved a hand around indicated the luxurious apartment. "I just hate the idea of you being forced into a marriage."

"Well, it wouldn't be the worst thing that ever happened to me," Bria said with a smirk. "He is quite handsome and if you got to know him you would like him. I guarantee you Olivia would have traded Lord Druango for him."

Prince Justin chuckled. Turning back to being serious again he said, "We do need to have the option of revealing Olivia. It gives us the ability to declare any agreements null and void. But I am worried about what will happen when Tee learns the truth. He thinks he's marrying a queen."

"To be honest I think he would be delighted. Tee doesn't want to be an emperor. He doesn't want to rule a planet. He wants his simple life back. Reminds me a lot of my father. He's driven by an obligation to protect others and is willing to sacrifice everything to do it. His selfish desires are simple and meager." Bria said.

"It almost sounds like you're in love with him," Justin said accusingly.

"I almost am," she said, surprised at herself to have admitted it.

That evening Bria left her apartment and wandered through the expansive and opulent emperor's residence in search of Tee. She eventually found him in the pool swimming back and forth. He never sits still she thought. Bria sat down and waited for him to stop. When he finally finished she said, "where are the kids?"

"I decided to be selfish. Told them I would watch them tomorrow evening for as long as they wanted. That seemed to satisfy them. Needed some exercise after sitting all day," Tee said smiling as he got out the pool with water dripping in rivulets down his face and body.

She was glad when he dried off and donned a robe. Tee had been almost naked in his skimpy swimsuit. His body glistening from the water had caused a somewhat pleasant physical reaction. That was the last thing she needed right now. "I came to tell you we agree with the plan. Prince Justin has his script and won't deviate from it. It was difficult for them to agree to this. However, we believe the Commonwealth was the root of the problems in Liberty. Defeating their plans for us means we need friends. For that reason, we have decided to join in the pact."

Instead of being delighted Tee face took on a somber look. Quiet for a while he finally said, "I'm sorry you're being forced into this. I know you have agreed to do it based on what's best for your people. I admire that." He looked at her for a few moments and then said, "on Pacifica marriage is a choice but it's also a lifetime commitment. We believe this is best for the children. And what's best for the children is what's best for the whole community. When I marry I will work hard to be the best husband and father I can be. I won't give up on that." Tee hesitated then lowering to one knee he said, "Olivia Hastings, will you marry me?"

Bria was stunned. She had not expected him to formally ask for her hand in marriage. Tears started to form in her eyes as the seriousness of the situation hit her all at once. However, she was committed to this and would see it through, "yes, I will marry you Theron Stone."

He stood, hugged her, and then said, "let's take this slow. Perhaps things will work out, so we don't have to do it." He hesitated, and then with a roguish smile said, "I will admit it's not entirely distasteful." She laughed suddenly releasing the anxiety of the moment. As strange and unnatural as his proposal was, she wasn't sure she could have gotten a more romantic one.

They announced their engagement the next day to howls of protest from Prince Justin and Justice Roberts. Caius was actually the first to talk over the din to voice his disapproval, "your Majesty, marriage is a very serious move. It must only be done after understanding the political consequences. I can't object strongly enough."

"As much as I hate to say it. I wholeheartedly agree with Senator Cereo Your Majesty. You simply cannot agree to a betrothal with this man," Prince Justin said waving his hand towards Tee. "You will be subjugating your people to a brutal non-representative government. They don't even have personal rights protections in their constitution. Citizens are not protected. You simply cannot do this."

"I can and I will. You forget yourself uncle. We have agreed that while on Liberty Theron will be Queens Consort and on Arista I will be Emperor's Consort. We will alternate living arrangements between the two planets. You have proven you can act on my behalf while I'm away. Tee trusts Senator Cereo to do the same. What we do with our children remains to be decided. We both agree with Senator Cereo that changes to government need to be made on both planets." Bria was especially proud of her acting here. They gave the First Minister everything he wanted. She hoped it would buy enough time to put themselves in position to control the situation. As Caius had observed, "they only care about money. If we can deliver significantly increased tax revenues they will leave us alone." Bria hoped he was right. This tradeoff would come at a high cost for their citizens. But being poor was better than being enslaved. When the current governor was replaced, perhaps they could turn it back around.

"Would a marriage resolve all the issues between your two planets?" Jack asked clearly questioning whether it did.

Prince Justin and Caius both started to talk at the same time when Bria held up her hand. "First Minister, I appreciate your efforts to mediate our differences. You can report back to the governor that you have been successful. Theron and I will resolve this between ourselves. We are of like mind on the issues and don't believe we need further assistance." As she said this she looked pointedly at both Senator Cereo and Prince Justin.

As Caius was walking Jack out he said, "I'm sorry you've come all this way just to be told you're not needed."

Jack smiled conspiratorially and said in a low voice, "the governor told me what your plan is. It looks like everything is falling into place."

Caius lowered his voice as well and said, "we still have a long way to go. The Commonwealth has to approve the plan for Pacifica. Once that's done Pacifica's government will have to be convinced to accept Theron as their figurehead king. Their culture will rebel against having royalty. However, if it's announced as a requirement to be accepted as a colony we should be able to push it through. They should be so delighted that the GEM threat is being eliminated that anything is acceptable."

"But what about Liberty? Why not push for a quick marriage and then move to make constitutional changes? That's the question the governor is going to ask."

Caius showed some frustration at that point and said, "the two of you need to recognize that Pacifica is the prize here. Anything that slows down progress risks losing their human capital. You've seen the reports on GEM collaboration and the massing of their troops. Pacifica is running out of options."

"Yes we've both heard your thoughts on that. It doesn't

change what questions the governor is going to have," Jack said with an empathetic grin.

"As soon as I have approval I will get Theron and Olivia to Pacifica. After we gain colony status, and everything calms down, we will have a wedding on Liberty," Caius said.

"Why Liberty and not Arista?" Jack asked.

"Because Theron is an absolute ruler here and can do as he pleases. The queen has to have a good relationship with the House of Lords to run that government. To make changes to the constitution we can't start off by insulting everyone," Caius said. Then he stopped to consider something and added, "if I can get approval for Prince Justin and Chief Justice Roberts to travel with us to Pacifica we can finalize wedding plans. They will want to see Pacifica and meet members of their government to feel comfortable with this anyway. That will speed up the timeline for the wedding."

Jack was clearly not convinced. Caius knew Jack was concerned he didn't have a strong enough message for the governor. "What can you do to move the Pacifica timeline along faster?" Jack asked.

Caius pretended to give this some thought. He was thrilled that Jack had pushed on the topic. After enough time to convince Jack that what he had to say wasn't preplanned he said, "I've been suggesting to Theron and Olivia that an investment in a mercenary army could be lucrative . An army led by General Eastbrook that includes the Pacifica Guard could charge an enormous premium. His defeat of General Harris had to have been noticed across the Commonwealth. If I can get approval to bring the General to Pacifica he can evaluate what it would take to form such an army. That would push our plans forward faster. "

Jack mused over this for a while and finally said, "ok, you have my support. I'll let you know what the governor says."

"Safe travels Jack," Caius said with a convincing smile.

"And to you as well," Jack said shaking his hand then

climbing up into his carriage. As he drove away he thought Caius Cereo was up to something. It's certainly an aggressive plan with enormous potential. But what is he really trying to do?

CHAPTER 15

THE COMPLEMENT

Jack had mixed feelings as he left Julie's apartment. It wasn't how the evening had gone. It was another humiliating experience followed by the now familiar self-loathing. She had a way of forcing you to do disgusting things then feeling like you were a bad person for doing them. It was slowly destroying his sense of self-worth. What was unusual is how their business meeting had gone earlier in the day. As he walked out of her building and down the street towards home he reviewed everything they had discussed.

"Good morning Jack, you look really good in that suit," Governor Jacobs said.

Jack froze for a moment. She never complimented him like this. "Well thank you Governor. You are looking quite nice yourself," he said deciding to flirt a bit. Perhaps that's what she was going for.

The governor actually smiled and said, "give me an update on Liberty and the negotiations on Pacifica." She had not asked if he had 'good news'.

Jack put on his dutiful underling voice and body language and began, "I was able to get Prince Justin to release Harris and what was left of his mercenaries. A number of them had already been executed for crimes against civilians. Liberty wasn't happy letting criminals go free. But I got them to understand that relations with other colonies are important, even if they are located in another sector."

"Did they demand compensation?" She asked.

"No. Prince Justin said that no amount of credits could compensate people for the abuse suffered. He was quite forceful in saying that Liberty would not accept blood money," Jack replied.

"How sanctimonious," Julie said. "It's childish to take that sort of position. However, it's good since Overlord Bennett is already incensed. Executing perfectly good mercenaries has him demanding justice. As you know Bennett is well connected on the High Council. It would do Liberty good for them to make amends."

"I will mention this again when I meet with Queen Olivia on Pacifica," Jack said. "Our meetings went surprisingly well after an initial shouting match. What forced agreement was Theron and Olivia announcing their engagement and telling their advisors they would resolve issues between the two planets. There really wasn't much for me to do," Jack said.

"So Cereo's plan is evolving as he predicted. Good. I want you to support him completely. Our interests are in excellent alignment with his," She said.

"Cereo says he can move things forward faster if General Eastbrook is allowed to join the discussions on Pacifica. He asked me to make that request. Do you approve?" Jack asked.

"No, I think the original proposal is good enough. No need to make those discussions more complicated than they already are," she said calmly. "I have to congratulate you on how well you've handled Cereo. While he has done some surprising things, you responded to them in a way that maintains our control of the situation." The conversation went on to inconsequential details. Her parting comments had been warm instead of cold. Weird!

Jack realized he had been standing in front of his apartment door for a while just staring at it. Why does she want General Eastbrook to remain on Liberty? She had never denied a request that claimed to accelerate a plan. He was at a loss for words when she complimented him. And he was at a loss to explain it now. In the entire meeting she had not insulted or demeaned him once. And then an actual complement. Something was wrong, very wrong.

CHAPTER 16

MORNING RUN

Jack was insistent that discussions with the Pacifica government happen privately. "The Commonwealth's Edicts on non-interference of pre-industrial civilizations are rigorous. Until they agree they have a monarch, and that monarch agrees to accept our offer to join the Commonwealth, this must remain private."

"What if they agree to join but claim they are a republic?" Caius asked.

"Then they will either sit to the side and watch the GEM's take over or declare the government dysfunctional and invade. The key is whether they can justify knowledge of second-generation warfare or industrial technology. My guess is that they will invade. Their justification will be that the human capital on Pacifica is too valuable to waste." Jack looked at Tee when he said this with an apologetic smile.

"The Master Sergeant of the Guard knows all the politicians. If I can talk to him he can help," Tee said. Then he added, "He trains teams all the time, so we have a good chance of catching him away from the city."

It took nearly a week to make the jumps necessary to enter Pacific's orbit. Unfortunately, after locating and tracking Griff for three days the man seemed to be spending the majority of his time at the university. Way too many people around him to organize a private conversation. Even out of uniform Tee was too well known to show up in public. Then Tee recognized Jay while he was with Griff and told the Commonwealth crew to track him as well. The next morning, they were rewarded with a view of Jay on an early morning run up a trail alongside the Armstrong River.

"Tee?" Jay said with disbelief.

"Yes, it's me," Tee said.

Jay walked over briskly and picked him up into a bear hug. Tee hugged him back just as vigorously. After a few moments Jay put Tee back down. With his hands now on Tee's shoulders he asked with a face masked in confusion, "where the hell have you been?"

Tee smiled back sheepishly, "You're going to find the answer hard to believe. Pacifica is in grave danger, and we don't have time for a long discussion. I'll explain more later but you are going to have to just trust me for now."

Jay hesitated, then said soberly but with conviction, "I trust you Tee."

Tee then quickly described what had happened to him, why they were in a crisis, and what needed to be done quickly.

Jay listened without interrupting. Tee could tell it was difficult for him. When Tee was done Jay looked down at his feet for a while considering what he had heard. Then he looked up and said with a straight face, "let's see if I have this straight. Space pirates kidnapped you. They took you to a planet ruled by a sadistic emperor and sold you into slavery as a gladiator. The legendary Vic turns out to still be alive having suffered the same fate. You talk Vic into a scheme to kill the emperor with one of your crazy suicide plans. The plan works and somehow that makes you the new emperor of the planet. Then to protect Pacifica you enter into an engagement with the ruling queen of yet another planet." Jay hesitated a moment and then continued, "Oh, and I almost forgot. The queen happens to be smart, courageous, sweet, and drop dead gorgeous. So far so good?"

"That's about it." Tee said with a slightly embarrassed grin.

Jay just looked at him for a while. "The really weird part is that I believe every word of it. Only you could get sold into slavery and figure out a way to conquer the planet responsible," Jay said and then grinned.

Tee grinned back for a moment and then his face turned serious, "I would love to explain more and catch up, but we have to get Griff to set up the meeting. The GEMs are massing and unless we agree to the Commonwealth's terms their next attack will likely succeed.

"Ok, you stay here I'll go get him." Jay started to run down the trail, stopped, and then turned around and said, "I can't tell you how good it is to see you Tee."

"You too Jay," Tee said and looked away so that Jay wouldn't see his eyes misting up. Jay then turned and took off running but not before Tee saw the mist in his eyes as well.

Almost two hours later Jay and Griff came running back up the trail. Griff hesitated a minute standing directly in from of Tee. Then he stepped forward and embraced him. Well, that was a more emotional greeting than I expected Tee thought.

"God it's good to see you again Tee. Jay told me what I need to know for now and we don't have time to waste so let me explain what we're going to do. Professor Dacy has access to President Malrey. He lives in a house on the University grounds that back up to this river downstream. We're going to sneak you in his back door and then I'll go get him. He will know how to contact the President." Griff hesitated for a few moments and looked over at Jay. They both looked uncomfortable. He appeared to come to a decision and then said, "Your mother ought to be the one to tell you this but since everyone you'll be talking to knows I better tell you now. Your mother and I were married about a month ago." Then in typical Griff fashion he turned and started running back down the trail obviously expecting Tee and Jay to follow. Tee looked at Jay who simply shrugged and nodding his head in the direction of the quickly disappearing Griff ran after him.

When Griff said he had something to tell him Tee's mind had gone blank with terror. In a flash his mind had gone through all the terrible things the news could have been. Stuck in that reflection he wasn't sure if he had heard Griff right. His mother and Griff were married? Then he remembered when he had seen her talking to Griff at his graduation ceremony. His first thought had been that they were flirting with each other. But that seemed so ridiculous he dismissed it. Looks like I had that right after all he thought. Then to his horror he realized that Griff was now his stepfather. After they had been running for several minutes he finally calmed himself down. Under control now he took a deep breath and said in all sincerity, "congratulations Griff."

Griff turned his head around to look at Tee and with a tight grin simply said, "thank you Tee."

Glancing over at Jay he could see him relax a little. So, you've been worried with how I was going to react Tee thought.

The next morning President Malrey with an unreadable expression opened up a special closed-door session of the Pacifica Council. "Thank you all for being here today. I apologize for the cryptic description given to get you here, but you will soon understand my reasoning." She took a moment to look around the room and then said, "please bear with me. You'll all have questions, but it will go much smoother if I can explain what I know without interruption." She looked around the room and got head nods of acknowledgement then continued, "the civilization our ancestors left two millennia ago has colonized this section of our galaxy." A collective gasp went up from those assembled. Jennifer held up her hand and resumed, "many of the local planets originally surveyed have been colonized by what is now known as the Commonwealth. We have been left alone for the past few hundred years because we are what they consider to be a pre-industrial civilization. Those types of civilizations are protected from interference under their laws. The First Minister of this segment of the Commonwealth is here and would like to present the conditions under which we can be admitted as a colony. If admitted, the Commonwealth will protect us from the GEMs. They will grant us all the rights and privileges of their other colonies."

There was dead silence in the room as they all internalized this shocking development. Councilwoman Ricks was the first to recover. "Have you had discussions with the First Minister?"

"Yes, but only to organize this meeting. He requested that everyone hear what he has to say together," Jennifer answered.

Barlow in particular seemed pleased by that. He then said, "will he help us negotiate with them?"

"I don't know. He just said that we won't need to fear them after colony status is conferred. He said he has the authority to take immediate action to stop the violence once we agree to their conditions," Jennifer said.

"What do you think of him," Ricks asked. Ricks was a big advocate of listening to your gut.

"I'm not sure," Jennifer said, her face mirroring her confusion. "He's polite and considerate but seems overly anxious for us to agree with whatever their conditions are. But you can make your own assessment. I've spent little time with him and have as many questions as I am guessing you all have." She looked around once more and said, "if there are no more questions for me I'll go get the First Minister."

"Good morning. My name is Jack Spenser. I am First Minister for Sector 27 of the Commonwealth. The Commonwealth was born out of the horrible wars your ancestors successfully escaped. Our mission has been to provide intergalactic peace for all humans. Our analysis indicates your lives are in immediate mortal danger from Pacifica's GEM population. I'm here to offer you an alternative. That alternative is an invitation to join the Commonwealth as a colony." Jack paused for a few moments and looking around the room asked, "any questions so far?"

Barlow recovered first and asked, "our failure has been our inability to negotiate in good faith. Will you help us negotiate with the GEMs?"

Jack seemed confused by the question. He mused over it for a while and then said, "there is no need for you to negotiate with the GEMs. We have technology that can be used to deny incursions into or out of the peninsula. Think of it as a fence neither of you can get over. Since your populations are separated by clear and distinct territorial boundaries this will immediately put a stop to the bloodshed."

"You will give us this technology?" Barlow asked.

"No. This is something the Commonwealth can put in place and manage. Your question highlights one of the requirements for acceptance as a colony. Pacifica must restrict its technology to pre-industrial levels. This is basically where your civilization is today. This requirement is absolute. I'm sure you can appreciate that all advanced technologies can be used for war. By restricting technology use we have provided peace and prosperity for nearly two millennia," Jack said.

"What other requirements do you have for acceptance of a colony?" Councilwoman Ricks asked giving him a suspicious look.

"There is one that will likely cause consternation. We require that each planet have a form of government that has demonstrated the ability to survive the test of time. Democracies have consistently devolved into tyranny. They have all done this in a relatively short period of time. History has shown these types of governments to be warlike in nature. This is a threat to peace. Your republic has survived as long as it has because of a common enemy. We don't restrict colonies from having elected representatives or guaranteed rights for their citizens. However, we insist it be led by a monarch. All long living governments have been managed in this fashion. The Kush, Roman, Egyptian, Zhou, and Ottoman empires are just a few examples. The latest example is the Commonwealth."

The room was silent as each of the Council members absorbed this news. Jennifer finally said, "We don't have royalty on Pacifica."

"Not currently. But there are representatives from two of our colonies in the sector who have a proposal. The proposal team is led by Theron Stone of Apple Valley." With that shocking news everybody started talking at once.

Jennifer finally got the council under control. She did this by shouting at them. It was so out of character it successfully silenced the room. With her face flushed and eyes blazing she turned to Jack and said, "perhaps it would be good for you to back up and give us some background on this proposal. A description of the colonies and the individuals on the proposal team would be a good start. And we are all dumbfounded by the news that Theron Stone is involved? Please explain that in detail. He disappeared over a year ago. We have been assuming he was dead. When Professor Dacy showed up with you this morning the fact that Theron Stone is alive wasn't mentioned."

Jack looked a bit chagrined and said in a conciliatory voice, "my apologies. I am so concerned with your safety that I neglected to give you the background you need to make sense of all this." He spent the next hour giving a quick history of the Commonwealth and a more thorough one for Sector 27. He then moved onto Tee's kidnapping and the subsequent trial of the Chief Justice for Sector 27. Jack then explained Arista's challenge by combat secession law and how that made Theron emperor of Arista. This was followed by a description of the representatives from Liberty and

Arista.

Jack stopped at that point and said, "You're probably wondering why Liberty has chosen to be involved. The simple answer is that Theron Stone is engaged to be married to Olivia Hastings. Olivia Hastings is the queen of Liberty." Jack hesitated for a moment and then said, "You probably need time to absorb this. I have to admit it boggles my mind as well. We've never had so much political interconnection between colonies. Since the Commonwealth is dedicated to non-interference we simply want to mediate the discussions. My role is to provide support for your decision process. I hope you will agree to our conditions for acceptance as a colony."

Stunned silence. It was simply too much information at once. Jennifer recovered and said, "Thank you First Minister. We will need time to discuss this privately. Can you return at noon?"

Jack smiled and said, "Yes, I'll walk over and see if I can wait in professor Dacy's office for the rest of the morning."

As Jack was meeting with the Pacifica Council, Griff was sitting in Del's courtyard having a light breakfast. As he finished Tee and Jay walked out. The previous evening Tee had filled them in on everything that had happened to him since he was kidnapped. Griff would not have believed it except that all the evidence said it was true. He also knew Tee. He knew the boy wouldn't be part of a plan to deceive.

"When do you think Professor Dacy will be back with news from the council," Tee asked.

"Not until afternoon at least. Might take the entire day. It's an awful lot to absorb and near impossible to make sense of," Griff said as he finished his meal.

"Will you spar with me Griff?" Tee asked out of the blue.

Jay head shot up and looked surprised that Tee would challenge Griff like that. Griff grinned and said, "You sure you don't want to try Jay first?"

"I'm sure. How about we use wooden practice swords," Tee said and smiled.

"Ok, it's your funeral," Griff answered.

It was conventional for Newbies to challenge each other to spar. This was expected. It was usually painful to challenge one of the experienced Guard members. They considered it an insult. They usually made sure the Newbie would think twice before doing it again. It was unheard of for a Newbie to challenge the Master Sergeant of the Guard. Griff smiled to himself wondering why this had come about. Did it have to do with his marrying Tee's mother? Then he decided it didn't matter. Perhaps Tee has a big head from his successes in the Arena. He would put this pup back in his place. They faced each other and Griff gave Tee the hand signal to start. He immediately thrust in towards Tee's left side pressing the weakness of Tee's standard defensive position. Well, he has improved on that slightly, but not enough, Griff thought to himself. Remembering another of Tee's weaknesses he came down with his sword over Tee's left shoulder causing Tee to stumble backwards. Having confirmed what he remembered as Tee's major weaknesses he thrust weakly down low allowing his sword to be blocked, and then went in for the kill. The next thing he knew he was on his back with Tee's sword at his throat.

Tee smiled down at him, reached into his tunic, and pulled out an envelope. "This is from Victor."

As Griff got up he glanced at Jay and saw the smirk on his face. "You got something to say Jay?"

The smirk disappeared and he said, "No Master Sergeant." It reappeared once Griff's eyes left him.

Satisfied that he had regained a little of his dignity he brushed himself off and sat down on the bench. He opened the envelope and pulled out a letter. Recognizing Vic's handwriting he took a deep breath and started reading.

Griff,

If you're reading this I am dead, and Tee has figured out a way to make it back to Pacifica. I hope you've received this laying on your back in the dirt. If so, this is my final lesson. If not, then I'm impressed.

Let's assume I'm not impressed. You had two major faults the last time we spoke. I have recently become aware of a third deficiency.

Aggressiveness is your greatest strength and your greatest weakness. Don't hesitate to act. Continue to move quickly but always have a backup plan. Consider this and improve.

When you perceive a weak opponent you have a habit of probing twice and then going in for the kill. Your enemies are watching. Being predictable is not acceptable. Consider this and improve.

You underestimated Tee. He arrived as an embarrassment. I give you back an adequate fighter. Consider this and improve.

The student has become the teacher. I would not have seen Tee's immense value. You were right that the Guard needs to be more than brutes bashing about. Having spent much time with him I believe he is the leader we need for the future. I have considered my lack of vision at length. Thank you for helping me improve.

You started out as a Newbie project and became an excellent warrior. From my discussions with Tee, it's obvious you have become an exceptional leader as well. You are much more than adequate.

Most important to me is that you are my friend. I wish you love, happiness, and long-life. No one deserves it more.

Your brother,
Vic

Griff paused for a few moments, smiled, and then turned to Tee and said, "so Vic put you up to this?"

"Yes. He made it part of our daily practice sessions for weeks," Tee said. "It's still hard for me to believe how accurately he emulated your movements and predicted your actions."

"There will never be another Vic," Griff said wistfully. Then he hardened his features and said, "Now that you and Vic have had your fun, how about another bout."

Tee was startled. He hesitated, then he grinned and said, "yes."

After their session was finished, Griff held out his hand and helped Tee to his feet. He was battered and bruised but elated. It was just like sparring with Vic. He was badly outclassed but got instruction from it instead of frustration. I wish I could do this every day instead of sitting on my butt pretending to rule a planet he thought.

"Vic was right. You are adequate," Griff said with a knowing smile.

Tee heard echoes of Victor's voice. It was the way Griff said the word *adequate*. He realized Victor must have used it to acknowledge Griff's progress long ago. With that realization he smiled back at Griff and said, "well, it doesn't get any better than that."

Griff smile warmed in agreement. Then he nodded his head gravely in acknowledgment of their shared experience.

CHAPTER 17

BENEFACTOR

Julie's yacht was waiting in a que for its turn to transit the final wormhole from Sector 3 to Sector 1 and Earth. One benefit of being a Sector Governor was that the wait was measured in hours instead of days. Traffic between the home world and the rest of the Commonwealth was heavy. She looked forward to the day when she would jump past all these idiots to the front of the line. She had been making this trip twice per year since she was posted as governor of Sector 27. This would be her final meeting with her benefactor as governor of that Sector. She had exceeded her original commitments to the High Council and was near to delivering those she had boasted of. Rising to the top involved taking calculated risks. It was not a game for the weak. She was looking forward to her triumphant return to Earth in a few months to join the elite of the Commonwealth.

Chairman Amala had been her mentor since she was awarded her first promotion. He had noticed her unusual success in increasing tax revenues. He was especially interested in her ability to exceed goals through aggressive negotiations. She had initially been intimidated by the attention of one of the elites. The spotlight grew with his ascension to Chairman. Anxiety had lessoned over the years but had not disappeared. Having the favor of the Chairman of the High Council was exhilarating and terrifying. It meant she was close to the ultimate in power. I also meant she was only a misstep away from being just another bureaucrat for the rest of her life.

"Governor Jacobs, it's nice to see you," Amala said. Julie had been assigned one of the apartments usually reserved for the highest level of visitors to Earth. An opulent penthouse with a rooftop garden overlooking Central Park had greeted her. A bevy of silver-collared servants had provided for her every whim since she had arrived. It was an indication of Amala's approval, and of his expectations. Nothing was ever given without a cost.

"It's good to be back on Earth Chairman. The apartment you arranged for me was amazing. Thank you," Julie said smiling. As she beamed back at him she wondered what her amazing accommodations would cost her.

"If your plans are achieved I think you'll be back soon," Amala teased. He then transitioned into mentorship mode and asked, "give me an update. I hope you have some good news."

She had learned the technique of putting her underlings on the defensive from Amala. There was always an expectation of exceeding goals or at least achieving them faster than planned.

"I can commit to having the enhanced plan for Sector 27 wrapped up within two months," Julie said.

"You're late," Amala said bluntly. Frowning as his eyes bored into hers.

"I am," Julie said. After pausing for effect she continued, "Pacifica coming under our control will be added to my commitments. The opportunity presented itself and I decided it was worth the slip." She had learned long ago that Amala appreciated initiative and respectful defiance. Be accountable, but never act submissive.

"How will you get that past Justice? Pacifica remains pre-industrial in the judgement of those academic idiot's who own those kinds of decisions," Amala said.

"It was partly luck. Arista has an archaic law allowing for their emperor to be replaced via succession by combat. A Pacifica gladiator assassinated him in the one place, on the one day of the year, when that law would apply. Senator Cereo recognized that this gladiator was now a monarch who could submit legal requests to the Commonwealth. Since he is also a citizen of Pacifica he can request his home world be granted colony status."

"Has Justice approved this?" Amala asked.

Julie nodded her head and said, "they have given provisional approval with the understanding that the requestor be the legal ruler of Pacifica. This way the ruler of Pacifica is making the request. That satisfies the non-interference Edicts and bypasses the pre-industrial civilization protections. Senator Cereo is on Pacifica getting this accomplished."

Amala just stared back at her for an uncomfortable amount of time. She waited patiently understanding his intimidating management techniques having adopted them as her own. "That is good news. What financial return are you committing to?"

"The initial first year target is an improvement of 15%. An additional 10% will be delivered with the creation of a mercenary army incorporating Pacifica units. However, the value to the Commonwealth will be enhanced beyond Sector 27 revenues. The additional 10% will be flowing in from other sectors further enhancing Commonwealth tax revenues," Julie said her face and manner all business.

Amala nodded his head and favored her with the corners of his mouth slightly upturned. Then his face darkened in concern. "Since we're on the topic of mercenaries. Overlord Bennett is incensed with Liberty. Evidently they executed a number of General Harris's men instead of ransoming them back. He is pressuring me for Commonwealth support to extract revenge. He will fund an invasion from his own coffers if the Commonwealth agrees to provide transportation and stay out of the way. His only financial request is that he be allowed to recover his cost for the invasion from Liberty."

Julie gave that some thought, smiled, and then said with enthusiasm, "that works perfectly. I'll get back to you once I've discussed it with Bennett. When Pacifica becomes a colony there will be a wedding on Liberty with the leadership from Pacifica and Arista in attendance. This marriage will unite the three planets. Once united under one government a coup that originates from one of those three planets will satisfy Justice. I just need to connect the players."

Amala was visibly pleased. "Clever. That should simplify Sector 27 administration nicely. Bennett has two other requests. The first is that he be given the judges who passed sentence on Harris's men. The second is that the queen be given to General Harris as compensation. He originally asked for General Eastbrook, but I said no. I'm assuming you want Eastbrook to lead your new mercenary forces."

"Yes, his defeat of Harris will ensure a premium for his services. It doesn't speak well of Harris that he is motivated by something as unproductive as revenge. But he can have the queen as long as she never reappears in the sector. The last thing the next governor needs is a legitimate legal challenge to the rule of Liberty," Julie said.

"Harris has always had an outsized ego. Up to now it's been deserved. Let's throw him that bone but make it clear that General Eastbrook and his entire staff must be preserved," Amala counseled. He hesitated a few moments and asked, "Do you already have someone to lead the coup?"

"Magistrate Pluta of Arista. He is awaiting instructions."

"How will you control him?" Amala asked.

"I have evidence that his bank account was the true origin of the bribe to Evans," Julie said with a glimmer in her eyes.

"Well done Ms. Jacobs. Impressive," Amala said giving rare praise. "How is progress going with our other Justice issue?" he asked with a penetrating look.

"I have enough failures documented to send Spenser's son home in disgrace," Julie said, "He is currently mediating the three-planet pact on Pacifica. Once the coup succeeds I'll dismiss him."

Amala nodded his head in approval, "As we discussed don't let the son know you have documented evidence tying him to the Evans bribery. I want it to come as a complete surprise to Justice Spenser. He will be given the opportunity to drop his High Council corruption investigation. His alternative will be seeing his son with a silver collar serving the High Council. It should be an easy choice."

"Isn't it dangerous to leave Justice Spenser in place?" Julie asked.

"I've been unable to trap him into anything personally compromising. There are advantages to leaving him in place. He can hardly say no to reasonable requests," Amala said. "Going back to your plan. Do you intend on making Senator Cereo First Minister after you remove Jack?"

"I haven't decided yet. I lean towards having him die in the coup. He's much too clever and I don't trust him," Julie said.

"I am intrigued by your Senator Cereo. His rise from poverty to control of Arista speaks for itself." Amala paused and staring intently at Julie said, "As you rise in the Commonwealth you need to take advantage of clever people. Those who pose a threat to you professionally are the same as those who are the most useful. There are many uses for untrustworthy people Ms. Jacobs," Amala said making his message clear. Julie understood. He wanted her to utilize Cereo. Amala was making a not-so-subtle point. He didn't trust her. But he didn't need trust to take advantage of her capabilities.

"Understood Chairman Amala," she said.

Amala examined her again. And again, it was for an uncomfortable amount of time. Then he said, "Katanna will resign from the High Council in three months and Norden will be elevated. This opens up a High Council Advisors position." He paused and then said, "finish your work in Sector 27 quickly Ms. Jacobs."

His tone made it clear the interview was over. Julie rose to leave and simply said, "yes sir." There was never any chit chat with the Chairman. He had made it clear early on that his time was valuable and not to be wasted. As she left his office suite she wondered how she was going to get Harris's army housed in Sector 27 while keeping it a secret. A27 was off limits legally and Cereo's network would immediately discover something of this magnitude on Arista. Any of the other planets in the sector would require Pluta to negotiate multiple contracts. That would take too much time to execute. She would need to take some additional risk. A more aggressive plan was needed. As her air taxi left for the spaceport she allowed her anger and outrage to surface in her mind. Amala had humiliated and abused her as a wide-eyed young woman trying to make a name for herself. Once he was done satisfying his desires he never called her by her first name again. Amala will beg me for mercy someday she thought. And when he does I'll put a silver collar on him but leave his mind intact. She spent the rest of the short flight entertaining herself with all the degrading things she would make him do.

CHAPTER 18

REUNION

Tee started arguing heatedly with Del as soon as the professor got home from the council meeting. Griff glared at Del and said, "Tee has gone through hell. It's reasonable for him to see his family. They can be sworn to silence. Even if they spill, so what? It will be public soon enough."

Del glared right back saying, "All of this has to flow out in a way that doesn't cause panic. People are already terrified. They know another GEM attack is coming. We can't have uncontrolled rumors about the Commonwealth and other planets popping up everywhere."

"I'm going to go see my mother and other members of my family. I'm doing this whether anyone agrees to it or not," Tee said calmly but firmly.

"I'll go with him," Griff said defiantly.

Del huffed out a breath. He glared at both of them for a while and finally said, "ok, how about this for a compromise. Griff goes and gets your mother; you can see her here."

"No, not good enough. Jay told me Hestie, Quinn, and Diana are in town. They are all part of my family," Tee countered.

Del took a deep breath and wilted a bit. Looking defeated he lowered his gaze and shaking his head slightly from side to side said, "ok, but they all need to swear to keep this quiet until the President makes an official announcement." He hesitated and then said, "she's going to skin me alive for this."

"So, you come out ahead," Griff said, "I was going to do something far worse if you tried to get in the way."

The door opened and his mother hesitated an instant taking her first look at him in over a year. Then she flew into his arms and started sobbing quietly. Tee was worried for a second because this was so unlike his mother. She had always been a rock. But then his tears started to flow as well. Then he finally relaxed into the joy of really being home again.

"Let me look at you," she said wiping away her tears and examined him head to toe. "You're a little taller. You've put on quite a bit of muscle. It doesn't look like your little vacation was all that bad," she said with a tearful smile.

This was more like his mother, making light of difficulties. It warmed his heart. "It wasn't all horrible," he admitted, paused, and then added, "just most of it." Which made everyone laugh.

"Well, there are others here that want to get reacquainted," she said and stepped to the side. Suddenly Hestie grabbed him in a tight hug and said, "it's so good to see you Tee. Don't have to tell you we've been worried sick." Quinn stepped up next and gave him a quick hug as well. This was unusual, Quinn didn't tend to hug people. Tee could tell Quinn had been worried and was thrilled to see him. Then he was face to face with Diana. They both hesitated, locked eyes, and simultaneously stepped forward into yet another hug. This one lingered a little longer than the others. He noticed she hugged him straight on, a full body hug not to the side which made him wonder.

After they separated his mother looked suddenly grave and said, "before we start sharing stories we have some bad news. Grammy passed away a few weeks ago." This hit Tee like a thunderbolt. His elation at being reconnected with those he loved disappeared and was replaced by sudden bone numbing grief. His mother continued, "she didn't suffer and seemed to know it was coming. She wrote her own funeral service and individual letters to everyone before she died. Hestie has a copy of the funeral service and your letter."

Tee didn't know what to say. He just wanted to run away. As he wondered what to do his mother stepped in again, "here, take the funeral service and letter from Hestie and go out in the garden." She said pointing over his shoulder at Professor Dacy's small, enclosed garden. "When you are ready come back in, we'll be waiting for you. Take your time."

He was so grateful he didn't know what to say. His mother knew him. She knew he needed to be alone to process this horrible news. She knew being outside would help with that, even if it was just a small garden."

Tee walked out into the garden numb. He sat down turned away so nobody could see his face and cried for a while. Then he pulled out the funeral service and cried some more but not for long. Suddenly an image of Grammy shaking her finger at him and lecturing him on all manner of things came to mind. He laughed. With a smile still on his face remembering other endearing qualities of hers he pulled out her letter.

Dearest Tee,

I would have loved to see you one more time. Knew you would return. But it was not to be. I can't tell you how much joy you have given me in this life. Truly blessed to have had you as my grandson.

Not that you're perfect! And for that reason, I have one final piece of advice. TELL HER! You know what I'm talking about.

Love,

Grammy

How did she know I was still alive? How did she know I would return? Of all the things the Commonwealth had stolen from Tee this might be the worst. He never got a chance to say goodbye. His last memory of Grammy was waving to him standing on the porch, a concerned look on her face. He promised he would see her in a few days. He sat there thinking about Grammy until he realized everyone was waiting for him. So, he stood up and walked in to tell them his story.

It was an emotional story to tell. While he had told much of it before it hadn't been to those he had known his whole life. They were outraged with his captivity and being forced to kill innocent people. They were amazed that Victor had not died those years and years ago. They were proud Victor had looked out for him and had become his mentor. They cried when Victor sacrificed his life so that justice could be served. They laughed when he described waking up thinking he was dead only to find out he was somehow emperor of Arista. But the strongest reaction was when he explained that he was engaged to the queen of Liberty and was going to have to marry her.

"No!" his mother said. "You've given too much all ready. There has to be another way."

She had startled him because he had actually been watching Diana without looking directly at her. Diana reacted very strongly to this news. Was there something more than pity in her reaction? His mother's outburst had startled him back to paying attention to her. He took a breath and said, "Mom, Victor gave his life. Senator Cereo is gambling his entire family's lives. Liberty has been under constant attacks from mercenaries trying to enslave them. Our freedom and perhaps all our lives are at stake. It's a sacrifice I will gladly give. You and Grammy always told me that an opportunity to defend our people is an obligation not a choice. I have an obligation."

There was silence in the room. Diana looked like she was going to burst into tears when the door opened, and Professor Dacy entered with Queen Olivia. "I hope I gave you enough time to get caught up. We stayed at the restaurant as long as we could without drawing too much attention." Diana just stared at her seemingly in shock. Since she was standing closest to the door Del introduced Olivia to Diana first.

"Your Majesty, may I introduce Diana Wells," Del said.

"Please call me Olivia," she said looking around the room. "I don't want to be formal with people who are sacrificing so much," Bria said graciously.

Diana recovered quickly, a trait that had benefited her greatly as a Wall Archer. "In that case I really like your dress Olivia," Diana said brightly in an attempt to lighten the mood. Tee smiled seeing the old Diana again. Diana succeeded by making Bria smile.

"Thank you," Bria said and then added, "I feel like I already know you Diana. Tee spoke of you so often." She hesitated a moment looking Diana up and down and then smiled and said, "It's hard to believe but you're as beautiful as Tee described."

Diana blushed and said, "thanks. Tee does tend to exaggerate and it's nice of you to cover for him." Tee felt himself turning red. He guessed he had gushed about Diana more than once.

Bria smiled at Diana's deft deflection realizing she had made things a bit awkward. She had blurted out what she was thinking. The real Olivia would do such a better job she thought. However, in her own defense, Diana really was a beauty. Recovering she asked, "so you're an archer? Do you really fight on the Wall?"

"As you probably know we are all warriors. We have no other choice. But let me get out of the way so you can meet everyone else," Diana said gracefully.

His mother was tongue tied when she met Diana. This was not the way to meet a future daughter-in-law. He would get an earful later. He decided she really couldn't say much given how he learned about having a stepfather. After the introductions were completed Del said, "Sorry to interrupt Tee. But I thought everyone would want to meet Queen Olivia. I'll talk to you later about what to expect tomorrow." And with that they left the front room and retired to the back of the house.

Later in the evening Tee noticed Diana was out on the bench in the garden. He turned to Hestie and said, "I'm going to go out and talk to Diana for a while."

Hestie gave him a nod and said, "we'll leave you two alone." She then gave him a look that he interpreted as 'there are things the two of you need to discuss'.

Fantasizing about the impossible again, Tee thought to himself.

"Hey," Tee said.

"Hey," Diana replied. Then she gave him a weak smile and slid over to give him room to sit down next to her.

"I'm surprised Ansen isn't here," Tee said testing the waters. He was a little ashamed he didn't just say what he needed to say. Grammy shaking her finger at him popped into his mind once more.

Diana turned to look at him and finally said sadly, "a lot has changed since you've been gone. Ansen is up in Apple Valley with his girlfriend."

"Oh, I'm so sorry Diana," Tee said. But he was secretly thrilled with the news. Not that it mattered anymore.

"Nothing for you to be sorry about. I broke it off. I did it because I'm in love with someone else," Diana said and seemed heartbroken saying it.

"You seem really sad. Didn't it work out?" Tee asked.

"No, it's not going to work out," she said. "There is somebody I'm seeing though, and perhaps that will work out."

Tee was suddenly deeply saddened for Diana. Whatever she thought of him, he loved her deeply and always would. Olivia was a wonderful girl, and they would have a happy life together if it came to that. Well, he would be much more than just happy. But there was only one Diana.

They sat in an uncomfortable silence for a while until Tee decided he needed to follow Grammy's advice no matter what. He would always wonder otherwise. "Diana," Tee said and waited for her to turn her head to look at him. "I'm going to say this before I lose my nerve. I hope it doesn't ruin our friendship." Tee hesitated, took a deep breath, and said, "I'm deeply in love with you. I think I've loved you since you sat down next to me under that oak tree."

Diana just looked at him, searching. Then suddenly she wrapped her arms tightly around him and started crying. He didn't know what to do. What did this mean? He guessed it meant they could still be friends.

After a long time of just holding onto each other Diana gently pushed him away and wiped her eyes. She looked down, seemed to gather herself, and looking him in the eyes said, "I am deeply in love with you too Tee. Realized it way before you were kidnapped. Almost told you that last night on the Wall. I'm sorry I didn't come to you when Ansen accused you of being responsible for Tia's death. That was wrong. You always seem so solid. So able to take on anything and recover from it. I meant to come back once Ansen settled down. Then you were gone."

Tee just stared at her not believing what he had just heard. Then he leaned forward and kissed her deeply and passionately. She responded by pressing her body close to his. It was incredibly exciting and frustrating all at the same time. Heaven, if only for a moment. When they disengaged he said, "I've been wanting to do that for a long time."

"Me too," Diana said, and their grins turned into laughs.

They talked long into the night. Smiling at shared memories. Crying more than once over their lost future. They agreed that Tee had to go forward with the marriage. Pacifica's future depended on it. It was a sacrifice they both had to make. When the eastern sky started to lighten Tee wondered where the night had gone. They could talk for hours, or they could just be comfortable with silence. His heart ached. They said their goodbyes in the garden. Both knowing this was the end.

As they left the garden a curtain ruffled on Bria's

bedroom window. Sleep had evaded her. She had guiltily stolen a few looks at the two of them on and off during the night. She had convinced herself she had a right to know what her future husband's true feelings were. But it still didn't feel right. She had liked Diana instantly when she met her. From Tee's stories it was hard not to admire her as well. Imagine going to war alongside the men. It was all so confusing. Her feelings were ridden with guilt. She wondered what Tee would do when he found out the truth about who she really was.

Diana was walking close to Hestie on their way to her dorm room. Griff had wisely decided to walk well behind to give them privacy. Arti and Quinn had decided to go get some sleep earlier in the evening with Griff agreeing to walk Hestie and Diana home.

"He loves me," Diana said in amazement mixed with grief. "I love him too. I've kept it hidden for so long."

"You only hid it from each other. It's been obvious to everyone else for a long time," Hestie said softly.

"Really? Why didn't you say anything," Diana asked.

"If you didn't admit it to yourself it would do no good for me to point it out. You do remember me constantly reminding you to look deep into your heart whenever you used to talk about your future with Ansen. And why do you think Ansen was always trying to push Tee and I together," Hestie said.

"God I'm such an idiot," Diana said a little louder than she intended.

Hestie stopped and made Diana turn to her. Then she said, "no, you were confused, and you ran away from something that scared you."

Diana thought about that for a while as they walked through the empty streets, "Hestie you're the best friend a person could ever have." Then she hesitated and with a grin said, "We are both a mess aren't we?"

Hestie turned, grabbed her and they both hugged and cried while Griff stood off to the side looking uncomfortable. Shrugging his shoulders and rolling his eyes he said quietly to himself, "men are so much easier to deal with."

CHAPTER 19

THE PACT

Jack gave an honest smile and said, "I am pleased Pacifica has agreed to the Commonwealth's conditions. I will get the exclusion fence in place as soon as possible. Please warn your people not to cross those boundaries. Have them stay on this side of the moat and off the beaches. We don't want any unfortunate accidents." He looked around the table and concluded, "if there are no more questions then I'll leave you to your discussions."

Jennifer was still vibrating from the earlier session with the council. In the end they voted unanimously to accept the Commonwealths offer. They really didn't have a choice.

To Jennifers surprise the incorporation of a monarchy into their constitution was quick and easy. They would model the later part of 21st century Briton and create a figurehead. Jack made it clear this was acceptable with the provision that their monarch would be solely responsible for interactions with the Commonwealth. That included making commitments for the planet. This meant that they truly would have an all-powerful monarch as far as the Commonwealth was concerned. This had everyone worried. They would figure out how to deal with that later. The lone dissenting voice was Barlow's. He was adamant that, "we can't have a king who comes from the Guard. This will just perpetuate military solutions to everything." When it was pointed out that Pacifica didn't have a choice in the matter they were able to move on. Jennifer did worry once again that with every defeat of Barlow's strongly held opinions he would get more and more unstable.

Then the really difficult discussion. Arista and Liberty would have two attendees to the initial discussions. The planet's decision maker and an advisor. They had requested Pacifica offer the same. This flew in the face of Pacifica's republic form of government. There really was no one decision maker. That Tee as king of Pacifica could make responsible decisions was too silly to even consider. Councilwoman Ricks finally resolved the uproar by proposing that Pacifica counter with a negotiator and advisor. The idea being that negotiations could take place but would have to be ratified by the council. In the end the Pacifica Council agreed that Jennifer would be the negotiator and Griff her advisor. Since a military alliance was one of the key proposals it made sense for the Guard to be in attendance. Again, this passed with Barlow dissenting.

The meeting to negotiate the Pact started early the next morning. Jennifer looked around the table trying to judge the other participants. She was quite adept at reading people. She smiled grimly to herself realizing that the range of attitudes around that table were similar to a typical council meeting. Tee and Olivia were clearly fond of each other. But she didn't think they were the actual decision makers. She suspected this from the way they interacted with their advisors. Senator Cereo was the consummate politician. Polished, smooth, and engaging. She instantly liked him so she would have to watch him carefully. He could just be an accomplished con man. Prince Justin, Queen Olivia's uncle, was angry. Jennifer suspected this was disguised fear and who could blame him. She would tread lightly with him.

Prince Justin opened the discussion, "what keeps Pacifica from landing a few thousand warriors on Liberty and simply taking over?"

Griff looked like he hadn't slept in a while. He huffed. Then he said in an irritated voice, "nothing." Griff stared at Prince Justin for a few moments and then added, "we have to trust each other because we have no other choice." His voice and body language made it clear he didn't trust Liberty any more than Prince Justin trusted Pacifica.

Well so much for treading lightly thought Jennifer having trouble keeping a smile off her face.

"We talked about this on Arista Justin. We have no other choice than to trust each other. The Commonwealth is the real enemy," Caius said.

"That's rich coming from you. You've admitted you've been lying to everyone. You were advising the previous emperor on how and when to invade Liberty," Justin said raising his voice. "You've made recommendations to the Governor of how to turn Pacifica into a slave planet. Why should anyone trust you?"

"Enough!" Bria said firmly, surprising everyone. With her voice firm and unyielding she said, "I've spent a lot of time with Senator Cereo's family and with Tee. I'm not the most trusting person. But I trust them both." Turning to Prince Justin she said meaningfully, "You're right. It's time for the lies to stop."

"No Olivia," Justin said in a small voice beseeching her.

"It's what she would want," Bria said firmly. Then she looked around the table catching everyone's eye and said, "I am not Olivia Hastings. I am not the queen of Liberty. My name is Bria Eastbrook." Justin just looked down at the table in front of him. He was obviously embarrassed. Everyone else just stared at Bria. Jennifer noticed that Tee was as shocked as everyone else, perhaps even more so.

Eventually Jennifer found her voice and asked, "so, what does this mean?"

Tee looked at Bria for a few moments. His confused and suspicious expression gradually softened, and he visibly came to a decision. He looked around the table and in a calm voice said, "It means we need to trust each other. I've seen what the Commonwealth does to people. The Commonwealth is our enemy. Fighting amongst ourselves servers their purpose not ours." Then motioning towards Bria he said, "if Bria is an example of the people of Liberty, then I trust the people of Liberty." Turning his head to look at her he hesitated and as a mischievous smile started to form he said, "I'm guessing this means the engagement is off."

There was a hesitation. Then the room rang with laughter. Prince Justin was laughing along with everyone else. Jennifer noted that the mood in the room had changed. The tension had broken. Griff had told her Tee was a natural leader. He predicted the boy would eventually be the CGG. Here was proof of that claim. When the laughter died down Prince Justin said, "Ok, you're right. I don't like any of this, but we do have a common enemy." He stopped for a moment and looked at Caius, "I apologize. We've been at war so long it's hard not to see threats everywhere. But that is no excuse to accuse you of something I'm just as guilty of." Caius nodded graciously. Prince Justin continued, "as you can guess I can't legally agree to anything on behalf of Liberty. We need Queen Olivia for that."

While the negotiation of a Pact was taking place, Jack wandered around until he found Barlow sitting on a bench in front of their government building. "Good morning Mr. Barlow. Is there somewhere we can talk privately?"

"Sure, we can talk in my office," Barlow said pleasantly. They walked in silence into the medium sized marble-faced building and up two flights of stairs. Barlow finally noticed that Jack was huffing and puffing as they reached the third floor. "I'm sorry First Minister. I know you aren't used to Pacifica's gravity. That was inconsiderate of me. We should have taken a break on the second floor."

Jack caught his breath before answering, "Don't worry yourself. Being here takes the place of my usual workout. Better even."

"Well, no more stairs for now. My office is just down the hall," Barlow said with a guilty smile. After they entered Barlow's office and closed the door they sat down at a small table. Jack was impressed with the workmanship given it must have been done with hand tools. Simply amazing he thought. It was the little things the colonies did that were impressive.

Barlow smiled and said, "what can I help you with First Minister?"

"As I mentioned in the council meeting the Commonwealth is dedicated to peaceful coexistence. I am concerned that a majority of your council is going to struggle with this given the history with your neighbors," Jack said. He was quite proud of how he framed it. He had often gone fishing with his grandfather as a child and knew the importance of choosing the right bait.

Barlow visibly reacted. He had to collect himself before responding. When he did there was still an abundance of passion in his voice, "They would commit genocide if the opportunity presented itself. They have no interest in peace. The Guard is a collection of homicidal maniacs. They even altered our history to hide the fact that we are the cause of our never-ending wars." Barlow took a deep breath further calming himself and observed, "with a fence of sorts in place I guess it's not really an issue anymore. I'm pleased the Commonwealth has invited us to join as a colony."

Well, that was certainly the right bait thought Jack. I'll press and see if anything interesting comes out. "My concern Mr. Barlow is that when there is no longer an external enemy, an internal one will appear. Our experience with warlike cultures is that the fighting never stops."

"That's exactly my concern as well," Barlow said with a frown. He hesitated and then asked, "are there examples of where the Commonwealth has helped cultures mature?"

Jack smiled to himself. He would have to tread carefully with Barlow. The man was smart. He already understood the non-interference Edicts and was looking for a way around them. "The non-interference Edicts are absolute. This governmental innovation is central to insuring peace across the universe. The Commonwealth will do nothing to interfere in your government as long as it has the correct form. As First Minister I am expected to offer advice and consultation. The more I know about your situation the more I can help." Jack paused pretending to be concerned and searching for a solution. Then he said, "the Commonwealth does have an opportunity to help guide your government formation. I have to sign off on the form of government. Given Pacifica's preference for a monarchial republic a key role is advisor to the king. This should be someone from your council who can help guide him. Theron Stone is an inexperienced and impressionable young man. He needs proper guidance. The role of his advisor is going to be critical." Jack paused again and then said, "at this point I don't know enough to decide who would be best for that role."

Barlow's nearly jumped out of his chair to start talking. Hooked!, Jack thought gleefully. For the next 30 minutes Jack was subjected to every perceived sin committed by the President and council. It took great patience to nod his head and look concerned at the appropriate times. His patience finally paid off when Barlow said, "I shouldn't say this." Then he took a deep breath and lowering his voice to just above a whisper said, "President Malrey, our illustrious university dean, our financial controller, a medical researcher, and the Master Sergeant of the Guard are part of a secret group. They meet privately in hidden tunnels beneath the University. I don't know what they do down there. But I'm convinced it's not in the best interests of the people of Pacifica."

"How do you know this?" Jack asked quieting his voice as well.

"Councilman Rickets discovered it by accident. He inadvertently left a report in President Malrey's office and went back to get it. Her office door was locked. She didn't answer when he knocked. It was very suspicious because her secretary claimed she hadn't left. He started checking her door when her schedule said she was going to be unavailable and had last been seen entering her office. That led to discovering others on the council having the same peculiarity. We got access to Kevin Wises office, that's our Finance Minister, when he went on a vacation. After almost an entire day of looking, we found a hidden door in the back of his closet. A tunnel led to a locked steel door. There were other tunnels we suspect lead to other offices in the Administration building and the University. When leaving we noticed a key hanging on a hook just inside the tunnel entrance. We think it fits the steel door. We made a copy but have been too cautious to go any further."

"Why are you afraid to go further with your investigation? You're both council members and nothing should be off limits," Jack said.

"These people are homicidal maniacs. They have a secret. It's reasonable to worry that they would kill to protect it," Barlow said in a whispery voice.

Jack pondered this for a minute and then said, "can you show me the hidden door and give me the key? It's my responsibility to make sure the Commonwealth understands what is actually going on before it approves membership for a new colony. I will not reveal you or Councilman Rickets involvement in any of this."

Barlow considered this and then said, "they tend to have early morning meetings the day after something of consequence has happened. My guess is that we'll find Finance Minister Wises office locked early tomorrow morning. If you meet me here at 5AM, Rickets and I will get you into the tunnel system."

As Jack walked to Professor Dacy's office to wait he wondered what the extreme secrecy was all about. He could certainly understand wanting to have meetings without Barlow. The man was paranoid, conspiratorial, and perhaps even a bit delusional. Hidden doorways and secret tunnels suggested a need to hide something significant. There was more to this than mere political disagreement. Hopefully, something he could play to his advantage.

CHAPTER 20

DISCLOSURE

The money had shown up. All of it. She was rich. Filthy rich. She carefully used a variety of agents to convert most of it into land, small private business ventures, untraceable precious metals, and Commonwealth certified bearer bonds. Nothing worse than keeping all your money in one place. By the time the money stopped moving it would not be traceable to her or her holdings. It wouldn't even be possible to figure out which planet it was on. It was important to stay out of the view of colonial governments and the Commonwealth. She had decided years ago to retire on Athena. It was a pretty place that was sparsely populated. It was an agricultural planet with excellent soil and predictable weather. But it was a relatively poor planet given it had few other natural resources. That meant nobody cared about it. The other nice attribute was the lack of corruption. A corrupt government is a good thing if you need to bribe someone. It is generally bad if you are hiding from powerful people. They had money for bribes too.

She wondered if Pluta would be satisfied. Not that she feared him. He would be stupid to try and do anything to her. She had been careful to build up favors, overpay for information, and make sure those who crossed her were never seen again. It tended to make decisions easy for those who were inclined to sell information. They could safely sell the inquiry to her at a premium instead. But you never knew what men like Pluta would try. She would keep her eyes open and her spies well paid.

Pluta could not believe his good luck. Cara had asked for a fortune; it was worth five fortunes. This information would destroy Cereo's political power. It would make his family social outcasts and ultimately drag his business into ruins. There was one earth-shattering revelation after another. The one he had to read twice was the news that his wife was a slave. She had always seemed provincial and unrefined, but he never suspected she was anything other than a well-to-do rural farmer's daughter. The story of her father's land being next to the Cereo estate was believable. That one of the elites of society would marry such a girl made sense given how poor Caius was after his parents lost their fortune. The common people loved the story. Pluta had all the documentation detailing how a birth certificate of a local girl who had died as a baby was used to create a false identity. His valet turned out to be his half-brother. Not that this by itself was all that unusual. Slave women had their uses. But it turned out Leo was the one making all the business decisions. Caius was little more than Leo's mouthpiece. Slaves could easily be denied access to business meetings. That should make life difficult, perhaps even crippling. This was enough for him. The information confirming Cereo was behind Trajan's assassination was too risky. Pluta thought he could control Theron once Cereo was out of the way. He had suspected the boy was an unenthusiastic ruler and that was now confirmed. The last thing he wanted to do was initiate a succession debate. They might end up with an emperor who actually wanted to rule. As he was gleefully considering what to do with the information there was a knock on his office door.

"What is it?" he snarled, irritated that his good mood was being interrupted.

"There is a woman who insists on seeing you immediately sir," Candice his receptionist said, her voice quavering.

"Tell her to request an appointment and I'll review it later. You should know better than to interrupt me," Pluta said angerly.

"I'm sorry sir but she said to tell you her name is Julie Jacobs. She was sure you would want to see her. She is quite forceful sir." Candice said clearly distraught.

Pluta's mind went white with terror. Cara's report started shaking slightly in his hands as he attempted to collect himself. After he somewhat gained control of his panic he said, "I'll be right out Candice." He immediately took Cara's report and put it in his desk drawer. Wondering how to handle her arrival he decided to let the governor lead the meeting. If she asked about the report he would admit he had just received it and was about to report back. He stood and went to greet her.

"Ms. Jacobs, what a pleasant surprise," Pluta said with his best false smile. He had immediately noticed she was disguised and played along. She obviously had contacts in to hide her mismatched eyes. This couldn't be good he thought.

"I hope you'll forgive me for the surprise visit. But I was in the city and decided to come by and see how you're doing. It's been much too long since we've seen each other," the Governor said with her own false smile.

"Please come into my office Julie, I would love to catch up," he said noticing Candice's alarm turning to confusion. Pluta was never this nice to anyone. He could see the wheels spinning as she tried to make sense of it. He would have to invent some story about a distant relative or long-lost friend.

After the office door closed the governor said coldly, "well at least you had the intelligence to not call me Governor in front of your doxy." Pluta just nodded in agreement. He didn't dare tell her that Candice was just an office worker and nothing more. She stared at him with her inhuman eyes for what seemed to be an eternity. He was surprised to discover that contacts making them the same color didn't change their chilling effect in the slightest. Finally, she said, "when were you going to inform me you had a resource at Cereo's villa?"

"She was an assassin I placed there almost a year ago.

Given our latest conversation I changed her assignment to gathering information and hadn't gotten around to telling you yet," Pluta lied.

"If you lie to me one more time it will be the last time," she said. The threat was clear and Pluta had no doubt she would carry it out. His hands started shaking again. If he hadn't just used the toilet he thought he might pee his pants.

"Yes ma'am," was all he could manage.

"You're fortunate I don't have time to replace you. But let me be clear. This is the last time you do anything independent of me. Is that clear?" she said.

"Yes ma'am," Pluta said thinking once again that this was the one thing he could say that seemed to mollify her.

She stared at him for another uncomfortable period of time before saying, "tell me everything you've been keeping from me." The dam burst and Pluta confessed everything. He even told her why he had been keeping Cara a secret and that he was surprised when she claimed to have information damaging to Senator Cereo.

"And what are you going to do now that I know?" she asked with a threatening half smile.

"Whatever you direct me to do?" Pluta answered.

"An intelligent decision. One you claimed to make before but didn't carry through with," she said and just sat there watching him as he grew more and more uncomfortable wondering what she would make him do. Then she said menacingly, "it's too bad you're not as competent as your assassin. Now there is someone with potential. She kept her fee reasonable so you would have no reason to be resentful. She did an admirable job of anonymously getting off planet and diversifying her money in a way that was near impossible to track. But what was really impressive is how she took the information she gathered to discover documented evidence that could be used against both you and Cereo. I especially like the seating charts based on tickets to the New Years festival purchased by a servant of Vicentius Cereo. It shows twenty experienced soldiers under his command directly adjacent to where Theron shot his arrows. She has put information in your hands to destroy Cereo politically, socially, and bring him up on charges of high treason. My only question is whether you have the intelligence and balls to take advantage of this?"

"Yes ma'am," Pluta said relying on his mantra when it came to the governor.

"Ok, I'm doubtful, but this is exactly what you're going to do," she said with a threatening smile. Then she described precisely what was expected of him.

CHAPTER 21

REVOLUTION

The committee started especially early that morning. They were all yawning. Jennifer bit back yet another yawn and decided to get things started. There was a lot to do outside of the committee today.

"Thanks again for coming so early. The Commonwealth showing up is a blessing for our people and a crisis for all of us. Before we get to a discussion of how we dissolve this group let Griff and I review the decisions that were made yesterday." Jennifer was proud of herself for calming referring to the dissolution of the Committee. Everyone knew she mean 'when we all commit suicide'. It just sounded better and more abstract.

"The three planets have decided to form an alliance. We've agreed to a framework of the major issues. At some point we'll have to formalize a treaty. But for now, we'll keep it at a high level. The council will meet today to hear all of this as well. I don't expect much disagreement as we really aren't agreeing to anything controversial." At least for everyone except Barlow she thought to herself. "The one odd wrinkle is that the woman we thought was the queen of Liberty is actually her best friend. The kidnappers mistakenly took her instead of the actual queen and she didn't inform them otherwise."

Del raised his hand and was acknowledged with a nod, "Does that mean that Tee isn't marrying the queen of Liberty?"

Jennifer smiled, remembering the banter around that

topic the previous day, and said, "no, the plan for all of us to retain some semblance of freedom is to have the wedding. Tee has agreed to marry the real queen."

"That sucks," Griff said angerly. "The boy should be able to choose his own wife for God's sake."

"I agree. It's an incredible sacrifice. Tee said that being a member of the Guard meant he would do whatever was necessary to protect Pacifica. You would have been proud of him. You've told me he's a natural leader and I saw that yesterday," Jennifer said mollifying Griff.

"Other than that, our agreements are fairly mild. We agreed in principal to negotiate a peace agreement that states we will not war on each other. The other two planets are very intimidated by us. I can see their point given how much more robust we are. But they should realize we have been yearning for peace for almost two thousand years. The last thing we want is war. They also proposed eliminating import and export tariffs. Since we have no trading experience I have no idea if this is a good thing or a bad thing. Del, can you have someone in the history department investigate it before we sign any agreements?"

"Sure, not a problem. To be honest Barlow might be a good resource for this. He used to teach a course on the history of economics. I know he's a pain in the rear, but he is knowledgeable and insightful as long as the topic doesn't get ensnared in one of his conspiracy theories."

"I'm fine with you using Barlow as long as it doesn't create more confrontation in the council." There she thought proud of herself, batted that ball right back to him.

Griff raised his hand and said, "my understanding is that mercenaries actually invaded Liberty. Is this something the Guard is going to have to learn how to deal with?"

Jennifer sat back in her chair and in frustration said, "the First Minister talks eloquently about how the Commonwealth has provided peace. But in talking to Senator Cereo and Prince Justin it seems they do everything but that. I…"

Just then the conference room door opened. The First Minister entered holding what appeared to be a weapon in his hand. He quickly cautioned them saying, "stay where you are. This is a stun gun. I will put you all down the instant I pull the trigger" With a tense expression he slowly backed himself into the furthest corner of the room. He motioned towards Griff and said, "I've seen you spar and know how fast you can move. Please no sudden movements."

Jennifers gut turned into ice. They had been caught. Worse, there wasn't time to eliminate knowledge of their origin. They had doomed their people to extermination. As her mind screamed for an opportunity to turn the tables on the First Minister he continued, "the four young people in the computer room were not harmed. They are sleeping and will stay that way for a few hours. I have some questions."

Jennifer thought perhaps I can talk him into solving our problem for us, "the general population knows nothing of what's down here. No harm should come to them. You've made the consequences of violating technology restrictions clear. Why not execute our sentences here and now?"

The First Minister looked surprised and a little confused. After a moment he said, "what are your real plans with Liberty and Arista?"

Jennifer took a deep breath and let it out. Then she said, "exactly what you've been told. Theron Stone and Olivia Hastings marry. We cooperatively work on increasing tax revenues from all three planets."

"Why hide all of this?" He said clearly indicating their hiding of technology.

Never the most patient of people Griff said, "so we can destroy the Commonwealth."

Jennifer actually smiled. Griff consistently said that Pacifica should go down swinging. She found herself caught up in his defiance and said sternly, "why don't you grow yourself a pair and get on with it." Jennifer was oddly delighted to notice the rest of the committee was shocked at her words. She never said things like that. Her mother would be horrified she thought and smiled again.

Jack just stared at her for a few moments. Then with an amused expression beginning to show he said, "that might just be the advice I needed." Another pause then he explained. "Uncovering hidden technology and a plot against the Commonwealth would make my career. At the very least I can be sure of being assigned First Minister of a much more lucrative sector." He hesitated again, and with a determined look said, "the truth is that I want to help you."

There was a long period of stunned silence. Finally, Del asked, "why would you want to do that?"

Jack huffed out a nervous breath and said, "Its complicated." Pausing a few moments to collect his thoughts he said, "no that's not true. It's actually very simple. I can't continue to do what the Commonwealth asks me to do. I've done horrible things in the name of the Commonwealth. I can't justify what I've done with that excuse any longer."

The committee members all looked at each other with surprised hope in their eyes. Jennifer then said, "so how can you help us?"

"I've been working with Senator Cereo for quite some time now. It's clear his strategy was to slow things down while generally giving the governor what she wants. It's a good strategy. Most of the Commonwealth's Governors just want to maintain the status quo. Most of them got their jobs because of political influence, not merit. Her replacement should be vastly easier to work with. I can assist you through the transition."

"What do you get out of this?" Del asked bluntly.

Jack just stared back at him for a few moments and finally said, "self-respect." Then in a sad voice he added, "as soon as the current governor has transitioned, I will resign my position and leave government. I'm not sure what I'll do. But it will be something I can be proud of."

Jennifer noticed that Griff and Del were giving each other looks. Griff then nodded his head and Del spoke up, "How far are you willing to go? Would you act against the Commonwealth? Are you willing to strike a blow?" Del asked

Jack considered this for a long time. Then with firm conviction he said, "the Commonwealth is corrupt from top to bottom. Its original founders had good intentions. But it has evolved away from those good intentions. It is an amoral system completely controlling humankind for the benefit of a few power-hungry people. My father is a high-level bureaucrat in the Justice Ministry trying to fight corruption. He is an idealist. I believe the Justice Ministry is supporting him as a way to gain more power on the High Council. They don't want to eliminate corruption. They are as corrupt as everyone else. If there was a way to revolt against the Commonwealth I would join the revolution."

Del smiled at Jack and said, "there is a way." He stopped, frowned at Jacks weapon, and added in the haughty professor voice he used with undergraduates, "if you're joining the revolution please put your weapon away and sit down." Looking over at Jennifer with sly smile he said, "Griff and I have a secret we need to share.

CHAPTER 22

FORT PACIFICA

Jacks' shuttlecraft landed at the designated location on the largest of Pacifica's two moons. He had informed the survey ship that he enjoyed visiting moons as a hobby. It was a ridiculous excuse for the shuttle craft to be there. But being First Minister meant that nobody would questions his right to have a crazy hobby.

Large enough to be a small planet it was perfect for hiding what they believed was there. From the outside it appeared to be a naturally formed cave. In fact, the opening seemed too small for what was described to be inside. Donning spacesuits the team walked into the cave which enlarged past the opening. At the end of a corridor sized cavern was a large metal door. Quinn located a touch pad alongside the door and entered a code. To everyone's amazement the door swung open to reveal an airlock. This was the tricky part. If the airlock didn't work the warships said to be within the base would likely be damaged. If that were the case their gamble would fail. When the next keypad code was entered the first door closed, lights came on, and a whooshing noise was heard. Quinn checked a readout on his space suit arm and after a few minutes announced with glee, "One atmosphere, seventy eight percent nitrogen, twenty one percent oxygen with traces of argon and CO_2. It's still very cold so don't take your suits off."

Del added, "The entry door to the base will unlock when temperatures match. Let's keep these suits on until we are on the other side with the airlock completely closed."

After shedding their spacesuits, they ventured down a hallway and entered what appeared to be a small reception area. A large screen on the back wall suddenly came to life. A GEM was looking at them. The group gave a collective gasp. Everyone except Griff and Tee stepped back. The two of them reached for nonexistent weapons at their belts. Just when they all wondered if they should run the GEM smiled and began to speak in a warm and rich voice.

"Welcome. I hope this greeting is being received by the descendants of Ships 1 and 3. If not, I beseech our own descendants to search for their humanity and honor your ancestor's greatest desire. Peace for all.

My name is Donald Pearce. I am a direct line descendant of the original genetically enhanced research team given asylum by Ship 2. Our team was given asylum because we refused to participate in a plan to eradicate unmodified humans. We strongly believe there is no justification for genocide. We believe all life must be honored and protected.

I am first generation which means I was genetically altered physically for life on Pacifica. Those likely still alive on Pacifica are second generation. Those alterations were intended to make them stronger emotionally and mentally. As you surely know, those alterations went horribly wrong. Most of the first generation volunteered to remain in orbit once it became clear what we had created. We told our offspring we were doing it to support them. In reality we were debating what to do. Our shared goal had been to enable our descendants to enjoy all the fruits of Pacifica. And to do so in peace. We intended to live alongside the inhabitants of the peninsula in harmony, honoring our common roots. It became clear this wasn't going to happen.

Our paranoia was justified. Autonomous shuttle craft pretending to be carrying supplies were used to destroy ships 1 and 3. Their plan had been to simultaneously board Ship 2 while launching an invasion of the peninsula. We uncovered their subterfuge and with great reluctance destroyed the shuttlecraft approaching our ship. We did not realize the danger to Ships 1 and 3 until it was too late. For that failure we are deeply sorry.

We now faced another difficult choice. We could have used our technological capabilities to wipe out our progeny. But then we would have been as immoral as the civilization we escaped. They are human, perhaps with the worse attributes of our race, but human, nonetheless. We knew about the secret bunker beneath Landfall Valley. After witnessing the devastation of the civil war, we knew it would be many generations before that technology would be useful. We were extremely concerned that remnants of the civilization we escaped would discover our technology. Some advocated destroying it, but others, including myself, advocated storing it away in the hope that Pacifica could someday use it for peaceful purposes.

The research project the original modified colonists were working on was QW, or Quantum Warfare. Allen's Law laid out the groundwork for making incredibly sensitive measurements of gravitation. So sensitive in fact that locating and identifying objects in the vastness of space was possible by simply looking for emanations from concentrations of mass. Not only could minute concentrations of mass be located, but their nature could be determined. For instance, a spaceship is easily identified given its three-dimensional distribution of mass compared to its volume. Our original goal was to confuse these measurements. Our research turned out to be much more successful. Not only could we confuse measurements, but we also found we could create false readings. We have the means to present whatever we want our adversaries to see. Including nothing at all. This means a QW enabled warship can travel undetected and deliver a QW enabled warhead that is similarly undetectable. The warhead seemingly detonates out of nothing. If our technology had been intended to defeat those who wanted to eradicate us we would have enthusiastically supported that effort. However, it became clear that hatred had infected our leadership and QW technology was going to be used for genocide. We simply could not contribute to that cause. Our hope is that this technology will be used to protect all forms of human life, not destroy them.

To enter we ask that everyone individually pledge to use the technologies within for the betterment of all of humanity. Please say your name and make your pledge. When all pledges have been accepted you may enter. Every time you reenter you will have to make your pledge again. Whomever you have chosen to lead should go first. After entering merely state your name and what you would like to accomplish. Automated systems will do the rest.

May peace be with you.

They all looked around at each other in wonderment. After a few moments Del stepped forward and said, "my name is Delvin Dacy. I pledge to dedicate my life to the betterment of humanity. This pledge includes all humans whether genetically altered or not."

The voice from the video simply said, "you speak the truth. Your pledge is accepted."

The rest of the group stepped forward individually and repeated the same pledge Del had made. Quinn was the last one to make his pledge. After his pledge was accepted the voice said, "welcome to Pacifica's archive of technology." A hidden door in one of the side walls popped open.

Even after three days of discovery the group was still in awe but wary. This seemed too good to be true. Everyone had a sense that disaster must surely be just around the corner. Well almost everyone. Quinn seemed to be on his dream vacation. It would be nice to exist in such a state of bliss all the time thought Del. While he had seen Quinn nervous or uncomfortable at times, these were rare and never lasted for long. It was a good thing the boy wasn't moody. He was key to unlocking this technology. While Hestie was also capable of understanding it she wasn't as passionate about the engineering side of things. Her passions were focused in other areas. Quinn's contributions were critical in protecting them from the Commonwealth. Del was very happy he did not have to deal with someone as irrational as he had been at that age.

The three warships were much bigger than they had guessed. They were designed to be operated by six crew members. But they were outfitted to comfortably hold twelve for long periods of time. There was a shuttle craft on board each ship for planetary excursions. These were small but could transport a crew of up to six for short distances. They were not equipped with jump capability. The warships had clearly been intended to do everything from destroying planets to boarding spaceships and performing limited scouting missions on planet. "Where are we in getting the warships operational?" Del asked.

"Donny says all calibrations and tests have been completed on Gerty. It's ready to go. The Aguila has an issue with its propulsion system. It's repairable but we need to create replacement parts and perform a full service. I recommend we leave that for later. Peregrine is currently being calibrated," Quinn said.

One of the political agreements was that each planet would crew one of the three warships. They committed to making sure these vessels were only used for sector defense and not planetary war. Pacifica did this with the restriction that they alone controlled the technology. The Liberty and Arista ships maintenance and support would be solely provided by Pacifica. Jennifer asked Tee to name Pacifica's ship. He named it after his grandmother. Prince Justin and Senator Cereo named the other two. Donny was what they had all taken to calling the voice that seemed to control everything. It was the same warm and friendly voice that had originally welcomed them. It had a calming nature and by now seemed to be part of the crew.

"I've finished testing our inventory of fusion and anti-matter munitions. They are all QW enabled," Quinn said smiling.

Del wasn't sure how anyone could talk about that kind of destructive power and not seem concerned, but again this was Quinn. "What are they designed for?" Del asked.

"There are two types of fusion devices. The first is small and would destroy a building, bridge, or spaceship. The larger would incinerate an entire valley on Pacifica. The anti-matter devices could destroy an entire planet. We only have five of those," Quinn said with a smile still intact.

Del shuddered to think they had the means to destroy five entire planets. "How many of each type of fusion device do we have?"

"One hundred and twenty of the small and thirty of the large. We also have full production capability to build more. The limiting material is anti-matter. If we keep in reserve what has been set aside for munitions we can build approximately one thousand more devices. The triggers for the fusion devices use a tiny amount of anti-matter. We can also produce more anti-matter but would need to invest quite a bit of time and resources to build that capability out," Quinn concluded.

In other words, we have way more than we should ever need Del thought. "How about crew related activities? When will we be able to launch Gerty?"

"Communications, propulsion, environmental, and ordinance have reported they are ready to go. Hestie has the navigation system up and running. I need to finish here and go through the navigation checklist with her on Peregrine." Quinn said.

After deciding Quinn had everything under control he went looking for Griff. He finally found him on board Gerty checking ordinance. He said, "for a man terrified of the Tram, you seem to have overcome your fear of technology."

Griff grinned and replied, "knowing you had nothing to do with designing any of this gives me great comfort."

Del smiled back and then changed to a serious tone. "Griff, is Tee really ready to take this on?"

Griff stopped what he was doing and looked calmly at Del. After a few moments he said, "yes. The boy has many lifetimes of experience in highly stressful situations where judgement and timing are critical. He is Pacifica's best military strategist. There isn't anyone I trust more to lead this, including myself." Then Griff smiled and said, "plus, he'll have the benefit of my vast knowledge and experience to fall back on."

Del retained his serious expression and simply nodded his head, "that's all I needed to hear Griff."

Griff seemed surprised at the lack of a comeback. "Were you thinking of using your authority to make a change?"

"I was. He just seems so young. It's also clear he doesn't desire leadership," Del said.

"He is young. But after Arista he is far older than either of us. While he doesn't pursue command, he never hesitates to take it on and excel. Having power over others isn't important to him. He's the kind of leader the Guard and Pacifica needs," Griff said with conviction.

Just then Donny's voice permeated the inside of Gerty saying, "we have detected movements of two Commonwealth warships that appear to be offensive in nature. Of immediate concern is a Commonwealth warship on a vector to Pacifica utilizing fast jumping. This warship will arrive in the vicinity of Pacifica in approximately twenty-seven hours at their current jump rate. A second Commonwealth warship together with three large transport vessels are vectoring for Liberty. This configuration is typical for transporting an invasion force. Given its current standard jump rate, an invasion force could be on the ground in three days."

Fast jumping was dangerous. By shortening the processing time to generate a wormhole you increase your risk of miscalculating. While rare, ships have simply disappeared forever when operating in this mode. This meant the Commonwealth was suspicious of a threat from Pacifica and decided to take aggressive action. "We need to get everybody together and decide what to do." Griff said with worry in his voice.

"The governor has obviously decided to accelerate the plan," Jack said. "If she understood what we're doing she would send more than one warship to Pacifica."

"But why send a warship here at all?" Jennifer asked.

"She doesn't like loose ends. Having legal authority for three planets in one location would be seen as a risk. It might look like an overreaction, but this is typical of her," Jack said.

"So, we still have the opportunity for a surprise attack," Griff said.

"In my opinion, yes." Jack said.

"What about providing immediate support for Liberty. You've agreed to provide for the defense of Liberty," Justin said suspiciously.

"We've all agreed to support each other," Griff shot back. "We will get to Liberty as soon as possible but it has to be in the context of an overall battle strategy."

"Gentleman, we are all friends here. We have a common enemy. Can we please discuss alternatives in an atmosphere of trust?" Cereo said. "Griff, you've told me that Tee is our best strategist. Perhaps we should listen to his council on what we should do with our warships."

They all looked at Tee and he momentarily leaned back in his chair. He looked down and said, "I've been giving this some thought. "We need to maintain the element of surprise as long as possible. This should drive our decisions until we decide to reveal ourselves. The first priority is to keep our base of operations hidden. That means this moon."

"But what about Liberty!" Justin blurted out.

"Give me a few minutes to describe what I think our strategic priorities should be and then I'll make a recommendation on how to achieve them," Tee said looking calm and confident. Jennifer smiled to herself. He really is quite mature for his age she thought.

Justin took a deep breath obviously settling himself, "I'm sorry Tee. My anxiety over the queen is making me crazy. I need to trust everyone here which is obviously still a challenge for me." Jennifer was starting to like Prince Justin. He might be overly emotional at times, but he owned up to it and made the necessary changes in his behavior.

Tee continued, "we are badly outnumbered and that suggests we cut their military supply line as soon as possible."

"What does that mean?" Del asked.

"It means we control movement through the Sector 27 wormhole. Cut them off from the Commonwealth," Tee explained.

Del scrunched his eyebrows together obviously giving this some thought. Then he said, "we can also shut down their ability to communicate. Quinn told me we could capture key nodes in their network and control communications. If we do this properly we can communicate

185

with ourselves and the Commonwealth, but they can't communicate with each other."

Del noticed that everyone was giving him confused looks. He hesitated a few moments and then added, "I know all this technology is confusing. Let me explain a bit more. The way real time communications happen across the sector is through permanent stationary artificial wormholes that are enlarged just enough to transmit optical information. A very thin beam of light. As we've discussed with the warships, the energy required to grow and keep artificial wormholes open is tremendous. By keeping the distances between nodes reasonable, and the size of the wormholes very small, a real time network can be built and reasonably operated. To control information flow, we simply select key nodes in the system and replace them with our own. Quinn built two of these long ago as a hobby project. He can build more if we need them."

Tee nodded his head at that information and continued, "the lowest risk short term move is to leave one warship here and take the other straight to the wormhole. However, that is likely just going to end up in a war of attrition. That is a war we will lose." Tee stopped and looked around the table. Then he said, "are you willing to gamble?"

CHAPTER 23

SIEGE

Olivia knew they had been extremely lucky. Without warning troop transports had landed just outside the capital. The luck was having the Royal Castle currently overcrowded with Colonel Peters Rangers. If they had landed a few days later most of those men would have been on their way back to their barracks near Perry's ranch. They were cut off from the main Royal Army units. But they had an adequate number of defenders to withstand a lengthy siege. The castle had its own well, so water wasn't an issue. But they only had about three weeks of food stored away. Perry had immediately issued orders for reduced rations but that would only add another three weeks best case.

Perry had been shocked to see General Harris riding up to the main gate with four armed guards under a white flag. He asked to speak with whomever was in charge. Perry walked out the gate to meet with him. He had Colonel Peters and another robust Ranger as his only security. Olivia smiled to herself. She remembered Perry had been outnumbered two to one in his previous confrontation with General Harris. Well, that's a creative way to insult him without saying a word, she thought.

"General Eastbrook and Colonel Peters. So good to see you both." Harris said jovially.

"What are you doing here Harris?" Perry asked sternly.

"I've come to take control of Liberty for its rightful ruler," Harris said with his smile still in place.

"Queen Olivia would never engage mercenaries," Perry said dismissively.

"Queen Olivia is no longer Liberty's rightful ruler," Harris countered, paused, and then with an evil grin said, "why don't I explain what's happened. That will speed up discussions of your surrender." Harris paused again then continued, "Arista's Senate has determined that Theron Stone and Olivia Hastings are legally married. They met the three qualifications of a common law marriage on Arista. They both had the legal capacity to enter into a marriage. They expressed an intent to be married. And they were engaged in cohabitation at Theron's private residence in Arista's Palatium. Once married under Arista law, Olivia Hastings falls under the authority of her husband. That means he became the legal ruler of both Arista and Liberty. Theron's chief advisor, Senator Cereo, was discovered to be secretly fomenting a slave rebellion. This was known to Theron and is in violation of the articles of property in the Arista constitution. This enabled the Senate of Arista to issue an arrest warrant for Senator Cereo and declare Theron unsuitable to rule Arista. Magistrate Pluta, in the name of the Arista Senate, now claims authority over both planets. The Commonwealths Justice Ministry supports the legality of Arista's claim."

Perry just stared at him for a while. Just as it got uncomfortable he said, "I don't believe you. Pack up and leave or this time the courts will decide your fate." Then he turned around and walked back into the castle.

Harris shouted at him as he strove away, "It's just a matter of time General. Something I have in abundance. My men will simply enjoy all your planet has to offer until you accept reality. Your only decision is to decide how much suffering you want the citizens of Liberty to endure."

Perry walked directly from his confrontation with Harris to Olivia's quarters. She was currently hiding away in the old apartment he had occupied for a number of months. As soon as he walked in Olivia could see his anxiety. She said softly, "I heard everything. What do you think we should do?"

Perry took in a deep breath and said, "It's time to reveal that they kidnapped the wrong person. The welfare of

Liberty must come first. It may put Bria in danger, but it's what she would want us to do."

"Agreed. How do you propose we announce this?" Olivia asked.

Perry steeped his hands together and said, "I recommend we tell Harris we're willing to discuss surrender if the First Minister mediates the discussions. Harris insisted on this the last time so he can hardly object now. We'll need to prove you are the queen. Pretty much everyone knows what you look like so it shouldn't be difficult. It's why it's been so hard to hide you. If we don't get the Commonwealth involved Harris will just claim you're a fake."

Olivia looked troubled. She gave it some thought and finally said, "I don't like leaving our people defenseless against that army. Perhaps it's better to declare it now. It might cause enough worry that he controls his men until the First Minister shows up."

"It will likely cause him to storm the castle instead. If he suspects that he has no legal authority he will take steps to change that situation. I have no doubts he will kill everyone in the castle to cover this up. Given the Commonwealth is involved anyone who knows the truth will be hunted down," Perry said firmly.

Olivia's expression grew firm and raising her voice she said, "I am not willing to hide behind these walls while our people are murdered and abused."

As Perry opened his mouth to respond they heard a loud whooshing noise outside the window. Both walked over to look outside and froze dumbfounded. Perry recovered first and shouted, "Peters! Full complement on the main gate walls. Assemble a raiding party for an assault in case hostiles emerge from that shuttlecraft." And with that he briskly followed Peters who was running to comply.

Olivia joined him a few minutes later in the watch tower above the main gate. Everyone she had walked past to get there had recognized her. Shouts of "Queen Olivia has returned," were ringing in the courtyard below.

"I guess you've made your decision," Perry said with mild sarcasm.

"You always told Bria and I that sometimes you just have to make a decision," Olivia said.

Perry frowned at her and looking back to the shuttlecraft said, "what do we have here?"

Just then the door to the shuttlecraft opened and a man walked out.

"It's Uncle Justin," Olivia said in surprise. A woman exited next, "and Bria!" And with that she ran down the stairs and out the gate to greet them. Colonel Peters quickly detailed his Rangers waiting by the gate to surround the queen. She ran and jumped into Bria's arms, both of them laughing and crying all at once. Perry joined them and pulled Bria into his own tight hug rocking her back and forth.

"I can't believe you're back. I've been worried sick about you," Perry said.

Justin smiled broadly watching the reunion and then looked towards the shuttle door and said, "come on out."

The three largest people Olivia had ever seen stepped out of the shuttle, "Surround." Colonel Peters barked out as his Ranger pulled their weapons and keeping their distance quickly encircled the newly embarked passengers.

"Stop!" Justin yelled, "they are friends. Put your weapons away ."

Olivia noticed the rangers didn't comply with Prince Justin's order. Only when Colonel Peters ordered them to 'stand down' and 'escort' did they put their weapons away. Even then they kept their hands on those weapons. They closed in around their queen but maintained their encirclement of the group.

"Your Majesty, would you allow me to make introductions," Prince Justin said. After she gave him a nod of approval he continued, "first let me present Theron, First of his Name, Emperor of Arista."

"It's a pleasure to meet you Your Majesty," Olivia said smoothly, which surprised even her given the shocking news she was talking to the emperor of a planet she thought utterly immoral. She paused and then said, "do you realize the mercenary army camped out on the plain believes they are acting under orders from Arista?"

Tee smiled grimly at her and said, "we suspected that was the case when we arrived. We saw the Commonwealth troop transport vessels and decided to come straight to your castle. There is much to discuss but know we are here to support you," Tee said quickly. Then he stopped and grimacing in embarrassment said, "it's nice to meet you as well."

"With Theron is Griffith Ricks, Acting Commander General of the Pacifica Guard, and Diana Wells, Captain of the Apple Valley Wall Archers. I'm sorry to rush introductions but can we retire for a private conversation?" Looking over at Perry he said, "I will vouch for Theron and his companions. They are our friends and as Theron said they are here to help."

"What about the rifles?" Diana asked Griff.

"Keep them in the shuttle for now. We'll offload them after we've explained everything to Her Majesty and General Eastbrook. In the meantime, if the army camped out there attacks take off and dissuade them with the shuttle's armaments," Griff said with a grin.

"Yes sir," Diana said smiling.

As they were walking to Olivia's reception room Perry turned to Justin and said in a hushed voice, "What's this all about?"

Justin turned and looked at Perry warmly. He grinned and said, "I've joined another revolution. I'm hoping to do a better job of recruiting you this time."

The next morning Olivia, Justin, Chief Justice Roberts, Bria, and Perry met to discuss what they had learned the day before. Justin started the conversation, "I've asked Bria to join us because she has spent considerable time in Senator Cereo's household and knows Tee well." He hesitated and continued, "our path forward has much to do with our level of trust in these people."

191

"And where do you stand on the trust issue," Olivia asked.

"Senator Cereo has a golden tongue which makes me nervous. He's been a master manipulator in Arista politics and with the Commonwealth. But I've become convinced he has helped Liberty in the process. I'm convinced he has good intentions." Justin stopped for a moment and looked around the table, "The real threat is Pacifica. A more warlike culture is hard to imagine. They control military technology that appears to exceed even the Commonwealth's capabilities. That combination terrifies me."

Olivia pondered his answer for a few moments and then turned to Bria, "would you tell everyone what you told me about Tee last night?"

"Terrifying is a good description of Tee. I saw him kill three of the guards on the slave ship without seeming to exert any effort at all. It happened so fast I can't tell you how he did it. As I'm sure you've noticed, he is smaller than others of his race." Bria then took a breath, smiled slightly, and said, "On the other hand, I'm convinced Tee is a man of honesty, integrity, and compassion. I trust Tee." She twitched a little mentally at the conflict that remained within her. She had come to realize she was scared of what Tee could do, but she did trust him to do the right thing.

Perry spoke up at this point, "Early this morning I watched Tee and the one they call Jay spar. We teach smaller soldiers to take advantage of their quickness when fighting larger opponents. The unusually large can be a bit ponderous. That is clearly not the case with these two. They are lightning quick and extraordinarily skilled." Perry smiled grimly and said, "and then there are the women. If Diana is typical, they are equally impressive. The men heard Prince Justin introduce Diana as a Wall Archer. While we were meeting yesterday they challenged her to a contest. They gave her one of our siege bows thinking to have a little fun. These bows are intended to launch heavy bolts over high walls from a distance. The bolts generally have large glass vials for arrowheads filled with a flammable liquid and are used to start fires. Very few are strong enough to use them. They confused pretty with weak. She used it effortlessly. She humiliated our best archers. According to those who were there it wasn't even close to competitive."

Olivia sighed and then said in a quiet voice, "Can we trust them?"

Justin nodded his head and summarized, "I think the best evidence of trust is what they have offered us. Instead of demanding concessions they will share their technology. The only restriction will be military technology. Medicines, transportation, power generation, and computer knowledge will all be available. They are asking Liberty to join Pacifica and Arista as equal partners in managing and disseminating it. The only price is that we join the revolution."

Justin hesitated clearly going through a checklist in his head and then said, "one more thing. Senator Cereo proposed that Pacifica announce they are the ones behind this. That Pacifica is merely evicting squatters. They will claim they achieved ownership of the sector by discovery when they arrived almost two millennia ago. It's a good idea because if this doesn't' go our way Liberty can claim we were forced to comply. Gives us an opportunity to avoid having our planet cleansed."

"It sounds too good to be true," Olivia said, "But then again I don't see how we have another choice. If we sit on the sidelines, and the Commonwealth wins, our people will still suffer. Their actions over the past few years proves that." She looked around the table and asked, "Does anyone disagree that our best option is to accept the offer?" Olivia looked at each person and received head nods from each. "OK, it's decided. Justice Roberts would you see what they have written down?"

Justin spoke up quickly, "Olivia, we don't have time to argue over wording. Events are unfolding quickly. We have to act immediately. If we agree then Perry will join one of the warships as its commander. And..."

"Wait a minute. I don't know anything about space travel or modern weaponry," Perry said with exasperation.

"You don't have to. The ships operate on voice command. There is a crew of five that will propose actions, and the commander simply gives the command to execute or belay. I observed this on the trip here. You will have no trouble with it. This is all part of the sharing. We have two warships currently operating. One will be commanded by Tee, and the other by you. The third once it's up and running will be commanded by Senator Cereo until he can retrieve his son Vincent. All are staffed by Pacifica for now. In the future we will have our own operators. Our warship is named the Peregrine by the way."

"Peregrine?" Perry said, "you didn't!"

"Yes I did. If you didn't want to be constantly reminded that you saved the life of a young and stupid Prince you never should have done it," Justin said obviously pleased with himself. "One more thing. You heard Diana mention rifles yesterday. With something called an optical scope they can accurately hit a target from over a mile away. Fifty of these are being loaned along with Diana for training. This should keep General Harris at bay until we can spare one of the warships to come back and mop up. It should only be a few weeks at most. The other item we'll leave behind is a communications console. For now, it's been set up so you can call any of the three warships or President Malrey. Diana will train a couple of operators for you." Justin hesitated and then said, "I know this is difficult. I had a hard time accepting it as well. But time is critical, we need to let them know we agree. Once that's done Perry must get with Tee and Griff to agree on a battle strategy."

Tee greeted Perry warmly, "I'm happy Liberty decided to join General Eastbrook."

"Call me Perry, we aren't much on formality Theron."

"Then call me Tee," he said smiling. "Let me give you a summary. You'll get a chance to get a more in-depth understanding once onboard and on your way. The advantage we have is invisibility. The Commonwealth warships can't see us or our munitions until they explode.

They can't hide from us. But we can hide from them. When we arrived at Liberty we destroyed the Commonwealth warship that accompanied the troop transports. The transport ships were then boarded and disabled. The Commonwealth is so worried about their own citizens revolting they do not allow anyone but the military to have weapons of any kind. The transport vessels are in stable orbits but unable to do anything until we return. The Commonwealth will think their sector communications network has gone down. They will eventually figure out its sabotage. General Harris has certainly realized something is horribly wrong at this point." Tee waited to see if Perry had questions then continued.

"Did you offer to let the Commonwealth warship surrender before you destroyed them?" Perry asked with a frown.

Griff looked surprised. He considered the question then nodded his head and answered, "It's a good question. Prince Justin recommended this when we arrived. However, we didn't know what action the warship might take. It might have used the demand as an excuse to attack the planet. He eventually agreed it was a risk we couldn't afford to take. Griff hesitated and then sheepishly said, "don't think badly of us. We've been fighting a never-ending war against an enemy where surrender wasn't an option. We've never been in a position to consider humanitarian alternatives."

Perry gave that some thought and then nodded his head in understanding. Then he looked at Tee and asked, "what do you propose we do next?"

Tee looked a bit guilty as he said, "my thoughts are that we need to cut their supply lines and blockade A27."

"That makes sense," Perry said nodding his head in approval. "Are you suggesting we try and stop all traffic into and out of the sector? Is that even possible?"

"Yes, we think so. We announce we are embargoing Sector 27 and then destroy anything that enters or tries to exit through the wormhole. We do the same for A27. We need to be careful with communications anytime there is a nearby threat. This is because our location is revealed when we transmit. In those situations, the recommendation is to only communicate when it's an emergency. In that case the process is to send short messages and then move immediately. They can't tell where we are if we just receive messages from the network."

Perry considered this and said, "so one of us goes to the wormhole and the other to Planet 27?"

"Yes," Griff said, "Our suggestion is that you proceed to A27, and we'll take care of the wormhole. You have much more experience with offensive warfare than we do. A27 is where we believe we might need to go on the offensive. The wormhole is a defensive action that we feel we are best suited for. Tee and I propose you take the lead on military decisions. Our experience is one dimensional while yours is not. All three planets have agreed to this."

Perry was pleased. These are reasonable people he thought. Their proposal makes sense based on experience and relative strengths and weaknesses. Giving up the lead on military decisions says they will do the right thing even if it's to their disadvantage. "Well, let's get going then. We can discuss this in more detail once we're on our way. The warships can communicate with each other right?"

"Yes sir, except when we're transversing a wormhole." Tee frowned slightly and continued, "I wish I could explain this better. Quinn started explaining radio communications to me, but I didn't have enough time to spend with him to truly understand it. I don't understand everything Quinn tells me, but I believe everything he says."

"Ok then I'll believe him too," Perry said and gave Tee an approving nod of the head.

CHAPTER 24

TRESPASS

Gerty's main console came to life with an image of President Malrey sitting at her desk. Griff noted wryly to himself that they had done a good job of cleaning off the top of that desk. It was normally piled high with paperwork. Quinn was explaining in excruciating detail how video cameras work when Jennifer started talking.

"My name is Jennifer Malrey. I am the duly elected President of Pacifica. This message is a declaration that we will no longer accept the Commonwealths trespass in our sovereign domain. Our ancestors discovered this sector one thousand eight hundred and fifty-three years ago. At that time, our ownership of all planets within the sector was established. We desire to live in peace with other like-minded people. It is clear from our observations of the Commonwealth that this is not possible. We believe that all people are created equal. That the form of government people live under is one they have collectively agreed to. We believe that tyranny is an abusive form of government. Our belief is that slavery is an expression of the worse attributes of the human race. It's become obvious from our observations that the Commonwealth does not share these values. We have decided that peace and freedom can only be obtained through separation."

Jennifer paused, glanced down at her notes, and then continued, "we feel it is important to give examples of why we have come to this decision. The Governor of Sector 27 has violated the Commonwealths non-interference Edict.

This is just one instance of the corruption that appears to be commonplace. She coerced the Arista government to declare war on Liberty. The people of Arista hold no blame in this. Their government was clearly under the duress of a tyrant. A puppet government controlled by the Governor was established for the purpose of enslaving the populations of Arista, Liberty, and Pacifica. This is an act of war."

Jennifer paused and changed her tone to one of triumph saying, "Pacifica has come to the defense of Liberty. The Commonwealth warship threatening that planet has been destroyed and the troop transports orbiting the planet have been boarded and placed under our control. Pacifica has no desire to oppress the citizens of Liberty or any other Commonwealth colony. They will be offered the opportunity to join a Confederation of Planets and live in peace, freedom, and security."

Jennifers face took on a firm look and continued, "due to the tyranny and lawlessness of the Commonwealth we require all Commonwealth citizens to leave the sector. As of this time forward, no vessels will be allowed to enter our sovereign domain without permission. This includes any traffic through what is commonly referred to as the Sector 27 wormhole. Any attempt to do so will result in those vessels' immediate destruction. A27 is similarly embargoed with the same result to any vessel attempting to land or leave the planet. We also control communications within the sector and through the wormhole. You may request permission to communicate so that plans can be generated to expedite your travel back to the Commonwealth. These communications will be individually reviewed and approved if we deem them appropriate."

Jennifer then paused and softened her expression. "Our hope is to live in peace with the Commonwealth. We ask your government to reply with its compliance so we may assist you with safe transportation back to your homes. May peace be with you."

Griff had a slight grin on his face as he turned to Tee and

said, "well that does it. It's official. The next ship that comes through that hole in space gets blown to hell." As soon as he said it a large Commonwealth warship appeared.

"Detonate S1," Tee ordered and after a slight pause the ship's sensors were overwhelmed with energy blinding them momentarily. After the sensors recovered there was nothing left to see but debris.

Jay immediately announced, "Device S2 ready for launch." Jay had only gotten one day of training to be Gerty's munitions officer. It was a simple job but given the requirement for human interaction for every step it was vital. The AI debacle in ancient times altered for eternity what computers would be allowed to do on their own.

"Destination match," Quinn said, indicating that the jump for Device S2 was ready for launch.

"Destination approved. Launch Device S2," Tee ordered, and the device immediately arrived at the mouth of the wormhole awaiting a detonation command.

Two more ships appeared and were added to the cloud of debris when Quinn said, "that last one didn't have any occupants. It was an empty vessel."

Tee considered this for a few moments and then asked, "can we determine if there are any occupants before they have time to jump?"

Quinn considered this and then with a frown said, "Probably not. The minimum processing time for a fast jump is roughly the same as the time to analyze the contents of a ship."

Tee frowned and gave this some thought, "Is the Aquila fixed yet?" Tee asked. The Aquila was the third warship and Caius named it after the Roman symbol of authority. Caius told him that he thought Arista's senate would feel pride with that choice and wanted to do everything possible to mollify them. When this was over Caius had an insurrection to deal with. The more he could bow to the senate's vanity the better.

"No. They sent me test data and their conclusions. I'm not allowed to respond to them this close to the wormhole. I don't agree with their conclusions so I doubt Aquila will leave Fort Pacifica anytime soon," Quinn concluded.

Tee sighed, frowned, and then said, "Colonel Peters you are in command until I return. Continue to destroy anything that comes through."

"Yes sir," came the response.

Griff can you join me in the dining room?" Tee asked. With a quick nod Griff turned and walked from the bridge with Tee close behind him.

As soon as the door closed Tee said, "we're screwed. They can continue sending junk vessels until Gerty runs out of munitions. We can't rely on Aquila for resupply. The danger has always been that we get overwhelmed. If they don't care how many vessels they lose it's just like fighting the GEMs. Eventually they will wear us down. If they can flood the sector with warships they will eventually find Fort Pacifica. If that happens we lose."

Griff just smiled at him and said, "You have some crazy plan you're reluctant to share."

"You've been listening to Jay," Tee accused with a weak smile.

Griff narrowed his eyes at Tee and said, "I've been watching you closely since you were stupid enough to challenge someone twice your size on the playground. You don't give up and you always have a plan. Sometimes the plan is insane. Your insane plans tend to work more often than not."

Tee shrugged in a self-depreciating way and said, "we have to change the rules. It might get messy."

CHAPTER 25

THE BUNKER

Governor Jacobs mismatched eyes were bugged out more than Jack had ever seen them. Even parsecs away it frightened him. He wasn't sure he would ever get over the trauma of working for her. "How dare you broadcast your ridiculous message directly to the Commonwealth and our A27 citizens," she said loudly glaring out from the monitor.

Jennifer stared back at her confidently and said in a calm matter of fact voice, "I don't have time to waste on inconsequential banter. We simply need to discuss your surrender and exit from this sector." Jack had become tremendously impressed with Jennifer Malrey. He had watched her orchestrate the Pacifica Council with graceful collaboration. He thought Julie Jacobs would chew her up and spit her out. But instead, she was showing a spine made of steel.

"Let me tell you what is going to happen. The Commonwealth will spare no expense to wipe out your pathetic little revolution. You might blow up a few transports trying to take off or land. But it doesn't change the outcome. The Commonwealth has hundreds of warships with nothing else to do. They will love having a conflict to resolve. It will temporarily relieve them of their boring lives. I've always thought the military was grossly bloated. A waste of credits. But I have to admit they are capable. I don't care what technology you have hidden away on Pacifica. You will be completely destroyed," Jacobs said with an evil smirk as Jack imagined a cat tail twitching behind her.

"If you are unwilling to recognize reality then we will have to introduce it to you in a more dramatic fashion," Jennifer said confidently.

"Spare me your empty threats. If you surrender I will see what I can do to ensure your people are enslaved instead of exterminated. Otherwise, you can go to your grave knowing you've caused their extinction. You'll be on your knees begging for mercy before this is over," Jacobs said with the intense stare of a cat ready to pounce. She hesitated, seemingly gathering her thoughts, and said, "By the way, what have you done with Queen Olivia, Senator Cereo, and my First Minister?"

"Queen Olivia and Senator Cereo have been offered sanctuary. Your First Minister is in a holding cell awaiting your surrender. We can negotiate his release once you've agreed to our terms," Jennifer said.

"Do whatever you want with Jack. It would be kinder if you simply eliminated him. Failure of this magnitude is dealt with harshly by the Commonwealth," Jacobs said and then her face took on a smile that caused chills. "Tell the queen and senator to start practicing their begging. It's going to have to be good." Then she severed the link.

Jennifer slumped a bit in her chair, took a deep breath and let it out. "What do you think?" she asked Olivia, Caius, and Jack who were all shown on separate monitor windows.

"She believes what she's saying," Jack said, "Even if we invade A27 there is a bunker she can retreat to. Only the Governor and the local Commander know where it's at. She is probably already there. She won't care if we kill everyone on A27 if she wins in the end. Her stance that she has time is credible."

They were all silent for a while then Olivia said, "I have to commend you Jennifer. I'm not sure I could have stayed as cool and collected as you did with her."

"I agree," Cereo quickly said. Then he observed, "She was

right about one thing. The threat is empty. We need A27 to surrender but are likely to run out of time if something dramatic doesn't happen."

Coronel Askook was irritated with Governor Jacobs but decided to try and not show it. She didn't seem to understand that the Pacifica rebels had technology the Commonwealth did not have. "We can't detect them Governor. They're invisible. The only encouraging aspect is that it appears they only have two vessels."

Julie Jacobs starred daggers at the Colonel and in a sarcastic tone said, "if you can't detect their war ships how can you possibly know how many there are?"

Askook kept his face normal and his response professional although he couldn't keep the fire completely out of his eyes. "This comes from a well-reasoned military assessment. It's the best analysis we have. I agree with its conclusions. The assessment is based on the timelines of when various parts of the communications network went down. We first lost contact with Pacifica. Then seventy-two hours later we lost connection to Liberty. This is the proper amount of travel time between Pacifica and Liberty. The local A27 and wormhole communication paths were shut down as if two ships left Liberty at the same time, arrived on normal transit schedules, and shut down each of those communication links when they arrived. Could there be more than two? Yes, of course. But our current information suggests two ships."

"Why weren't we notified prior to Pacifica's broadcast that our communications network had been compromised," Julie asked as she continued to glare at Askook.

"We failed to consider the possibility of sabotage. The network support team believed this was a cascading systematic failure likely caused by the latest software update. In their defense, we haven't had anyone take physical control of a space borne portion of our communications network since the military took control of the networks after the Mutant Wars. However, this is clearly a failure of military leadership. We should have had a contingency plan assuming this would occur. It will need to be addressed once this crisis is over."

Chief Justice Reginald, the highest legal authority in the Commonwealth said, "I appreciate your candor Colonel. However, the hijacking of our networks is not the main issue here." He then turned his attention to Julie and said, "Administration is responsible for Survey operations. How was it possible for Pacifica to hide technology for seven hundred years?"

The room was silent while Julie fumed. She was visualizing the things she would do to Reginald if she ever got the chance when Askook spoke up, "the rebels clearly have technology we don't have. Our advantage is time. Pacifica can't possibly defeat the overwhelming number of warships the Commonwealth can deploy. Finding the bunker will be difficult and time-consuming. We just need to wait."

"What if they do find us Colonel?" Reginald asked.

"If they find us our only option is surrender. We have to assume they have disruptors. As you know these devices disable anything electronic. Gunpowder was obsolete as soon as a way was invented to remotely identify it and then cause it to explode. That means that unless we can isolate ourselves in a metal tube, like a warship, we are limited to hand-to-hand combat. The few shielded assault vehicles we have on A27 would get instantly vaporized from the warship currently in orbit. Having seen videos of Pacifica warriors in action, I can assure you we have no chance to defeat them."

"Colonel Askook, do you have any idea of where their stealth technology came from?" Justice Reginald asked.

Askook nodded his head slightly and said, "We've had little time to investigate but there is a theory we're running with. There was a rumor of a Mutant military research and development team that was never accounted for. They were supposedly engaged in a research project around the time the Pacifica emigration fleet left Earth. It's possible one of the three ships in that fleet had the Mutant research team on board. If so, they may have brought along a few military prototypes. What confirms this as a possibility are results from sequencing the Pacifica Mutants. What Pacifica calls GEMs seem to be based on a Mutant strain known to be associated with that timeframe.

Reginald lost his temper at that point. He turned and pointed his finger at Governor Jacobs and said, "another survey failure! How could you possibly miss that?" Reginald paused for a few moments clearly trying to calm himself and think through the situation. "Are the other Pacifica natives really true humans or are they GEMs as well?"

"They're true human. This has been analyzed by multiple expert's time and time again. Whenever there is a subject to sample, Survey fully examines their genome for any hint of genetic engineering. The latest sample analyzed was the Arista gladiator, Theron Stone. He is true human," Askook said with confidence.

With her unblinking eyes ablaze Julie said, "it doesn't matter if they are true human or not. Once we get control of the sector I'll lay waste to every single planet and start over with new colonists."

"You are no longer in charge here Ms. Jacobs," Reginald shouted at Julie. He visibly calmed himself and then said with distain, "As a representative of the High Council, I have the authority to dismiss Governors who exhibit gross incompetence. No Governor in history has lost control of their sector. Congratulations, you've made the history books." He turned to Colonel Askook and said, "as the representative of the Commonwealth Military you are witness to Governor Jacobs being relieved of her duties. I will take over responsibility for all decisions in this Sector including negotiations with the rebels.

"I verify I have witnessed this transition. The military will comply with your orders Chief Justice."

Sovereign

CHAPTER 26

INCURSION

This was the dangerous part in Tee's mind. They had to avoid the growing cloud of debris and enter the wormhole at an oblique angle with low relative velocity hoping they don't ram a ship coming through the other way.

"Destination match," Quinn called out.

"Destination approved. Launch Gerty," Tee ordered. He had gotten used to seeing the background star field abruptly change. But having six Commonwealth ships suddenly appear was discomforting. He hadn't gotten used to being invisible, so the sight caused a sudden internal panic. Calming himself Tee said, "analysis Quinn?"

"Processing." Then a long minute later Quinn said, "they don't know we're here. There are two warships and four empty vessels that appear to be transports. The way they are configured its likely they are queuing up to send the four empty hulls through."

"Ok, Good! Let's execute the two jumps to M26. We'll clean this up later. I don't want to alert them we've entered their space," Tee said as he relaxed. Ramming something by accident had been a real concern. If they had been sending one of the hulks through at high speed the Gerty might have joined the cloud of debris littering Sector 27's side of the wormhole.

Back on Pacifica Tee had questioned Jack on what lay beyond the wormhole. He learned that each sector had an additional planet on the Commonwealth side of every wormhole. This additional planet was dedicated to the military. Their wormhole led to Sector 26 and thus there was a military planet designated M26. Jack said that anything involving the military for Sector 27 would be managed from there.

When they came out of the final jump the sight was staggering. The planet had a huge space station in a high orbit teaming with Commonwealth warships. There appeared to be no room left to dock any more. There were several more warships scattered about that appeared to be waiting for an open dock. In addition, there were three large installations on the planet for God knew what. The scale of it was intimidating. Tee wondered how they could possibly win against something of this magnitude. After a few minutes of shocked silence Tee finally said, "Options?"

"One of our large fusion devices should take out the space station and connected ships. All of that is pretty fragile. We can clean up anything we miss with the smaller devices. The planet buster will take out everything on the planet. Probably make it uninhabitable," Quinn said clinically without his usual happy enthusiasm. They were discussing killing hundreds of thousands of people, and it obviously bothered him.

While he didn't like the idea either, these people had joined a military organization they knew oppressed the Commonwealths colonies. They had made a choice, and it was an evil one. The faces of those he was forced to kill in the Arena came to mind as he said, "we'll take out the space station first. We don't want any of those warships to escape. Jay, load up one of the large fusion devices. Quinn plot a destination."

The crew quickly went through their process and after the large fusion device had been placed Tee gave the command, "detonate L1."

Even though they were prepared for it, the result was almost incomprehensible. Large segments of the space station were slowly pinwheeling in random directions with fires clearly visible. Quinn had placed the device close to the center of the docking station side and whatever was left of the warships was hard to pick out in the flotsam. Complete and utter destruction.

"The local communications network is getting overwhelmed," Quinn reported.

Not that this affected them given they were in receive only mode. Tee thought everyone on the planet must be trying to communicate at once. Tee hesitated as he imagined what would be going on down there. The space station was so large that it would be visible from the planet's surface. The explosion must have been quite traumatic for those below. Families would be huddled together. Mothers would be rushing to their children's schools. Friends would be calling each other hoping they weren't on the space station. His heart went out to those who were probably just caught up in a system they had no part in building. He turned to Griff and said, "What do you think we should do now?"

Griff looked at Tee with surprise and said, "I think the entire planet is a military installation and we should destroy it."

Tee just looked at Griff for a while considering his options. Perry's lecture on not killing indiscriminately had resonated with him. He had asked Bria once why she didn't throw her knife at him on the slave ship. Her answer had floored him.

"I won't kill," Bria had said. "I would rather lose my life than live with the guilt of taking someone else's life." She had stopped after saying this realizing he might be offended and observed, "I might feel differently if I grew up on Pacifica. It seems the consequences of refusing to fight there are much greater than on Liberty."

That led to remembering Victor's comments about the Arista gladiators. They were victims not enemies. It made him pause. What were his moral responsibilities? Griff was right when he told General Eastbrook that the Guard had never been in a position to consider anything other than killing their enemy on sight. This was a different situation. There were other options.

"Quinn, what do we need to do to destroy the three large installations but leave the surrounding residential areas relatively intact?" Tee asked.

"One of them is a space port and one small device on the launch area should be enough. The other two are spread out and will require larger devices. Since those two are remote from the major city we can minimize casualties," Quinn said.

Tee was once again surprised by Quinn's insight. He had correctly guessed what Tee's concern was. "Quinn, Jay, execute to that plan." He looked over at Griff and saw he was confused and a bit miffed. Griff wanted to see the whole planet destroyed. Tee thought that was the best purely military solution, but he just couldn't do it.

They destroyed all the military spacecraft they could locate in the vicinity of M26. They had seen a few wink out hopefully heading away from Sector 27. Then they jumped back to the wormhole and took out the lone warship there. Once back in Sector 27 they contacted Pacifica.

"Gerty, you were under orders not to transmit close to the wormhole," Jennifer said with a questioning look.

"There isn't anyone left to listen," Tee responded. "I violated one other order as well. A video file with commentary is being sent. It explains everything. The summary is that we've destroyed the Commonwealth's military capabilities on M26. Jack can explain what that means." Tee hesitated a moment and then said, "General Eastbrook did say to use my initiative if I saw an opportunity."

On the Peregrine they watched the video, and the crew broke into applause. Perry turned to Colonel Peters and dryly said, "I'm going to like our Mr. Stone. I think we'll go easy on him at the court martial." They both laughed.

Jennifer looked shocked and turned to Jack with a

questioning look. He smiled and said, "I think we just bought some time. Commonwealth citizens think the Commonwealth is invincible. Showing this will prove they are not. I have an idea."

President Malrey's image suddenly appeared on the Gerty's main screen. Sitting once again at her desk she looked confident but stern, "good morning, this is President Malrey with an update for the Commonwealth and inhabitants of A27. The response to our offer for peace has been rejected. Instead, an attack on our border security was made by the Commonwealth. Our response was the utter destruction of all military facilities orbiting and occupying M26." A video showing the orbital platform and multiple military bases on M26 as they were being destroyed took the place of Jennifers image. "We had the capability to destroy the entire M26 planet but refrained from taking this action to show that we can be merciful. It is a mistake to underestimate us. We can strike anywhere in the Commonwealth with impunity." An old picture of Earth taken in antiquity from its moon briefly made its appearance. The image quickly went back to Jennifer. She hesitated a few moments and then said, "let me repeat what I've said before. We desire peace with all our neighbors. Our only demand is that you vacate our sector." Jennifer stopped and with a look of regret said, "I don't like to threaten. But it seems your government doesn't understand peaceful negotiations. The Pacifica Guard will arrive at A27 within a week. If your government doesn't surrender before that time we'll take the planet by force. The Pacifica Guard does not take prisoners." The image switched to a still photo of Rilla in battle gear covered in gore and affecting a crazed expression. Then the monitor went black.

They had all been disgusted when Jack explained that the Commonwealth secretly recorded Arista gladiatorial events and the Pacifica wars. They consider it entertainment. They even had something called fan clubs who would gather to watch and root for whomever caught their fancy. Griff was a favorite. Tee had become quite popular after killing Trajan.

Those who enjoyed these sorts of things would replay his bow work on the Wall. Even Arti had her followers. Rilla had recently become popular because of how berserk he had gone trying to save Moose's life. His killing spree had recently been replayed over and over on the feeds. Jack thought his image would have a gut level impact on the ordinary citizens of not only A27 but the whole of the Commonwealth.

Later that evening Jennifers monitor signaled that a connection was requested. She sent out permissions for the rest of the group to view and then allowed it. A harassed looking middle-aged man greeted her. "My name is Jackson Depond. I am the mayor of A27. We only have a single city on this planet. There is a small military facility but that is different. I um, well this is quite unusual."

Jennifer interrupted him since it seemed he might just keep blabbering, "what do you want Mr. Dupond?" she asked.

The question caused him to blanch. He visibly settled himself and said, "we would like to discuss your terms for surrender."

"Where is Governor Jacobs? Isn't that who I should be discussing this with," Jennifer said.

"She is, um, she is indisposed at the moment," he said, clearly uncomfortable discussing the governor.

"Well, have her call back when she isn't indisposed," Jennifer said and acted as if she was going to break the connection.

"No, wait," Jackson said desperately. Then he took a deep breath. "A member of the High Council is on A27 visiting his daughter and decided it was best for him to take over decision making. He's asked me to negotiate on his behalf."

"I'm not going to negotiate with intermediators. Have him call me when he's ready to discuss terms," Jennifer said and cut off the connection.

An hour later another connection request was made.

When Jennifer accepted an older gentleman appeared and said with annoyance, "hello, I am Justice Reginald a member of the High Council for King Archibald. We will vacate A27 and leave the sector. We require all transport ships to be released immediately. It will take six months to pack up our property which will be taken with us. I have no authority to surrender the Commonwealth's claim on this sector. I wouldn't do that even if I could. This is the best offer you'll get."

"Thank you High Councilperson Reginald for your offer. I will consider it. If I don't get back to you within the next five days you'll know I've rejected your offer. In that case you can expect the Guard to land. Those negotiations won't be pleasant," Jennifer said curtly and cut off the connection.

Jack immediately spoke up, "This is really good news. I was hoping for a grass roots coup. Reginald is the leading Justice Minister on the High Council. He is not going to risk himself or his daughter for a minor backwater sector."

The next call was from Governor Jacobs, "I would like to speak with my First Minister."

"Ok, hold on a second," Jennifer said and passed the connection to Jack.

"Hello Governor," Jack said with a stone face. She just stared at him for a long time.

"If you can't think of anything to say please call back when you do," Jack said coldly.

"This isn't making anything easier for you when we get back," Jacobs said threateningly.

"I've been offered sanctuary and have accepted it," Jack said bluntly.

She showed some surprise at his news. Unusual for her to reveal anything. After a few moments she smiled evilly and said, "I'll be sure to say hello to your mother and father for you Jack."

"If you do that, it will be on A27. Commonwealths'

citizens who are granted sanctuary will have the opportunity to offer the same to their close relatives. None of the high-ranking members of the Commonwealth will be allowed to leave until this happens," Jack said and forced a triumphant smile on his face. He would be damned if she saw any fear in him.

"This isn't the end Jack. Remember that," Jacobs said and cut the connection.

In the end Reginald agreed to all of Jennifers demands. They would leave everything behind and evacuate as soon as possible. A surprisingly small number of Commonwealth citizens requested sanctuary. Those who did had few relatives so getting them to A27 was done quickly. Jacks' parents reluctantly agreed to sanctuary recognizing their life in the Commonwealth was over. When the last Commonwealth transport disappeared through the wormhole Jack breathed a sigh of relief. Now all he had to do was ask for forgiveness. That and spend the rest of his life trying to repent for all the horrors he had helped inflict on his new friends.

CHAPTER 27

BLUE HERON TAVERN

Jay and Hestie both arrived at the Blue Heron early. Their greetings were cordial but strained. After sitting for a while in silence Hestie finally said, "I think it's time to tell you why I pushed you away."

"That would be nice," Jay said with a mildly biting voice.

"I found out about our military technology when they needed help with navigation. I volunteered with the understanding that I would have to commit suicide if the Commonwealth gained control of Pacifica. They would have killed everyone if they knew. They call it cleansing," Hestie said with a look asking for understanding.

"Go on," was all Jay said.

Hestie continued, "I couldn't take our relationship further knowing you were going to discover I had committed suicide with no explanation. I just couldn't do that to you."

Jay looked down at the table in front of him and pondered that for a while. Then he looked up and said, "So you didn't trust me."

"I do trust you Jay. More than anyone else in my life," Hestie said with tears starting to form in her eyes.

"You didn't trust me to survive. Instead, you took what should have been months of happiness away from us both. When the world was coming apart, you took away my refuge," Jay said. Then leaning forward he added, "my purpose in life is to risk it saving others. I could have died at any time. But I trusted you to carry on, to survive."

"I'm sorry Jay. I hope you can forgive me," Hestie said with her voice trailing off and her eyes looking off to the side.

"How can I trust you when you don't trust me. How can I know I can depend on you when life gets difficult," Jay said. When she looked back at him he added, "I also think something else is going on. You have some other secret you're not telling me about. You might be able to hide from others Hestie, but you can't hide from me."

Hestie just stared at him for a while wondering what to say. Then she decided to stop pretending, "I do have another secret. A terrible one. Something I cannot and will not tell you or anyone else. I'm sorry Jay but there are things more important than our happiness."

"A secret that protects us all?" Jay said adjusting the Guard credo.

"Yes," Hestie said,

"That's all you ever needed to say Hestie. I wish you had said it months ago," Jay said with sadness in his voice.

As Hestie started to answer him Jay looked up in recognition. With his frown slowly turning into a grin, he said loud enough for the whole tavern to hear, "Theron, First of his Name, Emperor of Arista, Liberator of Worlds. Your Eminence, have you come to mingle with the common people?"

Hestie face transformed into a smile, and she laughed. Tee turned bright red as the entire Tavern turned to look at him. A few people chuckled recognizing Jay and the sarcasm. More than a few people simply smiled to see him. Tee had become a celebrity.

Tee walked over to the table and standing over Jay said quietly, "did you really have to do that?"

"Yes, I did. If I don't make fun of you you're likely going to get a big head," Jay said continuing to smile.

Hestie got up and gave Tee a big hug. "It's good to see

you. You've been gone too long."

Tee sat down in front of the beer Jay had already ordered for him and said, "I've been on Arista this whole time. I am no longer the emperor. The new emperor is Caius, Third of his Name." This was said with a hint of sarcasm.

"How did you pull that off?" Jay asked.

"By their constitution, an Emperor can abdicate to any blood relative of any of the previous Emperors. I could have abdicated to my cousin Pete. He would have loved that. Well, at least for a few days," Tee said smiling. "Senator Cereo is a distant relative of the emperor Trajan, the previous Emperor."

"The one you murdered," Jay said. Hestie punched him lightly in the arm for that comment. He grinned and rubbed it as if it were painful.

"Yes, the one I murdered." Tee said smiling at them both. "I had to go to their Senate one more time to officially abdicate. But the real reason Cereo wanted me there was to threaten people."

"Why did you need to threaten anyone?" Hestie asked.

"Cereo's main rival is the magistrate of their senate. He's the one who headed up the coup resulting in mercenaries invading Liberty. His argument that the Commonwealth forced him to do it had enough truth in it to absolve him. The elite are all former slave owners, and the majority support him. While the Emperors authority is absolute, it is tenuous. Civil war is a very real possibility. I met individually with many of Cereo's opponents before abdicating and told them I would be back if they caused trouble. They naturally assumed that meant with the Guard. They've seen Victor and I in the Arena and black-market videos of our GEM wars have been circulating recently," Tee said.

Jay looked at Tee with concern and asked, "Do you trust Cereo?"

"No, I don't trust him. He's too manipulative. But I like him which is weird," Tee said with a confused grin on his face.

"How can you like him if you don't trust him," Hestie asked with concern. Then she glanced over at Jay with an odd look. That's strange, Tee thought.

"I don't know, I just do. It's probably because every time I've seen him manipulate people it's for good reasons. While that isn't a good enough justification for me, he's been in a pretty extreme situation his whole life." Tee said, and after hesitating he added, "his situation has improved enormously but it's still dangerous. The magistrate's supporters now know he counts slaves as his family. They know he was secretly working to free them. They suspect he talked Pacifica into supporting him."

"It makes sense to me," Jay said, "Sometimes people you don't trust can be appealing." Giving his own odd look back at Hestie. Definitely something there thought Tee with some concern.

After a few moments of uncomfortable silence Tee decided to change the subject, "Where is Diana? I thought she would be here tonight."

Well, that didn't calm things down he thought as he saw Hestie react strongly. She just stared at him for a moment and then said, "she said she was meeting Glenn tonight."

Tee's brain boiled over with that news. He had been extremely busy with commitments since the warships were revealed. There had been no time to have a private discussion with Diana since their night in the garden. She knew the engagement was off and he assumed she would just wait for him to return. Not wanting to talk about it he quickly changed the subject. "I've been court martialed," he said.

"What!" Jay said loud enough for people in adjoining tables to look over at them.

Tee just smiled and said, "General Eastbrook turns out to be a practical joker. He pulled President Malrey, Queen Olivia, Emperor Cereo, Griff, and a few of his top officers together and put me on trial for disobeying orders. I was found guilty and sentenced to 30 days restricted duty. If I complete the 30 days successfully then the guilty verdict will be expunged. In other words, it's like it never happened. I've basically been sentenced to take a vacation. After that, Queen Olivia awarded me their Royal Cross, Emperor Cereo pined some olive leaf thing on my uniform, and President Malrey gave me a hearty handshake."

Tee took a deep breath and said, "I was hoping to talk to Diana tonight." He hesitated and then said, "General Eastbrook offered to take me hunting with him in the mountains close to his ranch. I wasn't going to go, but I think I'll accept. Will be nice to see Bria again." And with that he got up, hugged Hestie once more, slapped Jay on the shoulder and said, "will see you both in a couple of weeks."

Tee walked out of the Blue Heron with Jay and Diana staring at his back with open mouth surprise. Jay recovered first, "what the hell is going on between him and Diana?"

"I don't know. She seems confused and this will just make it worse," Hestie said.

"I know that look from Tee. He's decided something," Jay replied. Then they just sat in silence for a while.

Finally, Hestie said, "Do I have a chance to fix things?"

Jay huffed but his angry face from before had disappeared. He mouth went from relaxed to firm and he said, "can I trust you to trust me?"

"I trust you Jay. Maybe the problem is that I didn't trust me," Hestie said. "Anyway, if you'll give me the time to prove it I'm willing to wait. As Grammy said, some things are worth waiting for."

CHAPTER 28

FINAGLED

It was early in the morning with mist heavy in the air. The day would end up being hot and dry. Perfect for growing grapes Caius thought wryly. The sky was just starting to lighten, and the birds were waking and giving their opinion of the morning. The air was full of the earthy smell of vegetation. Caius was deep in thought on his favorite bench in the family vegetable garden. It was here he had spent a good deal of time as a young man desperately dreaming up schemes to protect his family. In some ways nothing had changed. There were still great dangers that would need to be navigated. There was no margin for error. The elite of Arista hated him. They would find a way to channel that hate.

He knew their hatred was well earned. The elite had retained their wealth. But they did not wield the power they once had. A power they believed was their right by birth. In their minds outrageous changes had been forced upon them. Slaves had been freed. Private armies eliminated. But what caused the most angst was the elimination of corruption. Government funded projects were not for sale anymore. Legal matters could no longer be settled with a bribe. A whole new way of life was being shoved down their throats. It was too much change too fast.

He was proud of what he had negotiated. He had been the one convincing the Confederation of Planets that Pacifica should appear to be acting alone. An outraged property owner dealing with squatters. The idea emerged when it became clear Pacifica would retain control of their military technology. Pacifica standing alone had its merits in dealing with the Commonwealth. But it wasn't the primary reason he had proposed it. No, his real purpose would come later.

Caius wanted drastic change on Arista. One way to accelerate change was to convince Pacifica to set conditions for joining the Confederation. Any planet declining would get an eviction notice. Their alternative would be to fall on the mercy of the Commonwealth. Everyone knew the Commonwealth would show no mercy. The challenge was to get everyone to agree that slavery would not be allowed anywhere in the Confederation. There was a strong bias that each planet guide its own future. He agreed with this bias, but he had to find a way for an exception. The key was gaining agreement from Pacifica.

His mother, his real mother, had given him excellent advice once. If you want people to agree with you, get them used to saying yes. Once they get in the habit they are likely to continue. He found this to be surprisingly true.

So, his first proposal to the Confederation was that A27 be recognized as belonging to Pacifica. The people of Pacifica were insistent that the GEMs be left alone which meant they had no room to grow. This was wildly popular with everyone. Jennifer had reported that Councilman Barlow in particular had been effusive in his praise of the idea. He even pulled out the original surveys and declared this would have been their home had they not lost their jump capability. They even named it all those years ago. It had originally been named Eirene after the Greek goddess of peace. There was no controversy in retaining the name.

At their next meeting he proposed that Arista provide significant funding for two new schools on Eirene. The first was an extension of the university on Pacifica and the other a technical training school. These schools would be open to applicants from all planets in the Confederation. It was an extremely popular proposal with Liberty immediately agreeing to match Arista's contributions. With those pledges

Pacifica committed to making Landfall University an extension of what would become the main university on Eirene. There wasn't anyone happier with this than Del. That evening after a few too many whiskeys, Del had slurred his thanks to Caius over and over again. "All I ever wanted to do was research and teach. Being told about our hidden technology was the worst day of my life. This is the best day."

Now with two yes votes under his belt he proposed the Confederation of Planets adopt as constitutional law a prohibition on slavery. Since no law is valid without enforcement he proposed that the Confederation Defense Force be tasked with compliance. That required Pacifica support.

Liberty quickly agreed. They had a prohibition of their own in the Liberty constitution. Having the same for the Confederation aligned with their beliefs. Although Pacifica had the same prohibition in their human rights clauses they were not in favor of interfering in other planets' politics. They saw the hands-off intention of the Commonwealths non-interference edicts as one of the few good things about that system. After much debate, Caius asked Jennifer to be allowed to directly address the Pacifica Council. She agreed.

The Pacifica Council was just as reluctant as Jennifer had been. "I don't like telling people what to do in their own homes," Councilwoman Ricks had said.

"Your own constitution prohibits slavery by declaring that everyone has the right to freedom," Caius countered. "How is this different?"

"It's different because we have control of military technology and it's a slippery slope towards becoming just another tyrannical Commonwealth," Ricks shot back.

"I agree," Barlow said forcefully. "We need to keep the military tightly reined in."

After a couple of hours of this Caius was exhausted. He had complimented, disparaged, pleaded, and appealed to their humanity. All to no avail. He was out of ways to manipulate the situation. When his efforts to get his way ran out of steam, June used to smile at him and say, "when you don't know what to say, just tell the truth."

So, he told his story. An hour later there were tears on a few of the council members' cheeks. He had told them everything about his family. Confessed that he had used every manipulative trick in the book to change things. That he was out of tricks.

The vote was three for and three against. Surprisingly, Barlow was the one who had switched sides. "Yea. I am voting for this because I believe he's telling the truth. And it's a compelling truth. My only request is that the constitution clearly state that this is a singular exception to the Confederation Defense Force non-interference rule."

Barlow's addition was unanimously added to the vote and again the result was three for and three against.

Jennifer took a deep breath and said, "the vote is deadlocked and there is no proposal for an alternative." She looked around the table and as her eyes met with Barlow's she said, "I vote yea."

He had been stunned. Given Jennifers strong disagreement with this at the Confederation of Planets meetings Caius thought he had failed.

The garden workers arriving to start the day brought him back to the present. He realized he was very satisfied with his life. Who would have guessed that the ragged farm boy who knocked on Mr. File's door would end up realizing his dream. Being distrusted by most in the Confederation and hated on Arista was a small price to pay.

CHAPTER 29

JACKPOT

Grant had been terrified when the small shuttlecraft docked with their survey ship and demanded they open the hatch. The communications network had gone dark a few hours before. It had done this just as a Commonwealth warship entered orbit. As soon as it arrived the ultimate symbol of Commonwealth power simply disintegrated into billions of tiny pieces. Data from their sensors identified the cause of its demise as a small anti-matter triggered fusion device. War was thought to be a thing of the past. Commonwealth citizens knew their government was all powerful and citizens had nothing to fear. Well, nothing except the government itself. The shuttlecraft claimed to under the command of the Pacifica Guard. It was all too surreal to be believed. Their captain was told his options were to open the hatch or suffer the same fate as the warship. It was an easy decision. Enormous human beings with frowns on their faces and swords in their hands entered. They looked so much bigger and deadlier in person than they had when viewed on a video screen. Grant was certain they were all about to be slaughtered. He knew the Pacifica Guard didn't take prisoners. He just hoped they would make it quick.

Grant chuckled to himself thinking of how he had gone from utterly terrified to wildly ecstatic. He had initially dismissed sanctuary when it was offered. He was a Commonwealth citizen and didn't want to live in some backwater Sector. Then he remembered what was waiting for him back home. Grant made the decision to request sanctuary fairly quickly after that.

When the Dean of the newly formed Eirene University found out he had a doctorate in anthropology he was offered a teaching position. It even paid more than his old job of survey anthropologist. When you looked at the whole thing it was like hitting an enormous jackpot. His luck had turned just like he knew it would. Now he just had to find a good local bookie.

CHAPTER 30

CLOSURE

Jennifer, Del, Caius, and Olivia were viewing the cockpit of Gerty.

"Destination match," Quinn said.

"How certain are we this will work?" Olivia asked.

"I am confident it will close. I'm less certain if it will close permanently," Quinn answered brightly.

Del added, "nobody has ever explained why permanent wormholes exist. Where they get the energy to stay open or how they are formed in the first place. We've learned how to create temporary ones of our own from analyzing them. But our artificial ones are simply not the same. Since permanent wormholes are viewed as immensely valuable, nobody has been motivated to find a way to close them. Until now."

"Does that mean it could come back at any time?" Olivia asked.

"We don't know. It could disappear forever, or it could come back instantly. It's possible that Quinns hypothesis is wrong, and nothing happens. Although I doubt it," Del replied.

Jennifer looked at everyone and said, "I would feel a lot better if it disappears and never comes back. If everyone is in agreement then I'll give the command." She looked around the table and got approving head nods. Then with a slight nod of her own head she said, "Tee, give the command to launch."

They all heard Tee say, "destination approved. Launch Closure Device."

A few seconds later they saw the magnified wormhole on their screen simply wink out. After a full minute of anxiously watching the screen the room slowly broke into applause and then congratulations. They were finally safe from the Commonwealth.

CHAPTER 31

EPILOGUE

Griff entered the Hall of Hero's and was struck by the silence. It seemed he was the only one here this morning and was glad for it. The display case wasn't large, but it certainly caught your attention entering the hall. Urns had never been displayed out here before. They made an exception for Vic. Eventually Tee would be housed right next to him. There was an impressive gold-plated plaque detailing how peace and freedom had been won for Pacifica. They were doing the same for all the war rooms detailing the story for each battle. The Hall of Hero's was turning into a museum.

"Well old friend. You never got to enjoy the fruits of your labor," Griff said quietly. Then he just stood there as if searching for more to say. "I came to thank you. Have regretted not doing that before you disappeared. It feels good that you knew I was made Master Sergeant. That would not have happened if it wasn't for you. Your obsession on excellence is what kept me alive." Griff paused and then said, "You were right about Tee. He was capable of being a much better fighter than I imagined. That was quite the dramatic final lesson." Griff paused, smiled, then continued, "it reminded me of all the times I ended up laying in the dirt during your training sessions. You'll be pleased to hear Tee's been promoted to CGG. Our President had to negotiate hard to get him to accept. He truly does not seek power or influence. One of the reasons he should have both. She had to supply a shuttlecraft so he could travel back and forth to Apple Valley. He says it's his home and he's never living anywhere else. The wonders of technology. She felt compelled to do this because Pacifica may need his influence. There are challenges with the Confederation of Planets. Tee has become somewhat of a legend across the confederation. Arista calls him Theron the Great. The former slave population there seems to think he personally freed them and then abdicated in order to ensure slavery is stamped out everywhere. Liberty calls him Theron the Liberator." Griff smiled a little broader and said, "Pacifica is not so grandiose. We just call him Tee. But he is rightfully viewed alongside you as Pacifica's liberators. Speaking of Tee, I'm married to Tee's mother. Yeah I know, she could have done better. Should have done better." He hesitated again and said in a hushed voice, "I'll fill you in on a secret. Arti is pregnant. Dr. Espers says the medical knowledge in the archives will eliminate most of the risk to a woman her age giving birth. She did some sort of scan and said the baby is healthy. She was even able to tell us it's going to be a girl." His smile faded and he said, "It's not all good news. The Guard is changing. There isn't as much motivation to excel. The fear and anxiety of the GEMs is missing. That would piss you off. I know it pisses me off. But in my opinion being able to bring up my daughter in a time of peace is worth any price. I just have to accept things for what they are. That doesn't mean I'll let the Guard get complacent." Griff took a deep breath and let it out. Then he said, "I'll stop in from time-to-time Vic. I hope you'll look in on me as well. Again, thank you for everything my friend." Then Griff wandered off to visit the other ghosts of his past.

Olivia and Bria were sitting on the porch of the Eastbrook ranch house enjoying their afternoon tea. It was sunny, hot, and muggy. But they were enjoying the House of Lords summer break. Getting the kingdom back in order meant the two of them had had no time until now to get caught up. But being best friends since childhood meant being together was instantly comfortable.

Olivia frowned and said, "I'm worried about Gloria. Her relationship with Jack seems to be getting serious. She told me he's the only man she's met who understands what she's been through. She says he doesn't look down on her because of it. She says he's patient, kind, and gentle with the girls. Treats them both like princesses."

"I can testify that princesses don't always get treated well," Bria quipped trying to lighten the mood. She had been struggling to get Olivia to relax. She was stuck in problem solving mode and needed to come up for air.

"He's done some horrible things Bria," Olivia said ignoring her efforts to avoid the subject.

Bria saw that Olivia's eyebrows were scrunched together when she turned to look at her. "Well, Grace likes him," Bria replied, refusing to get into a discussion of Jack's prior life as she worked to get Olivia to settle down.

Olivia frown softened a bit at that. "You seriously think everyone that dog likes is a good person?"

"Yes I do. She's got some sort of sixth sense about people. She even likes you," Bria said with a smirk locking eyes with Olivia.

That caused Olivia to roll her eyes and crack a smile. Then she asked, "Does she ever leave your side?"

Bria's turned her head towards Olivia and said seriously, "No. She saved me on Arista. I saved her. We're both grateful." After a few minutes of the comfortable silence best friends enjoy Bria suddenly smiled and said, "seems to me the ruggedly handsome Colonel Timothy Peters is never far away."

Olivia's eyebrows scrunched together again, and she looked troubled. She took a breath and sighed. Finally, she said, "yeah, that's a problem I'll have to deal with." She hesitated a few moments longer and then said, "I asked him to marry me."

Bria's tea went down the wrong pipe and came back out through her nose and mouth in a spray. After sputtering for a few seconds, she said dumbfounded, "you did what! Why?"

"I asked him to marry me because I love him. He never would have asked me," Olivia said in all seriousness. Bria just stared at her obviously at a loss for words. So, Olivia continued her story. "It wasn't very romantic. Instead of saying yes his answer was, 'I can't do that to you', and then he just stared at me. Kind of like what you're doing now." Olivia smiled and continued, "After a long and arduous discussion of what was in my best interests, he reluctantly agreed to marry me. Something I'll remind him of from time to time."

"But what about the House of Lords? What about your Uncle? I thought he was looking for the best political match?" Bria asked.

"Well, sometimes you just have to make a royal decision. We don't really have any serious political problems right now. So, I've decided to be selfish," Olivia said smugly. She then looked thoughtfully at Bria and said, "Were you really going to marry Theron Stone to protect me?"

Bria smiled reflectively for a few moments and finally said, "you and everyone else."

"You know I spent time with him when you were off catching up with your father. I don't think that would have been much of a sacrifice," Olivia said, and they both laughed. Bria was happy to see the old Olivia again.

Bria's smile turned wistful as she said softly, "It wouldn't have been entirely distasteful." Catching herself she forced a grin and said, "my dad is still rooting for it. Tee is everything he ever wanted in a son-in-law." They both chuckled.

"Well now you get to choose," Olivia said looking a little concerned. She had finally picked up on Bria's mood.

"Yes I do," Bria said softly. Then under her breath she added privately to herself, "if only it were that simple."

June was working in the garden when she heard someone approach. A man's soft voice said, "June?" She turned to greet him, started to reply, then stopped. She studied his face for long moments as she tried to figure out what to say. Then with tears welling in her eyes she simply said. "Henry." They both stepped forward and wrapped each other up in a long embrace.

They eventually separated but held onto each other's hands. "You've left your position," she said.

"I can't believe it, but here I am," Henry said with a relaxed smile. "Although I could have continued to provide useful information Leo and Caius insisted."

"Your sacrifice has already helped free millions," June said firmly.

"Leo told me the same thing. I told him it was a small part compared to what others have done. He's an impressive man June; you must be very proud," Henry said.

"Just as proud of my little brother," she said with warm light dancing in her eyes. She hesitated a few moments trying to decide whether to open up. Then remembering how Henry was the one person she would share secrets with as a child she finally said in a quiet voice, "I'm very proud of both my sons. I will never disrespect Caius's mother by claiming that honor in his hearing. But between us, he is as much my son as Leo is. Let's go in and have some tea. We have fifty years to catch up on."

Tee and Diana were married under the large oak tree where they had met as children. Representatives from all confederation planets were in attendance. The Guard showed up in force along with what seemed to be the whole of Apple Valley. The public reception took place on the school playground and spilled out into the streets. It would be talked about in Apple Valley for decades.

The private family reception started at sunset with a bonfire on the beach. Late that evening Tee was standing off to the side watching his family and friends laughing and having fun. It was as if no time had gone past. Ansen was entertaining a large group with one of his outrageously funny stories. Jay and Hestie were sitting on Grammy's bench where they had been for quite some time. They seemed to be going back and forth between a serious conversation and laughter. He noticed they had been slowly inching closer together as the evening progressed. It was obvious by the way they were now pressed close together, and the way looked at each other, that they were getting past whatever it was that caused their problems. Then he caught Diana looking at him. She smiled and nodded her head slightly in a gesture that said it was time to retire for the evening. He needed no encouragement. In that moment he thought he would like things to stay like this forever. Then he remembered the last time he had wished for that on this very same beach. Smiling, he reminded himself once more that Grammy was wise. Everything changes and it's best to simply enjoy whatever fate has in store for you. The good, the bad, and yes, even the regrets. He took Diana's outreached hand and as they walked around saying their goodnights he thought to himself, thanks for everything Grammy.

A young and vibrant woman sat on the front porch, surrounded by those she loved. She was wearing a self-satisfied smile as she enjoyed the dance of the fireflies. They had read their letters and followed her advice. Her work was truly finished.

ABOUT THE AUTHOR

Tom Burrell resides with his wife in Northern California. When not writing, Tom is busy with their five children and five grandchildren. He has a degree in mechanical engineering from Cal Poly San Luis Obispo. Before becoming an author, Tom enjoyed a career in the electronic test and measurement industry.

Prior to becoming a responsible adult, Tom spent a decade of his youth wandering aimlessly working a long list of jobs. These included lifeguard, swimming instructor, janitor, security guard, grill cook, painter, greenhouse worker, midnight shift convenience store clerk, residential liquor delivery driver, waiter, too many factory jobs to count, day laborer when immediate cash was required, and maker of handmade deer skin cowboy hats. These custom hats were sold by traveling around California to county fairs and other events where people tend to drink too much.

If you enjoyed Sovereign please consider giving a review. Feedback is a generous gift.

This completes The Revelation Trilogy. More stories from this universe are forthcoming.